TIME WILL BURY YOU

Also by the author:

THE COLD, COLD VOICE
NIGHT BRINGS NIGHT

TIME WILL BURY YOU

A NOVEL BY

KRIS LORENZEN

WOODSHED BOOKS
- Indianapolis -

Published by Woodshed Books
www.woodshedbooks.com

Copyright © 2024 by Kris Lorenzen
All rights reserved.

First Edition 2024
979-8-9869008-3-4

Designed by the author.
Printed in the United States of America

1 3 5 7 9 10 8 6 4 2

This is a work of fiction. All of the characters, organizations, locations, and events used in this novel either are the product of the author's imagination or are used factiously. The author forbids the use of his work in the training of "A.I." or machine-learning programs, as any such use is plagiarism.

*For Ben and Javier and Mark.
You know who you are, and you know why.*

THURSDAY

This was a couple years ago, when not much was going on.

Back then, I slept with my cell phone somewhere on the bed with me. It was my first one, and I guess the novelty hadn't worn off yet. It wound up under my pillow and the buzzing yanked me from black, formless sleep.

I flipped the thing open and said hello.

I hoped my nonchalant tone conveyed that I was already awake, and not stirred when the phone hummed. I felt awkward at being woken up, akin to fearing that someone didn't remember my name—my embarrassment was for them, not for me. What did that say about my defective brain?

Nobody answered.

"Hello?" I repeated.

Muffled whispers.

"What?"

Idiot. If you held the phone the right way—

I fumbled it around like I featured in a Z-grade *SNL* sketch.

It was Ben. He was halfway through explaining or asking me something.

"Backup," I said. "I, uh, dropped my phone for a second. What are we talking about?"

"Javier's wedding," he said. "I'm gonna drive down to Indy tonight. Bachelor party. There's a dress rehearsal and some other shit he wants to do early tomorrow. I figure we go down tonight, and we could hang out with Jake or Niedz before all the boring wedding shit starts. Or Estella."

"You wanna hang out with my ex-girlfriend?" I asked.

"Sure, but I was more thinking you might want to," he said.

I pictured his sly smile and his casual miming of various sex acts.

"Wait," I said. "You want me to go with you?"

"Yeah," he said, "why the fuck else would I call you? Aimee's gonna stay with the kids and come down on Saturday with Amy and Mark."

"You know I'm not in the wedding, right?" I asked.

"Kyle," he said, "are you new or something? Is this your first day? We're all in the wedding, but Lisa doesn't have any friends so only Mark and I are *in* the wedding. Officially or whatever. Javier won't care if you're there. He'll be stoked."

"Is Mark going with you?"

"Nope," he said. "Lucky bastard has to work and gets

to miss all the pre-wedding crap. He's coming down early Saturday."

Still foggy from sleep—I knew this. I was supposed to ride with Mark and Amy on Saturday.

Plus, maybe he had just told me this a few seconds ago?

"Right," I said stupidly.

"Well?" he asked. "Pick you up at six? It's about three now."

This wasn't my week off at the all-night drugstore but fuck it. I also got sick time.

"Yeah," I said. "It'll be fun."

"Dope," Ben said. "See you in a few hours."

"Wait," I caught him before he hung up. "Should I wear a tie?"

"Eh. I mean, it's just Javier."

This was five or six years after college.

After I glanced off the surface of the real world and fell flat onto my face, I moved back to my hometown, worked third shift in an all-night pharmacy, and had a quiet, one-bedroom apartment. I was *that* guy.

My friends settled into their grooves, too—either headlong into careers or returned to school. Some were married or nearly there, but they didn't need to see their partners all the time—hell, they lived with them. Might as well chill with your friends. So, I saw them nearly every day.

The wives and girlfriends hung around sometimes, too, but there wasn't dating-type bullshit. No drama. Comfortable and stable.

Even I found equilibrium. I didn't have one steady girl—there were a few and they didn't know about each other. I knew a lie of omission was still a lie, but what could I say? It didn't bother me then and there's much worse things I've got to apologize for than swinging my dick around in my late twenties.

So, yeah. I was that guy, too, and I thought: This is what my life is.

But how many times have I thought that?

It felt as if life had just begun, but that happened over and over. It changed in a second without warning. I stood and looked back at the ruins of what had been my life, and I still lived, so that must've been an intro, and this was the real shit here and now. This was my life.

Until something else upended it again.

It was February, and if you've lived in the Midwest through a winter, you know what that means.

Gone were the holidays, gone were the excitement and promise of a new year, gone were those resolutions. Well, I still wasn't smoking. Six weeks in. Maybe it'd stick this time.

The fresh, white snow and the silent dampening of the world were replaced by dirty gray sludge splashing and sloshing in the streets.

I had this friend in college who people used to call a wigger. As in a white N-word. I know. Casual '90s racism—it made me cringe too.

Whenever someone would give him much deserved shit for cultural appropriation, he would look at them solemnly and tap an index finger against his forehead and say something like:

"Black is a state of mind, brotha."

which trivialized the hard-earned pride of the group of people he attempted to emulate. I didn't know if he believed that state-of-mind crap, but I knew he never had trouble hailing a cab or being followed through a store. He never got hassled—or worse—by the cops.

I heard he taught English as a second language in Europe somewhere after school and maybe he's still there.

I suspected he said it as a joke to deflect from whatever insecurities drove him. Make a joke so you're not the joke.

Anyway, I won't condone his state-of-mind line, but February was that—a mental state.

It wasn't a month so much as a mood, a funk that descended and blanketed everyone with its gray. You couldn't escape it. It was the weather, the environment— it was the world surrounding and pushing down on you. You could stay inside, but for how long? Could you stay away from windows that whole time? Could you not feel it leech in through the cracks to touch you with the cold?

How long could you really keep the world away?

It was like leaving a light on. Eventually, it was going to burn out and it was going to get dark. Floor of the Grand Canyon dark.

I joked and fucked around but make no mistake—it was only to keep myself together. How I dealt with the darkness. Laugh along, sure, but never mistake comedy for tragedy.

I set the alarm on my phone for 5:00 pm and dove back in for more glorious, dreamless sleep. The kind of sleep that only came from working third shift.

I worked at the Walgreens up north and I got every other week off. I worked seven twelve-hour days in a row, and then had seven days off. Twenty-six weeks off a year, plus paid vacation, sick days, and holidays.

Other people I worked third shift with couldn't sleep right away. We'd get off at 8:00 in the morning and they'd busy themselves for four or even six hours before they crashed. Not me. I'd be home by 8:15 and asleep by 8:30. Never slept better in my whole life. Then I would wake up at 5:00 in the evening and meet my friends after they got off work for dinner or to hang out for a few hours before I had to clock in.

And then there were my weeks off, when I did anything I wanted. The perfect schedule for my bachelor lifestyle.

I woke back up at 5:00 and scarfed a cold pizza breakfast while standing in front of the sink. I tried washing it down with swigs of flat Diet Coke, but it was beyond cold, the way cans can get when left opened in the fridge, so I coughed pop and pizza crust all over myself.

I took a quick, hot and pelting shower. It woke me the rest of the way up.

I called in sick to work. I'd been there over a year and had never called in before so there was no resistance at all.

I heard a strange noise, something loud but muffled, maybe. Probably one of my neighbors getting home.

When I'd moved in, I met my neighbor across the hall, a recently retired woman who'd worked with my dad for decades.

My dad had just turned fifty and lived his whole life

within a few miles of here. School, church, work—couldn't go anywhere with the fucker without him knowing somebody.

This woman staggered out of her apartment, saw my dad lugging boxes, and assumed he was moving in. Another oldster like her.

"Nope, helping my son," he said nodding his head in my direction.

I imagined what she saw. Some young punk with uncombed hair in skinny jeans and an obscure band T-shirt moving in armloads of stereo equipment and drug paraphernalia.

I smiled and asked, "Is it quiet here? The lady in the leasing office assured me it was, but it's not like she wouldn't lie to me."

She visibly relaxed.

It wasn't entirely a put-on. Quiet was important to me—I needed to sleep during the day after all.

At his point, I had lived there for a year and she was the only neighbor I ever met, but who knew their neighbors anymore? There was this dude I'd run into at the dumpster or the mailboxes or the pop machine by the pool and exchanged nods with, but I didn't think that counted.

From under the bed, I pulled out my red-leather suitcase and started arranging clothes in it. My mom picked it up at an estate sale when she learned I traveled by duffle bag. I hated when she bought me stuff, but damn I loved that suitcase.

It looked like you'd pack your life into it, or the bare essentials for a life: some durable clothes, a bottle of Johnny Walker, a notebook and a thick novel you've been putting off for years. Zip it up and hit the train station. Roll traveling montage.

A decade or so later she bought me a vintage comic book spinner rack that read WHOLESOME COMICS ARE GREAT FUN on the top in a painted metal sign. So, of course I display classic porn mags in it like *Swank*, *Velvet*, or *Clyde*. This, clearly, is the best thing she ever gave me, but I still have that cool-as-Kerouac suitcase.

I finished with the clothes and threw in some books. I was paranoid about being bored when not at home. I smiled. Booze was a great idea, so I wrapped a bottle of Johnny Walker Black in a couple thick socks and secured it inside.

I finished zipping the suitcase and there was a swift couple taps on my front door, like the former caused the latter.

What the fuck, Ben? It wasn't even 5:30.

Maybe he wanted to grab a bite before we hit the highway. I wasn't even dressed yet.

I opened the door without checking the peephole and she stood there. She gave me that smile and brushed her hand lightly over the front of my boxers as she walked past me into the apartment.

"You cannot be here right now," I said.

"Sure," she said and took her shirt off in one fluid motion. She glanced at me from over her shoulder. "Unhook my bra?"

I turned her around at the shoulders so her back was against the wall. I remembered to shut the door and lock it behind me somehow.

"Or I can leave it on," she said, and looked up at me with her face tilted down, that goddamn smile on her face.

"Do you like it? It's new."

"It's lovely, but—"

"It's a set," she said. Magically, her pants were down around her ankles.

I shook my head and placed my hands back onto her shoulders.

"I'm serious," I said. "Ben's picking me up at six. You remember Ben, right? You cannot be here."

She stepped out of her pants and got even closer to me.

"There's no time," I pleaded.

She was on her knees suddenly, like she'd been there all along. She kissed my stomach and moved her fingers lightly along my legs.

"I'm extremely horny and exceedingly wet," she said, and my boxers vanished. "We have time."

. I staggered backwards into the bedroom as she followed on her knees with my hard cock in her mouth. Unwieldly, but less than ten steps.

I sat back on the bed and she slowed her mouth rhythm on my dick and added an accompaniment of a gentle tugging on my balls.

I made some sort of familiar noise and she stopped.

I scooted back so the rest of my body was on the bed. She kicked her panties off and climbed onto me and slid my dick into her. She told the truth about this anyway— she was exceedingly wet.

She looked down at her beasts.

"I am going to leave it on," she said.

"Take it off," I said.

"No," she said and squeezed me tighter with her legs.

I sat up slightly, flipped her onto her back and thrust into her, hilt deep. She gasped and her eyes were wide.

"Take it off," I repeated, pushing into her with all my weight.

"No," she said softly between pants.

I pinned both of her wrists above her head with one hand and pulled the bra down, exposing her breasts while continuing to thrust with as much force as I could.

Her legs were wrapped around me as tight as she could manage. She stared at me with wide eyes. She never shut them during sex. Her face was damp with sweat.

I sucked on her left tit and she moaned and wriggled one hand free and brought it down to her clit. I kept her other hand pinned. I stopped sucking and pulled back, I looked at the right one. She nodded at me. I smacked it instead. She increased her frenzy. I lowered my head and sucked on the right nipple. I came quickly and she was right behind me, attempting to buck my weight off her as I stayed hard inside of her, gasping into her chest.

I laid on top of her as our breathing and heart rates slowed and she ran her hands up and down my back, lingering on my neck and head, tracing the softness of those shorter hairs.

I rolled off her.

"Fuck," one of us, maybe both, said.

"Your suitcase fell off the bed," she said.

"I would imagine so," I replied.

Why did I quit smoking this year?

"Are you leaving town forever?" she asked like she was asking me to *Pass the salt* or *Do you know the time?*

Shit. The time—

"I'm going down to Indy for Javier's wedding," I said and groped around for my phone.

"Oh yeah," she said. "I'm going to that."

"Right," I said, "well, I'll see you Saturday then."

She made a disgusted snort.

"Are you kicking me out?" she asked, full of mock outrage.

It had to be fake, right? She must've been more aware than she let on.

She smiled at me.

"What if I want you to fuck me again?" she asked.

I got out of bed and found my phone against the baseboard across the room.

"Jesus," I exhaled checking the time. "Yes, I'm kicking you out. Ben's going to be here in less than fifteen minutes."

I grabbed her shirt and pants from near the front door and tossed them behind me into the bedroom. At least I heard her getting up and the clothes rustling.

"He might be late," she said, not bothering to conceal the smirk in her voice.

"Are you fucking kidding me?" I said. I knew she was baiting me, but I was in too much of a panic to stop myself. "Ben? He's never been late for anything in his fucking life."

"Ooh," she said or maybe moaned. "You keep saying fuck."

I was well past boner territory at that point and still searched around my apartment. Where the fuck were they?

"Did you…" I trailed off.

No. It was ridiculous. Not even she would—

She came out of the bedroom, pulling her hair back into that messy ponytail bun thing I hated, fully dressed except for shoes and socks.

"You came in here barefoot?" I asked. "It's February."

She shrugged and smiled. Not the fuck me smile, the one that radiated. The one that got her out of tickets and past velvet ropes and immediately sat at any table anywhere. Or whatever she did when she wasn't here causing trouble.

"It's nice out today. I'm enjoying it," she said. "I can't believe you didn't notice when I came in."

"Uh-huh," I said. "I was a bit distracted."

I looked at the clock on my phone, looked back at her. What, did I have to do, press it into her goddamn face?

She held her left hand up as if asking for a high-five, then she rotated it back and forth slowly, bouncing light off her wedding band.

"You didn't notice this either," she said.

"I don't notice things?" I said it like a question, but it was a statement. I've never been that aware of shit around me. Too much in my own head. Too many books, too many hours spent alone. Too much pushing the world away.

"We never reached a consensus on this," she said referring to the ring. "Is it hotter if I wear it when I come here, or is it…too much?"

I waved the phone screen in front of her face. Absolutely no time for this shit right now.

"Less than ten minutes," I said.

She looked at me more coolly even though her expression didn't change.

"See you Saturday," she said and walked straight out of the apartment with no hurry in her step. Just out for a barefoot stroll in February in northeast Indiana.

I shut the door and scrambled into my boxers.

I didn't bother with the bed and righted the suitcase on the floor. On my hands and knees, I scooped and shoved everything back into the suitcase. It wouldn't close correctly anymore, so I leaned on it until it I could make the damn zipper work. It shut but wouldn't stand on its side like normal. I leaned it against the wall. It looked lumpy and weird.

I wiped on extra deodorant and spritzed cologne while I pulled on pants.

I was buttoning a dress shirt when I heard someone wriggle the front doorknob unsuccessfully, then a quick, single knock on the door.

I should've noticed that earlier. Ben always just walked in here like he's the wacky neighbor in a sitcom, like I wasn't a single guy who shits with the bathroom door open. Or fucked other people's wives.

I should've noticed, but I didn't notice things.

I unlatched the door and opened it, walking away from it so when he entered, he saw my back, and I looked like I was scrambling to get ready. Which I was but I also needed just a bit more time to compose myself.

He said something I didn't catch. I finished buttoning my shirt and slipped into the bathroom and splashed water on my face.

I'm reminded of the first time I was with her. Well, immediately afterwards anyway. I'd made some comment about other people being able to tell.

She'd shrugged.

"Then wash your dick off," she'd said.

"I'm more concerned about your pussy all over my face," I'd said.

"Oh, no," she'd said as seriously as she could manage. "I ever catch you washing that off, I'll be very offended."

I walked out of the bathroom with my face in a towel.

"Barefoot?" Ben asked.

I decided not to push the towel down my throat until I suffocated to death. I looked at him, not knowing what else to do.

"What?" was all I could manage.

He pointed at my feet.

"You're barefoot," he said. "You put your pants on before your socks?"

"Um, I guess?" I said, still unsure I was momentarily safe.

He shook his head at me as if I'd just confessed to drinking pee or something.

"Heathen. See, Aimee and I have this argument," he said. "My pants are the last thing I put on. I'll walk around for hours in just my socks and underwear."

"Gross."

He grabbed his package at me and continued. "She thinks it's weird, meanwhile her feet are always freezing."

"OK." I was really utilizing my half-finished English degree.

"When you're married," he said, pulling up his pants and nodding in a manner that was partly a put-on and partly serious, "you find dumb shit to argue about. Little things that don't mean anything so that you don't kill each other over the big shit. Like, whether to circumcise your kids or something."

I blinked at him.

"You guys only have girls," I said.

"It was an example, dipshit," he said. "I'm not going to tell you something real we fight about."

I ran a hand through my hair.

"Sorry, third shift still fucks with me sometimes," I said. "This is my morning. Early morning."

He smiled and nodded his head at me.

"Your fucking weird life," he said. "Sleeping all day, having every other week off. Living alone. Fucking a different chick all the time. You make it easy to envy you, bro."

I picked my suitcase up.

"The bro thing loses its irony if you keep using it seriously, *dude*." I said.

He continued nodding and smiling at me, not getting out of the way.

"What?" I asked. "Third shift can really suck. And I'm not fucking different chicks all the time. Living alone is pretty sweet, I will admit."

With his smile still plastered on his face, he leaned his head to the side at an exaggerated angle. He broke eye contact to look past me to the floor in front of my bed.

At her panties that were, impossibly, still there.

Lying there as if in the middle of a photo shoot for how to make something so sexy appear the exact opposite. Like a dead supermodel in a brightly lit crime scene photograph.

"Right," I said.

He clapped me on the shoulder, about-faced and

opened the front door.

"Ready to go?" he asked.

We hit a Wendy's drive-thru on the south side of town before merging with the highway. I'm sure I haven't eaten at this Wendy's every single time before hopping on I-69 south to Indianapolis, but it felt that way.

"I used to grab this every time before I came to visit you at college," Ben said, sipping from his cardboard tub of chili one-handed.

"I was just thinking the same thing," I said. "Like I'd die if I didn't eat for the hour and a half it takes to get down there."

"Eh, any excuse," he said. "Aimee doesn't let me have fast-food. The girls and I will sneak Mickey Dee's sometimes, but they usually sell me out. Are these my fries or yours?"

"Yours," I said between bites of spicy chicken sandwich. "I didn't get any."

"Blasphemy. How can you not get fries with a sandwich?" he asked.

"Fuck you," I said. "I got fried chicken and a frosty. Breakfast of champions. You're the maniac who's drinking chili while driving."

"God, I wish they'd give this to you in a drink cup," he said, "but I figured they'd freak out and put me on some kind of list if I asked."

"So, you admit you're some kind of chili pervert?"

He made an exaggerated groan as he slurped more down.

"You know, I actually thought drinking anything

while driving was illegal when I was a kid," I said. "Those fucking commercials. Very unclear when you're six and you don't know what drunk is."

He laughed, dropped his empty container into the bag, and came back up with the fries.

"I used to drink a six-pack on the way to see you," he said.

"Fuck," I said. "In less than two hours while driving?"

"Yeah, I was an alcoholic," he said.

"And now?" I asked.

"Probably, that shit never leaves you," he said. "But I quit for five years, I don't drink and drive, and I don't black out anymore. I dunno. Trying not to be uptight about it."

I remembered when he got together with Aimee, I knew his sobriety wouldn't last. She drank, it was only a matter of time. He lasted maybe another year, then it was a beer here, bottle of wine there. But he was right. It wasn't like it was before. I had plenty of dumb-shit drunk stories, but I could never do it like Ben or some of our other friends. I could never drink two days in a row, let alone if I felt sick from drink. I wasn't committed enough to make a good alcoholic. I supported him when he quit drinking and, when he started again, I wasn't sure he could find equilibrium, but I guess I didn't understand it.

"Shit," he said and nodded at a sign, but it flashed by before I caught it. "There's a White Castle down here. We should've waited."

"I have something to confess to you, dude," I said. "I didn't wait. I had cold pizza before you came over."

He nodded thoughtfully.

"And pussy," he said.

Dammit. This is what I was trying to avoid.

"Let it go," I said. "Those were probably under my bed for weeks. I accidentally unearthed them when pulling my luggage out."

"I don't know, man," he said. "Your apartment was cloudy with fuck-fumes."

"What I was trying to say," I said, "is if you want to get a couple of sliders, I'm down."

"Maybe on the way back," he said. "You eat like a fucking trash-compactor. Where do you put this shit?"

"My grandma says I have hollow legs," I said.

"Uh huh."

I didn't say that the stress of lying—even through omission—was like a living thing, a fluid that coursed through my system and ate all the fat in my body. Probably muscles and other vital things as well. I couldn't bring myself to deal with it, so I pushed these things down until the next time I couldn't sleep or showered or ate alone or nothing was on TV or I couldn't focus on a book. Any time when the loneliness crippled and I couldn't escape my own brain, it would be there waiting for me with the rest of the poison thoughts, the shitty things I had done to other people, the things I should or shouldn't have said. Opportunities missed. Mistakes made. My impending and inevitable demise.

Nothing ever left you.

"We just missed the exit, anyway," Ben said. "No sliders sliding out of our assholes tonight. And since we're sharing a hotel room maybe it's for the best."

"That was the Daleville one anyway," I said. "It's always full of creatures from the outlet mall across the road. I'd rather eat at the Anderson one. At least those monsters are home-grown and live under nearby rocks."

"I thought it was Deanville," Ben said.

"Why would you think that?" I asked.

"Isn't that where James Dean was from?" he asked completely serious.

"You think James Dean is from a place called Deanville? You can't be that stupid," I said.

"Fuck off," he said. "They renamed the town after he died. Deanville or Deantown—"

"Deanton?" I tried.

"Or," he continued louder, "he had a weird name, so he took the name of the town when he went to Hollywood."

"Jesus, stay off the internet," I said. "Where do you get this shit? His name was always James Dean and he was from Fortville. We passed it, like, twenty miles ago."

"Shit. I should have snapped a picture of the sign for my sister," he said. "She loves James Dean."

"Megan or Ellen?"

"Ellie," he said. "She'd always say she had a huge girl-boner for him. She'd say this shit when she was like ten years old. My parents would go fucking nuts. They'd get so mad at her."

We laughed.

"I think they're both coming to the wedding on Saturday," he said.

"Your parents?" I asked. "Even your dad?"

"No, no. Of course not. Dunno what he's up to and I don't care. My sisters—Meg and Ellie," he said. "I don't know if they're coming down with the Redneck Twins or maybe with Aimee and Amy."

We called his sisters' husbands the Redneck Twins, not because they were related prior to marriage, but because they were redneck-y and eerily similar to each other. Like his older sister Meg made a stupid mistake and then the younger one Ellie thought, *Sure, I'll make the same one.*

"Remember when you slept with Javier's sister?" I asked. Seemed like a good time to fuck with him.

He looked at me for an uncomfortable amount of time. Like we were playing chicken. I pointed towards the road without breaking eye contact.

"Why would you bring that shit up?" he asked. "We're going to the man's fucking wedding. She's definitely going to be there. My wife's going to be there. Aimee fucking hates her."

"Yeah probably," I said.

"Jesus, why did I ever tell you that?" he grumbled.

"You were bragging?" I hazarded. "Look, no judgment. She's fucking hot dude, and she was smoking-hot then, I just wondered if you ever felt bad about it."

"Why?" he seemed shocked. "She was eighteen."

"Right, but she'd had a crush you forever," I said. "You were what? Twenty-four?"

He shifted in his seat.

"I'm pretty sure she was more mature than I was, at that point in my life," he said flatly.

"I'm serious. I'm not judging you or trying to give you shit. Well, not entirely," I said. "You know what I mean. It's not like when you turn eighteen a switch flips and, suddenly, you're an adult. I just wondered if you ever thought about it."

He softened in his posture slightly and exhaled.

"I, um," I faltered as I attempted to relate to him. "I had sex with a sixteen-year-old. She was my girlfriend and I was the same age. But it bothers me sometimes."

"Right," he said. "I get it. I don't really think about it. I was pretty fucked-up then. It's not an excuse, but you know what I mean. Plus, I try not to remember the act at all. She was so ... I lasted, like, two minutes."

I laughed.

"Oh, fuck you," he said. "You brought this shit up."

"Sorry, sorry," I said. Then after a beat, "Two minutes?"

"Jesus, God. At the absolute outside," he said. "Her pussy, fuck. That shit broke me. I tried to get her to stay and give me a little reset time, but she said Nope, I got what I wanted, and she just turned and walked out of there."

"Huh," I said. "Guess she was just getting you out of her system. Probably good for her that you weren't any good at it so she could move on."

He flipped me off.

"Does Javier know all this?" I asked.

"All of it?" his voice nearly cracked. "I hope not. I'm pretty sure he knows I fucked her, though."

"Yeah?"

"Yeah, I think she told him, or hinted at it or something," he said. "A couple months later, we were hanging out and he started joking about fucking Meg or Ellie, you know, how we do when we run out of material on our mothers. Anyway, I was playing along and then he swerved and caught me off me guard. He said, Why not? You fucked Gina."

"Shit," I said.

"Yeah, but even then, I think he was fucking with me, we were still joking around," he said. "Like maybe she told him, but he didn't really believe it, or she hinted at it and he wasn't sure. But I totally whiffed it. I should have agreed and been like Yeah, I fucked her just this morning, smell my finger. Instead I got defensive and started denying it up and down. I could tell. I could see it in his face that he was sure now."

"Ah, man," I said.

"Yup. We never talked about it again," he said.

"Did that bother you?" I asked. "It's the man's sister."

He shrugged.

"Fuck that," he said. "I feel bad lying to him, but that's it. Meg and Ellie can fuck whoever they want."

"They're both married," I said.

"Yeah, to couple of retards and I never complained," he said. "Well, not to them, anyway. Besides, the shit we know Javier's done?"

"That is true," I said.

We drove in silence for a minute or so. The sun was long down by now and in-between cities the sky was as black as the two lanes of the highway. The worn painted dashes chopped by at a rhythmic clip broken up every once and awhile by the soft, twin red dots of taillights. It was so regular, so automatic, we'd both driven this stretch countless times—separately, together, in larger groups—that we couldn't even really see it anymore. It flowed past us like air. If we were in some strange sci-fi simulation of this highway, a tight loop or Möbius-strip, a never-ending treadmill for Ben's SUV, I don't think either of us would notice until the sun came back up.

I worried I soured him with all my talk of Gina. All

my questions. Like a kid that comes home from school and says *They're going to tell you I did something bad, but I swear I didn't do it!*

I couldn't help myself. I was usually good at secrets, but this one ... I felt it unraveling.

"It's weird to me that you don't have your pickup truck anymore," I said. "This thing is so ... family friendly."

He made a little grunt. He either agreed with me or he didn't.

"I'm gonna put my iPod on," he said.

It was only thirty minutes or so, but we didn't talk the rest of the way.

We checked in at a Holiday Inn Express very close to where I used to live with Estella on the north side of Indianapolis. Not the suburbs like Fishers or Carmel, but in the city. Right at 86th Street where I-69 narrows into Binford and there's the interchange for the 465 loop. Pretty far north, but good access to different routes, since we had a bunch of different shit to do all over town for the next couple days.

Ben booked the hotel before he'd even called me and wouldn't take any money for it. He got some deal through his work or something. Whatever, I'd buy him a couple of drinks later to even it out. I didn't like owing people, even if they didn't see it that way.

We still had an hour or two before the bachelor party congealed, so we took our shoes off and stretched out in the room. Ben turned the TV on but muted the volume. I showed him the bottle of scotch.

He nodded his agreement.

"Nice," he said and leapt to his feet. "I'll get some ice."

Ben dropped in a few ice cubes and I poured a couple glugs of the good stuff into those shitty plastic cups they give you at hotels. We attempted to clink them anyway. It was extremely unsatisfying, so I said, "Clink," out loud before I took my first sip.

"You should text Estella," Ben said. "See what she's up to."

I fluffed a pillow behind me.

"It's a weeknight," I said. "She's probably watching TV before she goes to bed."

He laughed.

"Oh, did I bring up something you don't want to talk about?" he asked.

"I don't care," I said. "I'll talk about her."

"Just not to her," he said.

"What's the point?" I said. "We've got a bachelor party in like an hour."

"There's always afterwards," he said.

"Did you actually just fucking wink at me?" I asked.

"I thought you guys were still friends, is all," he said.

I took another sip.

"We're friendly," I said. "We're not really friends anymore. I wouldn't even know how to do that."

He gripped his Dixie cup in his teeth and mimed an index finger penetrating a circle of thumb and forefinger.

"You're cut off," I said, and pulled the bottle across the nightstand until it was firmly on my side.

"Well," he said, "You're going to have to see her at the wedding anyway. She's going right?"

"Huh," I said. "I don't know. I guess, maybe? She was going to at one point."

He took a sip, arched his eyebrows and pointed at my phone. I played dumb.

"Find out," he said.

"All right, all right," I said.

"Unless you want me to do it, like we're in grade school. Passing notes and shit," he said.

"Fuck off, I'll text her in a minute," I said.

He stretched over for the bottle, poured himself much less than I had given him.

"She seeing anybody?" he asked.

I sighed.

"Hey, you brought up Gina earlier," he said. "Comeuppance."

"Hoisted by my own petard," I said.

"Ah," he said, bowing to the better turn of phase.

"And yeah, I think so," I said. "She was anyway. We do talk on the phone occasionally. It does become difficult to fill two weeks off a month. Wouldn't Aimee know?"

"Probably, but nobody tells me shit," he said.

He got up and went into the bathroom. He pissed with the door open like we were in our teens again, staying in a much worse hotel after seeing a too-loud concert.

"You hear from Jake or Niedz yet?" I asked. They were friends, sorta, but of the extended kind so I didn't even have their numbers. A general rule: if I referred to a guy by his last name, then I probably didn't know him that well. Or care to.

"Nope," he said and flushed. I could hear him washing his hands, so he hadn't completely reverted into his teenage self.

I fired off a quick text to Estella before he came out of the bathroom, so I didn't have him watching me do it.

whats up? in indy for Javier's wedding. what you doing?

Then I followed it quickly with

down early w/ ben for bachelor party & rehearsal stuff

"What'd she say?" Ben asked, plopping down on his bed.

"Dude, I just fucking sent it," I said. But, of course, as soon as I said that, she responded.

He made a face like Well, look at that.

I poured myself another scotch.

"You have the most annoying text message sound in the world," he said.

"What, the meow? Yeah, my mom's cat fucking hates it. I originally selected it like a joke. You always hear people's phone chirping, so I thought the next time I hear that I'm going to turn the volume all the way up so I can piss them off too," I said.

"But?"

"It kinda grew on me," I said. "Like if you watch bad movies to laugh at them and then you soon realize all you watch is bad movies and you now enjoy them as cinema because you're not watching anything else."

"You should probably change that tone," he said.

"Agreed," I said, but knew I wouldn't.

I noticed that he'd mostly finished his second drink and had pushed it away from himself, out of easy reach.

Alright. Look at the damn thing before he starts in.

It read

cool. whatre you guys doin?

Then

they invited me but don't know if ill go.

Ignore that bit for now. I wasn't sure if I even wanted her there. Weddings tend to make ladies horny, everyone knows that, but I hadn't been with Estella since we broke up and I didn't really think I wanted to.

I mean, I wanted to, but it wasn't a good idea. We are still friends, even if I blew that suggestion off earlier, and we were friends before, and I fucked that up by sleeping with her. And then after a few years of dating and feeling suffocated I fucked it up again, so she'd have an excuse to leave.

"What'd she say, playa?" Ben asked.

I shrugged.

"Nothing," I said. "She doesn't know if she'll go on Saturday."

"Sure," he said, "I get it. She knows she wouldn't be able to stay off of you."

I laughed.

"Not really, man," I said. "That's over. It was a bad idea to begin with, I think."

"Didn't you guys date for like five years?" he asked.

"Eh, four-ish, I think," I said. "But we were friends for a while before that. Really close. And we lost that friendship or most of it and that was the important part. At the time, it finally seemed like serendipity. We'd never been single at the same time before. I was stupid and lonely, and I knew her very well. I should have gone somewhere else. It isn't hard to get ass, let's be honest. Everybody's looking for the same thing."

"I knew it," he said and shook his head at me, a

triumphant look on his face. "A different chick every week."

I tipped my glass at him.

"Sometimes," I admitted.

I didn't tell him how I found it depressing sometimes. Depressing because I didn't like myself very much and I felt like I was conning women into liking me, and then hating them a little because they were stupid enough to be duped. How could they really like me? How could anyone?

My phone meowed again.

"Ask her if we can get ready at her place on Saturday," he said and picked up the remote, absently flipping the channels.

"What?"

"Yeah," he said. "We gotta check out at noon on Saturday, grab lunch and then be at the church in a couple hours."

"She doesn't even live over here anymore," I said. "She's east off the loop somewhere, I think."

"Perfect," he said. "We gotta head that way to get to the church anyway."

"Why don't we go to Niedz's or something?" I asked, running out of excuses.

He made a face like somebody farted.

"Those fucking hedonists?" he said. "Wouldn't you rather get ready in a bathroom maintained by a lady than fucking Niedz or Jake? Imagine the smells."

I opened my mouth, but he cut me off.

"And I don't want to get ready at the church," he said. "There's always a suite for the ladies and then a drain on a bare concrete floor for the dudes."

I put my hands up in surrender. "All valid points."
I checked my phone. Estella had said
who you guys staying w/?
And
we should get lunch or something if youve time
"You're a fucking mind reader, dude," I said.

I told her the situation and asked her if we could borrow her nice flowery, feminine bathroom to get ready in peace and tranquility. Or whatever the hell Ben thought it was he was looking for.

I didn't think he was attempting to play a misguided matchmaker. Although I explained the situation after he suggested all this shit, so pride or simply being in too deep could've prevented him from backing off now.

I could see Aimee or Amy putting him or Mark up to it, but I could also see them making excuses or nodding in consent and then never going through with it. That was more of their respective styles.

I wished Mark was here too. Then it'd really feel like we were teenagers again road-tripping down here to see NIN or Tool or whoever. Ah. Nostalgia for the late '90s. I've become an old fucking man.

But Mark's not here for Javier's bachelor party or rehearsal dinner because he had to work. Meanwhile, I called in sick at the drop of a hat to hang out and see my friends. I'm not even the one in the wedding. I didn't know whose priorities are more screwed-up. It's not like he didn't have ample notice to take a couple days off.

So, what am I, the fucking groomsman-alternate? That's not even a thing, right?

Estella responded.

"She says yes," I said. "And, oh shit! She suggests

Yats for lunch on Saturday."

"Fuck yes," he said. "That'll make all this wedding bullshit worth it."

He'd get no arguments from me.

"I thought of the Chili Cheese Etouffee just now and my mouth started watering," I said.

"Jambalaya," he purred.

We both zoned out for a bit, fantasizing over Cajun food as the TV strobed in the background and the spent ice melted in our cheap plastic cups until Niedz texted Ben.

"I can drive," I said, "if you're tired from the trip."

He shook his head.

"They're gonna pick us up," he said. "We traveled. They get to schlep us around."

I nodded but would've rather driven. Now we were going to be at the mercy of someone else's timetable all night.

I let out a slow breath without drawing attention to it and tried to talk myself into being cool with the situation.

It was fine. It didn't matter where you went or how long it took. You had nothing to come back to but a gaudy hotel room. Stop worrying about shit. Get drunk. See your friends. Get out of your fucking head. Ogle strippers or flirt with club girls or whatever the hell you were going to do. It didn't matter. It was all either friends you've had for years or people you would never see again.

Relax, goddammit.

Ben went into the bathroom to check in with Aimee. I couldn't hear anything distinct in his bass tones rumbling through the thin hotel wall. It might've been a hushed argument. I tried to block it out. Not my business.

I didn't like eavesdropping.

He emerged after another minute.

"Stay single," he said.

If he wanted to tell me he would. Instead, he said, "They're five minutes away. Let's wait in the lobby."

In the elevator, we decided against a drink at the bar while we waited and then regretted it as five minutes became ten minutes and then fifteen.

"Well, these chairs are comfortable," I said, feeling like a child in the huge overstuffed lounge chairs. I imagined myself kicking my feet inches above the floor, a stupid look of wonderment on my face.

"Finally," Ben said, popped up and slid his phone into his pocket. He brushed past a flustered looking family with too many bags and out the doors. I followed him.

We clamored into the back of Niedz's SUV—does everybody have these stupid things now?—and time sped up.

We caught up and bullshitted as we drove into downtown, the music loud enough that we were all shouting at each other. We picked Jake up at his building. He was waiting for us—miraculously on time—and then we angled west towards Broad Ripple because, apparently, we thought we were still in college. We darted in and out of traffic and swerved around already drunk pedestrians and somehow found a parking spot only two blocks from our first destination. Jake had a flask with him, and we'd passed it around in the car even though Niedz was clearly uncomfortable with this but said nothing about it. We kept tossing it back and forth as we strolled. I tried not to think about how bad I wanted a cigarette. At least nobody else was smoking yet. Niedz coughed after taking a huge pull off the flask.

"This shit's terrible," he said.

Jake nodded.

"You guys don't recognize it?" he asked.

"Gasoline?" I guessed.

"Bum piss?" somebody else said.

He held it up to the sky with his arm fully extended.

"Ten-High Whiskey!" he shouted like a lunatic.

"Oh, OK, so only poison, then," Ben said.

"You're out of your fucking mind," I offered.

Jake laughed.

"You idiots are drinking it too," he said.

"Is that the shit you barfed on somebody?" Niedz asked, directing it towards Ben.

Jake laughed harder.

"It was a window," Ben said. "One of those half-basement things."

"Yeah," I said, "my fucking neighbor's window."

"It was so soon after I drank it, it was still cold," Ben marveled.

"Ten-High?" Niedz said. "Is that a poker reference? Because that's a terrible poker hand."

"Is that the same time you dumped a bag of garbage on that same neighbor's front-steps?" I asked Ben.

"Maybe?"

"I feel like a pussy admitting this," I said, "but I helped them clean the trash up the next day."

They all groaned at my sorta act of kindness.

"What?" I said. "I went out the next morning for a smoke after you motherfuckers all left, and she was standing there gazing down at it in disbelief. I had to pretend like 'Oh shit, that sucks, let me help you.'"

"Wasn't it a sorority or something?" Jake asked. "Did you bang any of them?"

"It was, and no I didn't," I said. "They were all irritating. That's why we talked Ben into dumping garbage on their steps."

Ben mimed pushing Jake away from him.

"Don't let me have any more of that shit," he said or maybe repeated.

We rounded the corner and arrived at Olde Point Tavern or OPTs as everybody called it. There were more people outside smoking than inside, but it was barely ten so that seemed about right. It'd pick up later.

Ben beelined to the bar and bought us all beers before anybody else could get shots or something worse.

We found Javier's younger brothers and somebody I think I recognized as his cousin playing darts in the back. Glancing at the chalk scoreboards, I assumed they'd never done this before.

"Where's Javi?" somebody asked.

One of his brothers shrugged. Chris? Brad? They both had Anglo-names so I could never remember who was who.

"He's late," the brother said.

"It's his fucking party," Ben said, unable to comprehend why any person was ever late for any reason. Well, men anyway. He's married, so he understood late women.

"He's always late," the other brother said.

They seemed overly focused on their darts, so I meandered towards a pool table and put a dollar on it and exchanged nods with the dudes currently playing. I went to the bar and drilled holes into the back of the bartender's head, willing the fucker to turn around. I scanned the bar and the room. Sausage fest.

I ordered a beer when the bartender decided I existed. Jake immediately sat next to me.

"Make it two," I said to the aloof prick's back.

Jake nodded thanks and clapped me on the back. "How was the drive?"

"Fine, not as boring when you have someone else to bullshit with," I said.

The bartender slid a beer in front of each of us. So at least he wasn't deaf.

"Nine," he said.

I had exact change, or I had a ten. I could've given him the extra dollar to try to grease any future transactions and get this guy to fucking pay attention to me. There were six of us there so I wouldn't be buying many rounds and when I did, I'd have had a group backing that were too rowdy to ignore. Plus, how long would we stay in this one place?

Eh, fuck him.

I counted out exactly nine dollars onto the bar top silently while eyeball fucking the asshole. He scooped them up and waltzed away.

"You know that guy?" Jake asked me.

"I don't think so," I said. "Maybe. I used to come in here a lot a couple years ago."

He made a face like *And?* to get more out of me.

"I don't like him," I said. "He's trying to ignore me."

"Great," Jake said and sipped his beer. "And now he associates me with your cheap ass. I'm fucked when I have to get my rounds."

"But he started it," I said in my best whiniest bitch-voice.

We both laughed.

I caught him up on my shit, he caught me up on his. I didn't remember the last time I saw him, so I was pretty sure I told him stuff he already knew. It seemed rude to ask as he talked about people and events as if I should know what he was saying, as if he was telling me the punch lines to jokes he'd set up months ago but I was too wrapped in myself to remember. Or maybe he was faking it too and he was plowing through his recent history in the hope I wouldn't notice.

"Where the fuck is Mark?" he asked. "Didn't he come down with you guys?"

I shook my head. "He had to work, I guess. Won't be down until Saturday."

Jake made a face like I'd just answered on *Jeopardy!* without forming it into a question.

"We all have to work," he said. "What kind of excuse is that? He's in the fucking wedding."

I shrugged.

One of the guys from the pool table threw me a friendly elbow as he went past. They were done.

I stood up. "Pool?"

"Yeah," Jake said.

"At least Mark's not here for this," I said picking out a cue. "We had a two-hour game one time because we were both so terrible."

"I see...you wanna make this one more interesting?"

I laughed. "Fuck you, no. I would like to play cutthroat if you wanna grab Niedz or Ben or somebody."

He made a loud yelping noise until Niedz was the first to look over. He acted out and shouted the word,

"Cutthroat!" until he finally strolled over and then had to explain it to him all again.

"It's the three-player pool one," I said, attempting to simplify. "You either get one through five, six through ten or eleven through fifteen. Try and sink the balls that aren't yours. If you scratch, the other two get to take a ball out of the pocket. Last one standing with any balls wins. You down?"

"Sure," he said without seeming like he really got it.

I racked while they chalked their cue tips.

"One of you break," I said. "And be gentlemen about it. Just decide. It's a friendly game."

Niedz's hand slowly retreated from his pocket. He wanted to flip for it, but none of this mattered. We were just fucking around. The last thing we needed tonight, when I was already picking fights with bartenders, were competitive dudes headbutting over a friendly game of pool. I mean, it was called cutthroat, so I guess it was kind of baked-in.

"Go ahead," Jake said and gestured his cue at Niedz.

While he was lining up his shot and taking forever, Jake continued our earlier conversation as if no time had elapsed. He always talked like this and you had to struggle to keep up and remember what the conversation was about. Sometimes hours or even days later.

"I just can't believe he didn't come down," he said. "And not even tomorrow for the rehearsal and everything?"

I shrugged. "I dunno, man. I agree it's a little thin."

Niedz broke. Nothing went in. I nodded at Jake to go.

"Thin?" he said. "It's fucking rude."

"What are we talking about?" Niedz said. It was

practically his catchphrase.

"Mark," Jake said, and sank the nine ball. "He's not here until Saturday and he's in the wedding. I'll take one through five."

"Isn't the wedding on Saturday?" Niedz asked.

Jake and I exchanged a quick glance. Niedz was an imposing and good-looking guy, but I could never tell if he spoke before he thought or if he never really thought at all.

Jake was more patient with him than I would've been. And Ben—he gave him constant shit.

"Yeah," Jake said, managing to not sound like he was explaining it to a child. "But he's missing all of this stuff. The real shit."

"Like stimulating conversation," I said, mostly to myself.

The five ball went in on my first shot and Jake casually flipped me off.

"I'll take eleven through fifteen," I said while scratching my nose with a middle finger in his direction.

"We all know the real reason he's not here," Jake said as Niedz was lining up his shot. "It's Amy. She keeps him on a short leash. She can be such a bitch."

Niedz whiffed and his cue bit into the felt. He made reflexive eye contact with me and then looked away quickly.

Jake laughed.

"Take another shot," he said. "you didn't hit anything in play."

If Jake noticed the look Niedz and I had just shared, he showed no sign of it. Why did we share a look? I've never really thought much of the big, handsome idiot, but there was something in his eyes just then. Some sign of life, even if I don't know what it meant.

Niedz shot again, barely getting the two ball to drop, but drop it did. Even ugly shots counted.

"Shit," Jake said. "And I told you to take the mulligan."

Lining up his own, Jake jumped back into it. "I'm serious about Amy. She's always picking at Mark and fighting with him and shit. I was in town and we went to see this band. I mean, we invited her, but she didn't wanna go. So, we went, and she was texting him and calling him constantly trying to get him to come home. What is that shit?"

Now Niedz was avoiding us. With his posture, he completely faced away from us, focusing on his beer.

Jake missed a shot.

"We've known Amy forever," I said. "She's always been like that. I mean I feel bad for the guy, but what was he expecting?"

I missed my shot too.

"Maybe he should just cheat on her, if that's how she treats him," I said. This was not the territory I wanted to dive into, obviously, but fuck it—let's see what kind of reaction it got. I also wanted to see what was bothering Niedz.

Unknown—his back was still to us.

"Niedz," I said.

"Huh?"

I pointed at the table.

"You're up, dude."

He turned around.

"Cheat on her?" Jake laughed. "He's too fucking

loyal. Plus, she probably smells his dick when he gets home."

Niedz white-knuckled the pool cue. What the fuck was going on in the big man's head? His raw nerves started to make me nervous.

"Alright, lay off," I said to Jake. "Amy's our friend, too."

Jake made a *So what?* face at me.

"You're hurting Niedz's sense of chivalry," I said because I couldn't help it.

Niedz ignored me, tapped the fifteen in and missed his follow up.

"Yeah," Ben said coming up from behind us. "Lay off my wife, asshole."

"Not Aimee," I said, drawling out the Es. "Y-Amy."

"Oh," he said and leaned against a tall table. "Then bitch away. And I'm sure you guys were badmouthing me before I strolled over."

I shook my head.

"It's not all about you, Truman," I said.

He made a jerk off motion in my direction.

In the late summer of '98, we'd piled in the back of Ben's old pickup and drove up to the Auburn drive-in for a double feature of *The Truman Show* and the first *X-Files* movie. After *The Truman Show*, Ben became convinced that it was like his life—that we were all actors and he really didn't have any friends. He wouldn't fucking shut up about it all night. He was impossibly drunk. I think he finally forgot this particular delusion when the Foo Fighters' "Walking After You" played through the *X-Files* credits and he started singing along and reminiscing about when we all saw them with Ben Folds Five a couple of months prior.

I reflexively checked Ben's drink.

I was pretty sure he was still on his first beer, and barely through the neck. He was getting good at nursing them. Better late than never.

Jake dropped three balls. Two of Niedz and one of mine. I only had thirteen and fourteen left, Niedz was down to just the six. Jake still had the one, three and four balls. Somehow, nobody had scratched yet.

Jake missed his fourth shot.

Jake and Ben laughed about something, general fucking around. Javi still wasn't around and I didn't see his brothers. They'd reeked of stogies when I said hi to them, so they were probably outside smoking. The cousin was at the bar chatting up some chick. She seemed impressed when he pointed to his Mets hat. That's right. He was from New York. I wondered where Lisa's brother was, whatever his name was—probably with Javier.

I could've probably taken Niedz out, but I needed him to help me take down Jake first. Eh, fine—the six was the easiest shot. And with my next shot I sent one of my own balls in and scratched.

"Dammit," I said. It meant Niedz was back in play and he could place the ball anywhere on the table.

He immediately sank my last remaining ball and smiled. I blew him a kiss.

I mimed washing my hands of the whole thing and turned towards the bar.

Ben made a pouty face and traced a single imaginary tear trickling down his cheek.

"Fuck you, it was my dollar," I said. "And you're not even playing."

It looked like they finally added another person behind the bar, so I angled towards her rather than my buddy at the other end.

She smiled back at me and gave me the *Just a minute eyes*. She got the relaxed *No problem* thumbs up from me.

She came over and I leaned in and posted up for a high five. She reciprocated with only the slightest of bewildered looks on her face. She still smiled though.

"Oh, I'm sorry," I said. "Don't I know you?"

"I don't think so," she said.

"Oops. I thought I've seen you in The Alley Cat a few times," I said, picking a dive-bar without a sign that usually fills up late into the night with bartenders and wait staff from other places around here.

This was not the first time I'd used this trick.

She nodded and tried to place me, but of course couldn't. I could practically see her deciding it was her own faulty memory.

"Yeah, OK," she said. "Sorry. Remind me of your name?"

"No worries," I said. "Kyle."

"Can I get you a drink, Kyle?" she asked.

"Killian's, please," I said.

She returned quickly with an open bottle. I slid a five towards her across the bar.

"This one's on me," she said.

I nodded at her.

"Thanks," I said, and nodded towards the bill on the scuffed and scratched surface of the bar. "Then I guess your next one is on me."

I turned around before we could have a playful argument about it and headed back towards my friends.

Niedz cut me off as soon as I'd cleared the bar area.

"Kyle," he said and nodded, the tone of his voice betrayed nothing. It was flat and cool.

I realized in that moment, that Niedz and I had never been alone together. Did that make him less than a friend? A friend of a friend or an acquaintance?

How many couple friends did Estella and I used to hang out with but the guys from those relationships and I never did anything else outside of those interactions? In fact, they were Estella's friends and I never saw any of them after we broke up.

Back to Niedz and I: had we ever had a one-on-one conversation? It seemed impossible that we wouldn't have, but I could find no evidence of one in my memory.

But I was thinking all this, and not responding to him and he was starting to look at me strangely.

"What's up, Niedz? Did Jake win?"

"You can't stop yourself, can you?" he asked me and pointed towards the female bartender.

I smiled.

"She's an old friend," I said.

"What's her name?"

I should probably figure that out.

I looked around like I was confused. "Are you busting my balls for flirting with a waitress? I'm trying to get us some service in this dump."

He nodded. He'd acquired Jake's flask somehow and he sipped from it nonchalantly, as if you're allowed to do that in a bar or as if it wasn't full of poisoned rat piss.

"Careful," I said. "Someone might see you."

He smiled and leaned forward, crowding me.

"You be careful," he said in a quieter voice.

I did my best to play dumb, but the big guy clearly knew something.

"I don't know what you mean," I said lamely, but looked him in the eye when I said it.

"What was that shit you were talking about Amy over there?" he asked jerking his head towards the pool tables.

"Uh, that was Jake, man," I said. "He just wishes Mark was here. He's blowing off steam. He didn't mean anything."

"Right," he said and kept staring at me. He was standing too close, I had to take a step away from him to sip my beer.

"I don't know what you mean," I repeated because I couldn't think of anything else to say.

He maintained eye contact for another beat, then tipped Jake's flask up and polished it off. He handed me the empty thing and I accepted it reflexively. He headed off towards the restrooms.

I felt worried for the first time since Ben was ten minutes from my apartment.

What did Niedz know—or think he knew?

Ben and Jake came over.

"Jesus," Ben said. "Did you finish that?"

I realized I was holding the flask upside down.

"No. Niedz," I said.

Jake laughed.

"That fucker can drink any and everything," Ben said, shaking his head. "And never seem drunk. Remember that lake party after high school when him and Mark took those double shots of One-Fifty-One? Towards the end of the night? Ha! I thought Mark was gonna puke his organs out. But Niedz? Nothing. A brick wall, that mother fucker."

We laughed.

"That was the first time I took Estella to a real party," I said before I could stop myself. "She tried to match me drink for drink that first night. She got so sick. She barfed when we tried to have sex."

"That could be from something else," Ben said.

I flipped them both off.

"It was your parents lake house, asshole," I said to him. "And I didn't clean any of that puke up."

"Aw, you probably got me grounded," he said.

"I don't think I'd met her yet." Jake said.

"That's right, that's right," I said. "You and—what was her name?—came up on Saturday."

"Jenny," he said, and put his head in his hands.

"Right, Jenny. What a fucking mess that one was," I said chuckling. "So, Estella has an all-day hangover Saturday and tries to recover in that room, while the cottage fills with more and more people and everyone's like, 'Is your new girlfriend here? Where is she?' and they just catch glimpses of her as she floats from the bedroom to the bathroom to puke more."

I pause and we all sip our beers and stare backwards through the years.

"Good times."

Jake nodded. "I hated her. I couldn't understand why she wouldn't come out and talk to us. Or even meet us."

"Yeah," I said, laughing. "I'm sure it tortured her for years."

"You should call her and see if she wants to come down," Ben said.

What was with him and this shit?

"Dude, it's a bachelor party," I said.

"It's a sausage fest," Jake said.

"It's after ten," I said.

"Javier's not even here," Ben said.

"I think his brothers left, too," Jake said.

I felt my phone buzz in my pocket. Then Jake said "Drinks?" and pointed at the two of us and raised his eyebrows and spun towards the bar without waiting for an answer. Ben said something like, "Drain the Entertainer," and loped towards the restrooms. I was alone in the middle of a public place without even a drink, so I checked my phone. It was Estella. *What are you bachelors doin?* and I told her and she said *Of course Javi's not there yet* and I said *I know, right?* and I asked her to come by *Everyone would love to see you* I said and there was this long pause and was it actually longer than any of the pauses so far? I was very alone standing there in the dimness of the bar without my friends and I knew even if they were there I would still feel alone even if I was among them even if I smiled and laughed and traded barbs and bought drinks and received drinks. I was alone and I always felt alone most in a crowded room. I also knew it wouldn't help to text Estella or to talk to her or see her or fuck her or fight with her or anything she could give me. I could feel these things in the middle of the night, woken up by these thoughts and feelings and existential dreads and I could wake her and she could hold me and tell me everything I needed to hear and listen to my ramblings and she could understand me as she was capable of and very likely there was no one else in the whole world that knew me as well as she did.

And it would not matter.

It would not be enough.

I would start to feel better, yes, with her touch and her soothing words and understanding face. But these are not the reasons I would feel better. I would feel better only because I couldn't feel that bad all the time. It wasn't possible to feel like this all the time and live through it. It would grind you to dust. It would pulverize you. It would crush you to a clump or burst you into pieces.

My phone buzzed again, and I checked it.

i'd like see you

she said. Then

but just you. meet me at Bruges?

"Fuck," I said to no one.

I shouldn't have said anything. She was already misinterpreting my intentions. She sniffed out my sad need to connect with somebody who sort of knew me.

I thought about earlier that day when I wasn't thinking of Estella at all, when I was sleeping with another man's wife and why I was so scared Ben would find us together. There were the obvious, practical, confrontational reasons I didn't want us discovered. But that really wasn't it, was it? Once that bandage's off then you're out of excuses to not be together, like a real couple. A choice must be made.

And then I'd have to really look at her and I'd see too much of myself and I'd run for my fucking life.

I texted her back

yup. leavin OPTs now

because I started it and what else was I supposed to do? Say *Psych! I was just fucking with you! Idiot!*

I slipped my phone back into my pocket and headed towards the door. I saw Ben and nodded at him. He weaved over.

"I'm gonna go for a walk," I said.

"Yeah?" he said slyly.

"Yes," I lied, "just a walk. I haven't been back down here since I moved home. I want to look around. See if that hotdog guy is still around."

He shook his head.

"Your fucking metabolism," he said. "Save room for Paco's later."

I cradled my stomach and pursed my lips. "Oh, I always do. Are we heading to the Vogue next?"

He shrugged.

"Let me know if Javi shows or you guys bail for somewhere else," I said and stepped out into the night.

I swerved around and stepped over people drunker than me, or at least pretending to be. I smelled weed from somewhere close—not as common of a smell in public then as it is now, reserved mostly for house parties and concerts or festivals.

I darted across the street, while a guy on a bicycle stood in the crosswalk shouting hard at a red-faced man in a Saturn, whose windows were rolled up tight.

I slipped between buildings, cut through a parking lot and picked up the trail that ran behind the classier side of this clusterfuck.

It was mid-February and unseasonably warm tonight, but still the patios remained mostly unused, a few stragglers here and there smoking, or speaking firmly into clenched cell phones.

I went in through the kitchen entrance because it was

closer to the bar and it avoided the waiting area and the hostesses. The bar was seat yourself but the tables in the bar were not. Most people didn't know this, and somebody was bound to open their stupid mouth and ruin my instant seating trick if a room full of idiots saw me waltz past them when they'd been waiting two or more hours. When I used to live here, they let me stand at one end or other of the bar without a seat and munch fries, but I doubt any of those late-night barroom heroes were still on staff.

Estella was somehow already here.

I saw her back as soon as I ducked in. She sat at the far right of the bar with her purse on the empty stool next to her. There were no other vacant seats in the place.

I tapped her on the right shoulder and then came in from the left. Miraculously, she always fell for this.

"How'd you beat me here?" I asked her after we exchanged a hug and pleasantries. "And are you drinking wine?"

She sipped from her glass daintily a pinky extended and everything.

"Fancy," I agreed.

"I ordered you a Guinness," she said. "And frites, if you want any."

"Fuck yeah I do," I said.

"I was already out," she said. "Like a block away."

"On a Thursday? When did you get so cool?" I asked.

She stuck her tongue out at me.

I reevaluated her clothes. Under her burgundy pea coat, she was sort of dressed up, especially for a weeknight. I raised my eyebrows at her.

"Oh shit. You were on a date," I said.

She wiggled her free hand back and forth as she took another sip of wine.

"Eh," she said. "It's not gonna go anywhere,"

"Sorry…?" I offered.

"It's fine," she said, "everybody's into these group meet-up things. Like, real casual so no one has to say it's a date. There're so many moving parts. Exhausting."

"Sounds awful."

"It really is," she agreed and nodded. "And my ex showed up and made everything worse."

My Guinness materialized in front of me, so I sipped it without tasting anything.

"Ouch," I said into my beer.

She laughed and put a hand on my arm.

"No, oh sorry. Not you," she said. "This guy I'd been dating recently for a few months. He just appeared at that group date thing I was at. And kept talking to me and hanging around me. Ruined the vibes."

I relaxed. She still had her hand on my arm, though.

"It's nice to see you," she said. "You're never in town."

I took another sip of beer.

"Alright, alright," I said. "Don't over sell it."

We chatted about boring work stuff and the like until the frites arrived. She'd ordered the big one that came with all eleven sauces because how could you not?

"Jesus," I said, "we're not going to make a dent in this thing."

She grabbed one and dunked it in the sauce closest to her—curried ketchup, maybe?—and popped it into her mouth.

"Let's try," she said.

The fries, or frites as they called them here, came served in a wire cone lined with parchment paper. If you sat across from someone at a table, it would eclipse them entirely. Fries protruded a good couple of inches above the rim of the receptacle. Around the base of the cone were the eleven different dipping sauces portioned out into little metal cups. Yes, eleven. If sauce is your favorite food group, these fries are for you.

I preferred the aioli-type ones—the real garlicky, mayonnaise ones—but there were some good spicy sauces and even a couple serviceable soy-sauce-based ones, but they didn't really adhere to the fries too well.

We munched fries mostly in silence.

"So, where's your new place?" she asked me.

"You remember where the mall is? A few blocks north of that," I said. "Pretty much behind the Lutheran high school where Mark, Ben, Javier—most of my friends went."

"You have to be dating, too, right?" she asked me. "With all that free time you have every other week?"

"Sorta," I said between mouthfuls of potato. "Mostly I'm just sleeping with people. There's a waitress I met in Ohio that lives near my mom so that's a good excuse to get away from there when I'm visiting. A girl I work with sometimes. We're just kind of friends. And, that's about it."

"About it?" she asked. But I didn't elaborate. "Do they know about each other?"

"Maybe?" I offered. "I'm not keeping anything from anybody, if that's what you mean. I'm not really, like, *dating*-dating anybody."

She gave me that *Don't shit a shitter* look.

"I'm serious," I said. "I'm going to all these weddings and seeing all my friends pair off or make these long-term commitments and everybody says shit like 'I'm marrying my best friend!' and I think that you were my best friend before we got together and I couldn't make it work. So, I just don't know if that kind of thing's for me."

She thought about it for a second and nodded. "That's fine for now, but you're going to be thirty in, like, a year."

"Year and a half," I said unconvincingly.

She made a *My point exactly* type of face.

"Right, so what happens when you're a year from turning forty?" she asked. "There's nothing wrong with what you're describing or doing but it gets sadder the older you get."

"For who?" I asked but knew what she meant.

"For everybody," she said. "Are you going to sleep around with women that have teenagers when you've never grown up?"

"Hey," I said mildly offended even though she was right. But who was ever offended by something that wasn't at least partly true? "I work full-time and have my own place and hobbies and shit. I'm not sleeping on a friend's couch or living in my dad's basement."

She put her hands up in surrender. My tone probably came off as more offended than I anticipated or even really felt.

"At least tell me they're all age-appropriate," she said.

"Uh, mentally or actually chronologically?" I asked.

"Kyle..."

"No, yeah they are. It's not like they're teenagers or something," I said and then thought about it for a second.

"Well, one of them is."

"Jesus."

"She's nineteen," I said. "She's in college and everything."

She shook her head at me.

I shrugged and drank more of my beer. She kept inadvertently touching my arm or leaning into me and it was starting to make me uncomfortable. I liked this. I liked us being friends again and I didn't want more than that. I mean, part of me did, sure, and if I thought we could sleep together like a couple of old friends exchanging a hug after not seeing each other for years then I would have, but it was too soon. I didn't think it could be done without meaning being attached to it. For me or for her. I cared about her too much and I believed she felt the same. It's hard for me to believe, to really trust, that someone feels something like that for me. I was sure it was because I didn't like myself very much. So, when I knew, when I was one hundred percent sure I'd achieved with someone a balance between what we're putting in and taking out, well... I didn't want to fuck it up.

So, I told her about my tryst this afternoon and who it was with.

I really hadn't planned on it but the vague talk about my casual fuck-buddies didn't turn her off like I intended. It seemed like it was having the opposite effect. I needed to make it real for her. She needed to know all the players in the drama, and she needed to realize I was the villain, so she'd stay the fuck away from me.

"You're not kidding," she stated matter-of-factly as I tried to find the bottom of my Guinness.

I shook my head no.

"What the fuck, Kyle?" she said, lowering her voice and absently scanning the room for anyone else we knew.

"I know," I said.

"She's married," Estella said.

"I know," I repeated. "It was her idea, if that helps at all."

"Uh, no. Not really," she said. "Christ, if Ben—"

I put my hand up and lowered it slowly to the bar top.

"Believe me," I said. "I think about it all the time."

She wouldn't stop shaking her head. She was not leaning into me or making physical contact with me in any way. Why did I think this would be better?

"Why did you tell me this?" she asked.

"I don't know. I guess I don't know anybody else I could tell," I said.

"Clearly not. Jesus," she said.

I stretched and cracked my neck. I wanted a cigarette so bad. Going on six weeks. When did cravings stop?

"Also," I said, "I didn't want you too taken with the roguish charm of other dalliances."

"Fuck you," she said. "Are you serious? Like I'm going to drop panties over your prowess. We slept together plenty of times, Kyle."

"That's not what I meant," I said, even though it was exactly what I meant.

"What is she thinking?" Estella said with disgust, which I tried not to take personally.

"I don't know," I said, starting to sound like someone hitting a repeat button. "I think she's getting to a point where she wants people to find out."

"You are going to lose friends over this," she said. "Life-long friends."

I thought about how when we were dating, she thought it was so weird that I still hung out with my friends as much as possible, seeing most of them nearly every week. She got along with everybody and they liked her, but it grated on her sometimes that I would drop everything or move our plans around to hang out with my buddies.

"Is it worth it?" she asked. I was uncomfortable with the specificity of this question. I was never really one to kiss and tell or go into detail anyway and I didn't really compare different women. Everybody was different. Why have preferences or things like that? Plus, it was a little like she was angling for me to tell her that No, Estella, you're way better in bed which is frankly beneath her to ask—and also not true.

"No," I said because she was looking at me and not going to let me get away without at least a partial answer to this question. "You have to blow your life up sometimes and not always for great reasons."

"That's bullshit," she said. "You're an idiot. You wanna be bad and this is as bad as you can be."

"That sounds about right," I confessed.

"Are you going to be with her, like if she gets divorced?" she asked.

I parroted her wiggly hand motion from earlier back to her.

"Maybe," I said. "Probably, I guess. It'll be a fucking disaster."

She waved the bartender away when he asked if we wanted more drinks. I mimed signing a check at him and he nodded. I needed to get back soon.

"I should call her," she said flatly.

"No," I said as firmly as I could without coming off as aggressive. I might've failed. "Do not do that. If she knows I told someone, she's going to tell someone."

"She probably already has," she said. "You know she's mostly crazy."

"'She's mostly crazy?' That's not very feminist," I said, but flashed onto Niedz from earlier and felt that sinking feeling again. But why the fuck would she tell him? They didn't even live in the same city.

"You know, you can be a better person," Estella said.

"C'mon," I said, but it wasn't much of a defense.

"I'm serious," she said. "You don't have to indulge in bad behavior to have an interesting life. You are a good person and you can be even better."

"You're getting into motivational speaker territory," I said. "Real self-help stuff. Vision boards and shit."

She looked genuinely disappointed in me for the first time all evening. Not the shock or revulsion of earlier but a real *You're wasting your potential* kind of look.

The bartender came with the check and handed it to Estella with her card. She must have opened a tab before I got here. I gave him a *What the fuck, man?* look but he pretended not to notice.

She signed the bill and waved me off when I tried to give her some cash.

"Are you going to tell me it's never too late to go back and finish school?" I said because I couldn't help it.

"It's not," she said. "You should."

I nodded and let out a breath.

"I've been thinking about an ethics degree," I said.

She blinked then laughed and the tension evaporated.

"Fuck off," she said and pushed my shoulder away

playfully. "Don't you need to get back to your friends?"

"I do actually," I said and checked my phone. Ben texted me two minutes ago. "Shit, they left OPTs. There's this hot bartender there."

"God, what is wrong with you," she said.

"Just trying to find the woman that can solve the mystery that is me. Ooh! The *me*-stery."

She sighed. "Why do I even know you?"

"We're going to The Vogue," I said, after checking my phone. Ugh. Too clubby for me when they weren't having a show and too packed when they were.

"Do you want me to drop you off?" she asked me, standing up and smoothing the front of her clothes and gathering up her purse.

"Thanks," I said. "That'd be great. I should've just driven myself, but Ben wanted to mini-road trip like old times."

"Yeah, and it'll probably be your last. With him anyway," she said, but there was no real malice in her tone. More of a gallows humor thing.

"I'll give you that one," I said, and we bounced.

I had her drop me off around the corner because she was headed that way anyway and I knew she didn't want to see anybody, not right now at least. Not like this.

And I didn't want Ben giving me knowing glances all fucking night either.

"Saturday?" she said when I was getting out of the car.

"Yup, lunch," I said. "Yats. At least me and Ben. Maybe Jake and Niedz too, I don't know. You coming to the wedding?"

"I still haven't decided," she said.

I nodded.

"Later," I said and waltzed.

I zipped through a throng of people and around the corner and ran into my friends piling out of a cab.

"How'd you beat us here?" Ben asked and I got this weird sense of déjà vu.

"I was already over here," I lied. "OPTs was dead."

He shrugged.

"That bartender wondered where you went," he said.

"Shit. Tell me you got her name."

He smiled.

"Maybe," he said and then changed the subject. "Javier's already inside."

He walked away from me and bypassed a section of the line huddling with somebody Jake or Niedz knew.

I double timed my stride to keep pace with him.

"Don't fuck around, dude," I said. "If you don't tell me now, you'll forget and then we'll end up at the Alley Cat later and I'll have to be like 'Hey...you' and she'll walk right the fuck away from me."

"I mean, you'd probably deserve it," he said.

"What the fuck are you, a priest now?" I said.

He made the sign of the cross at me as if I was an entire congregation.

"I get it," I said. "You want me to crash and burn so you can swoop in and make a play for her."

"What?" he said, offended. I was just fucking with him like he was fucking with me but now that I could see it bothered him, I couldn't help myself of course.

I shrugged and lowered my voice.

"You complain about Aimee a lot," I said. "I don't know your life."

His eyes became tiny triangles of suspicion. His nostrils flared and his mouth compacted into a tight line.

Shit. I pushed him too far. He's making connections in his brain, lining things up. He knows. I am fucked—

He relaxed suddenly and a smile cracked his face. He was Ben again.

"You're fucking with me," he said.

I conceded and smiled. He pushed me lightly on the shoulder. I let out a breath I hadn't realized I was holding.

"Fuck you, man," he said. "Don't joke around with that shit. Maybe I used to be a dog, yeah, but I take my marriage shit very seriously. If I ever did anything like that, and I never would, stop being my friend."

"That seems a little harsh," I said.

"No. It isn't," is all he said but he kept looking at me.

"Erika, with a k," he said after a minute, right before they let us into the club.

"Gracias, with a c," I said and bowed to him.

The Vogue was in full swing if you like that sort of thing. I didn't, but it wasn't my bachelor party so what are you gonna do? Javi or his brothers or somebody must have called ahead and reserved a VIP section. It looked like they had bottle service and everything which is fucking great because the two bars in the middle of the floor were completely mobbed from all sides. They were like little squares of an oasis in a desert of people. One of the bartenders was flipping bottles and another was blowing out fireballs of Bacardi or something. I swear I'm not making that up. People were fucking cheering. I felt like I stepped into another world or hit my head and woke up in Vegas or a dumb movie. Javier had wanted to do a Vegas thing—bachelor party and wedding out there—but Lisa had nixed it. She didn't think anybody would come and she was probably right. I'm not sure I would've. I'm pretty sure her family was dirt-poor white trash and Javier comes from poor Mexican stock, but he's got mad skills at selling cars, so he forgets that everybody else isn't doing so well like all formerly poor people. He lived like a fucking lottery winner. The last time I saw him, he bought me an eighty-dollar steak for no reason. I'm not complaining—that slab was delicious—but you see what I mean. He was in full Rastafarian look tonight, a mane of thick black dreadlocks and a huge beard. He was laughing and knocking back huge glasses of Johnny Walker. Maybe Blue? Holy shit, I needed to get in on that. He wore a white suit coat over a purple button down, opened down a few too many buttons. His taco-meat chest hair was on full display. He saw us and bellowed a laugh like he couldn't believe we were here, like he couldn't believe his cosmic luck. He bounced up and crushed each of us in turn with those insane bear hugs of his. I think my back even cracked and I know my feet lifted off the ground even though he's a good couple of inches shorter than me. Up close he smelled like scotch and cigars and something chemical I could not place. His eyes looked a little weird and darted around here and there and I started to feel anxious. He's been known to do things besides alcohol or tobacco but that's been years ago—or I assumed anyway. We didn't really hang out much these days. Drinks materialized in our hands and we shoved some coats out of the way and sat down. I didn't know everybody in here with us, but I scanned them and the coat I pushed away at least didn't seem to fit anybody here. It was an old well-worn camouflage type thing, huge and with dozens of pockets. It was extremely heavy for a piece of clothing. The VIP area was elevated over the rest of the crowd by a couple of feet and it looked like we had it to ourselves. There were women hanging around too even though this was a bachelor party and I certainly didn't recognize any of them. I think they were just club bitches who had been sucked into the orbit of Javier and his lavish spending at his own event. Everything immediately felt too large and too chaotic and just too much. It was all spinning out of control. I tried to sit but the bass was jumping the chairs on the floor or maybe it was the bodies moving. They were smoking cigars inside which is definitely not allowed anymore, and drinks just kept arriving and arriving and disappearing. I could stick my hand out empty and a drink would just be in it. One appeared but when I drew it to my lips, I thought maybe I saw a weird foam on top or something dissolving in it—some traces of sediment and maybe it was just the lights. Jesus—all the lights and the strobes but I set it down and it was gone and I didn't think I drank any before I noticed but I might have and that might not have been the first drink I had and it seemed a little like the room was moving like it was breathing but rooms didn't breathe but the bass and the people and the smoke and the lights and the strobes and I was on my feet because I was starting to feel panicky like the crowd was going to surge and I was going to be crushed and there was a strange buzzing in my leg but maybe that's the pocket where I keep my phone but I can't check it because it's so packed I can't get my hand into my pocket and back out again and look at my phone because there are people pressed all around and it's so loud that I feel like I can't even hear but there are noises inside the noise but my brain simply cannot make sense of them and the lights and strobes are starting to have the same effect on my eyes on my vision that there's so much happening so much stimuli that I'm not even processing it it's like all the colors are merging and layering on top of each other to white each other out to make one swath of nothingness that encompasses everything and what will happen to my other senses if I can't hear or see or think—

Two hands gripped my shoulders from directly in front of me. Ben's face loomed from out of the miasma and filled my vision and gave everything else scale and depth and I knew who I was and where I was and this was my friend and he was trying to help.

He was making eye contact with me and he was calm, so I calmed down and when I seemed normal again to myself and I guess also to him he leaned in and said right into my face

"Outside."

and he was leading me and pulling me and helping me and guiding me and we left the club and we were suddenly in a cold alley out back with a couple random smokers or other escapees.

"Fuck," he said.

"What the fuck was that?" I asked or thought I did or tried to.

I could see his breath and my own and I realized that inside the building it had been insanely hot like boiling because I could see our breath and we were just in shirts but the sharp February air didn't feel like cold—it felt like relief.

"Shit," Ben said and leaned against a brick wall, his knee bent supporting himself on one foot, his head resting gently against the brick wall like he was a cool teen in some movie. His breath looked like smoke and so did mine and it triggered something in my brain and for the first time in six weeks since I'd quit smoking, I had no desire for a cigarette because look the air can be smoke. I think I was unconsciously holding my fingers as if I was gripping an invisible cigarette.

"Fuck," he repeated.

So, I repeated myself, "What the fuck was that?" This time I was one hundred percent sure it was out loud and in the real world.

Ben shook his head.

"I dunno," he said, "I dunno. I think a lot of them on are on something. I think the drinks might be dosed."

"Yeah," I said, "I thought mine looked weird. I didn't drink it, but I think it touched my lips for a second. I felt weird for a minute there. I still feel weird?"

"You're talking weird," he said. "I didn't have anything. I don't think I knew any of those people and I've known Javier since middle school."

I leaned against the wall and sort of slid down it until I was on my haunches. I rested my elbows on my knees and my head in my hands.

"Thanks for pulling me out of there," I said.

He nodded and looked at the ground.

"We should go find Jake and Niedz and get them the fuck out of there," he said.

"Jake, yeah," I said, wondering if we abandoned Niedz to whatever the fuck was going on if it would make my shit with him better or worse. If he knew what he sure as shit acted like he knew. Could this shit fry his brain, or would it spill his guts?

"What about Javi?" I asked, to distance myself from the evil fucking thought I was having about Niedz in that moment, realizing the potential in myself to go way too far to protect a lie that already had too many moving parts. Had Niedz seen us? Had anyone else? Did she tell him? Did they have a thing? Had she told some other unknown third party who then told Niedz? How far down the grapevine was he? How many people were stumbling around with this information waiting to collide with someone that knew me directly, someone who mattered or who it mattered to? By accident or malice, how long would it be until they told someone who would do something about it?

Until someone told Ben.

Before Amy, Mark had dated a girl named Kat. She was hot but cruel. Most dudes would call her crazy, but she wasn't. It was colder than that, more calculated. She did crazy things, yes that's true, that's undeniable, but she did them because she was cruel.

They were supposed to come visit me down here a few years ago. We had tickets to a show at Birdie's, a small, local bar that got great musical acts because they were owned by a record store that was also a distributor. I saw Guided by Voices there for the first time and Mark, Kat and I had just seen Clem Snide (again, a first) there a few months prior and they fucking loved it. They couldn't believe how intimate the place was and yet how big the names were that came through—if you were into early aughts Indie Rock anyway. It was their first Birdie's experience and they were sold. They snatched up pairs of tickets for the following shows that interested them. The next one was The Apples in Stereo on tour for "The Velocity of Sound," a divisive record among Apples fans, but undoubtedly their hardest rocking one.

The Apples were also part of the Elephant 6 collective, a group of bands that shared musicians. This was of special interest to us because Mark's all-time favorite band, Neutral Milk Hotel, was also a member of this collective. At the time, the main creative force behind Neutral Milk Hotel, Jeff Magnum was entirely retired and completely reclusive.

Seeing any of their friends and label mates, specifically The Apples in Stereo (whose front-man Robert Schneider recorded and actually fucking played instruments on Neutral Milk Hotel's "In The Aeroplane Over The Sea"—the single greatest LP ever recorded by humans) was impossible to pass up.

We were not missing that show.

It was the first week in January a few years ago and if you've ever lived in Indiana you know this is when you typically start getting the first snowstorms of the season. This year was no exception. So, Kat refused to go. Mark is not a wasteful person. He's not cheap, but he's thrifty. He's not going to buy food and throw it out later. He's not going to own something and not use it. And he sure as shit isn't going to have tickets to a concert, specifically one he really wants to see, and not go to it. Rain? Who cares—get wet. Late on a work night? Guess I'm going to be tired tomorrow. Snow? Fuck snow—I drive in that shit three months a year.

So, they have a huge fight about it, and she won't go,

and he says fine I'll go without you. I'm sure Ben will take your ticket.

"I hope you hit a patch of ice and your car runs off the road and you die in a ditch," she said to him. She said that to another human being, let alone her boyfriend of five years or so at that point, someone she claimed to love.

She didn't yell it or even say it particularly harsh, in tone anyway, she just said it to him and hung up the phone. Cruel.

So, after that incident and about five hundred others depressingly similar ones, Ben, Jake and I, along with Amy (who was only our friend at that point) stayed up all night planning an intervention with Mark. Discussing how best to tell him he was dating a monster in a way that he could understand. In a way that wouldn't push him away from us and deeper into his shit with her.

We never figured it out and when dawn broke, we lost our conviction and Amy went home and Jake and I fell asleep on Ben's couch and floor respectively.

One theory was that all we had to do was tell him and he'd slap his forehead comically, like *Of course, how I could not see that she's evil. Gimmie a second to break up with her over text and let's all get some beers.* I didn't think any of us really thought this would shake out to be true, but it was the most straightforward, simplest and best-case scenario. Maybe he'd even change her contact name in his phone to BITCH or DON'T ANSWER or something awesome and apt. Maybe Amy believed in this proposal, I didn't know. It's clear now in hindsight that she already had feelings for him since they began sleeping together a short time later, when Mark did finally kick Kat to the curb, and they've married since. But us fellas didn't buy it.

We weren't divided on whether he would reject the notion that she was an evil whore—we knew he wouldn't be able to hear us, to see it—but we couldn't figure out how he'd handle it. Would he shrug and make excuses, and everything would go on as before? Or would he flip out on us, despite knowing in his heart that what we told him was true, and turn around and walk away from us? From there, would he tell her what we said or not? He'd have to, surely, if he suddenly stopped hanging out with all his friends, right? She'd notice that. Again, we were divided. Would she? Would she look that gift horse in the mouth when she could just have him to manipulate however she wanted, without any outside influence or competition for his time?

I argued that we lean hard into it, that we shit on her as much as we could until he has no choice but to go to her and tell her all the horrible stuff we said about her (things we knew he already knew, things he already believed) and then she could reveal her true thoughts about us, his friends who he loved and was loyal to, who were here before her and would be standing long after memories of her were forgotten.

I felt like that was the only way to show him what we meant, to get her to expose herself.

Jake loved it, but ultimately it was too theoretical, it was too much psychology, too Hannibal Lecter with nothing guaranteed.

Were we willing to risk our friendship with him to get rid of her?

We were not.

He broke up with her for the final time a few weeks

or months later without our open rebellion, even if he could feel the vibes of it wafting off us.

Towards the end of that long night of the soul, I mentioned that I could sleep with Kat in a bid to get Mark to finally leave her and it would only cost him one of his friends instead of three. They laughed but Ben was stone. He had, even then, a very black and white, cut and dry view on cheating. For himself, he always claimed. He said he didn't judge others, but he sure sounded like he did.

I had been joking, of course, I told them and myself. I would never sleep with a friend's girlfriend.

Now, here in the future, I think of the feel of another man's wife.

I got my phone out while Ben was still shell-shocked and opened a blank text message. I had received a different text, but it could wait. I needed to send this while my self-hatred and disgust were at its peak. When the juices had cooled enough, I could never see her again and mean it.

we can't do that again

was all I sent. I manually punched her number in from memory because I couldn't have her saved in my phone. She had me saved as Mamma Mia's Pizzeria or something, but she promised she deleted any messages after sending or receiving them.

I deleted it after it said it was delivered.

She quickly responded with

see you saturday

and then a serious of emojis like a peach and a flower and a pair of lips and a smirking devil.

I deleted it.

im really wet thinking of earlier

she said and I deleted it.

saturday

she said and I deleted it.

Then she sent a photo of her panties and her right hand resting near them on her leg and her index finger, reaching.

I deleted it and shut my phone and jammed it back into my pocket. It vibrated almost immediately. I couldn't deal with it.

This was crazy. She was crazy.

Of course, she was fucking crazy. She was fucking you and she was married to someone else, and I realized Estella was wrong earlier when she said I wanted to be bad. I didn't. I was scared—terrified—because this is what embracing bad behavior really looked like.

"What?" Ben asked me and I nearly yelped.

"What what?" I asked in return.

He pointed at my pocket.

"Your pager's blowin up," he said, cribbing some old Ice Cube lyrics. "And you said 'fuck this' out loud without even realizing it."

Shit, really?

"Work," I said without looking at him shaking my head to try and sell it.

"You work third shift at a Walgreens," he said. "What could the problem possibly be?"

I took in a breath.

"Well, a girl at work," I said. "Or maybe more than one, I guess."

He smiled.

"Ah," was all he said, and I watched him believe the mythology I was spinning about myself as it also dawned on me that it's hardly mythology if it's basically true.

He was still shaking his head.

"I didn't think you had women problems," he said. "I just assumed you bailed at any whiff of trouble."

"Don't call it women problems, genius," I said. "It sounds like we're getting our periods."

He laughed.

"And usually, yeah," I said.

"But you like this chick," he said. "Or one of them, I mean."

"No," I said too quickly and knew it to be true. I didn't like her. Well, why did I fuck her? Because I didn't like her? Jesus. How does that make any fucking sense? "Well, I mean I like her but not how you mean. It was a mistake. I never should have slept with her because now I still have to see her sometimes even if I don't want to."

"Don't shit where you eat," Ben said.

It made me think of another phrase:

No one is ever betrayed by an enemy.

Then someone, from the other end of the alley, said

"What are you faggots doing out here?"

and my night, or morning at this point, started to get much worse.

FRIDAY

Ben saw them first. He faced the direction of the voice.

I turned at the sound and only saw that familiar camouflage coat from inside the club. Dumb first thought: not that this was clearly the same coat, and this must be someone that we knew, but that what an insane coincidence that there would be two of these similar jackets in close proximity to each other.

I refocused and looked up. There were two of them and they grinned. I did know these fuckers. Whichever one had spoken disguised his voice so I, or even more likely, Ben, wouldn't recognize it. I did not want them here. Them being here was not a good thing for anyone, especially not for me. They knew Javier, sure, but enough to drive down here for his bachelor party?

"The Redneck Twins," Ben said under his breath so

they wouldn't hear him. Maybe I wasn't supposed to hear him either, maybe it was some way of psyching himself up to deal with them. Corey and Dustin. His dipshit brothers-in-law.

First Niedz knew something and then these assholes showed up? This was not good, and I needed to get the fuck out of here. I felt panic again but unlike whatever chemical enhancement caused the one inside—this one came from within me, from knowing I've done something wrong and knowing I was caught and feeling the trap sprung.

Would they tell Ben before or after they started beating the shit out of me?

Ben headed over towards them with a shit eating grin on his face. When he was past me, he glanced back at me and rolled his eyes.

He didn't know yet, that's for sure. He wasn't that much of an actor.

"Us?" he said to them and traded some half-hearted handshakes and pseudo-manly hugs. "Who let you hillbilly assholes into the city?"

My phone buzzed in my pocket again but there was no way I could check it now with all these extra eyes. I'd probably accidentally drop it face-up and it'd skitter across the ground and shine up at them from between their huddled feet. Or somebody would snatch it out of my hand as a joke that suddenly becomes anything but funny.

Or maybe they could just see it reflected in my eyes.

"You remember Kyle, right?" Ben said and waved me over away from the protection of the shadowy brick wall. A couple of giggling girls stumbled over each other and out of the door to the club Ben and I had exited from seemingly years ago and I briefly considered making a dash for it and trying to lose the guys inside the strobing psychedelic madness and shifting labyrinth of sweaty bodies.

I thought about it for too long and the smooth, handleless door slammed shut with finality.

I puffed out my cheeks, straightened my posture and walked over to them.

I exchanged firm and meaningless handshakes with the twins. Their grips were strong and their hands rough and calloused. I tried to match strength at least and looked straight at them and never broke eye contact. I wasn't resigned to my fate, but I would go down fighting. Or at least deny it until the end.

Corey was taller and wider with a thick stubble. Dustin was scrawny and shifty. They dressed the same, almost a uniform—jeans tucked into timberlands, flannels, heavy jackets, and worn-out, old baseball hats.

Their faces were entirely unreadable. Maybe they were content, maybe they were on something mellow. Their expressions barely registered to me as human, like they were posing as Ben's brothers-in-law to observe us and report back to their alien overlords with a shrug or a thumbs down. It was as if they believed themselves to be a different species.

Mostly, though, if I had to project onto them—and I couldn't seem to help it—they seemed bored by the whole thing, out of place in the big city and up too late and talking to us because they knew us and not because they wanted to.

"You dudes have been hanging out with Javier?" Ben said and I tried to make myself focus.

They nodded.

"Huh," Ben said seemingly a little wounded. "He never said anything to me about that."

They shrugged.

"Yeah, we've been coming down to Indy just about every week or so for a bit," Corey said.

"For business," Dustin added, and they exchanged an unreadable look.

I realized whatever weird chemical smell I'd smelled on Javi was also wafting off them. Maybe they had been the source and it had just been lingering around him.

"The ATV stuff?" I asked, partly because I was trying to remember what the hell these guys did and partly because no one else was saying anything.

Ben suddenly looked very uncomfortable.

One of them nodded while the other one spit off into the gutter somewhere.

"Yup," Corey said. "We branched out into some snowmobiles last winter and we're gonna add a couple more things this year, too. Javi's hooked us up with this guy down here. Selling cars—he knows all the mother fuckers around. You should come up and take a tour, Kyle. On the house, man."

"Yeah," Dustin said. "Maybe wait until the summer. We'll take you out on the lake."

They both laughed and I forced a smile. Pretend you were in on the joke so you didn't become the joke.

"Probably wait until everything's fully thawed," Corey said and the other agreed. "After they've fished all the bodies out of the lakes."

I glanced at Ben. *Bodies?* He nodded.

"Every year, they find one or two up there after the

thaw," Ben explained. "In the lakes. Unlucky snowshoers or ice fisherman."

"Sometimes," Corey said. "I know a state trooper who says Chicago is dumping them there."

"That's quite a trip for a Chicago gangbanger," Ben said. "What is it? Two hours with those back roads?"

They nodded in agreement.

"They don't always make it all the way to the lake," Dustin said, looking at me. "Sometimes, they find some poor mother fucker at the side of a two-lane in the bottom of a melting snow drift."

"All right," Ben put his hands up in mock surrender. "Stop trying to scare the city boy with campfire ghost story shit."

He laughed and they laughed and so I laughed, too, because I didn't know what else to do. Laughter seemed better than sprinting through the nighttime Indianapolis streets screaming in sheer panic.

Ben motioned to the club and started walking to the mouth of the alley.

"We should probably get back in there and see our buddy," Ben said. "It's his party after all and I only talked to him for five minutes."

They went blank. Stone-faced. They intentionally didn't glance at each other or exchange any looks. As if they thought we'd read their minds though their volleying expressions, which meant about as much to me as birds exchanging songs.

"Yeah, tell Javi we're out here," Corey said. "He's supposed to help us out with something."

"Now?" I said when I should've said nothing.

They nodded.

"Right," Dustin said. "He knows what it's about. We gotta pick up a bunch of Sea-Doos from that guy he hooked us up with."

"You guys should come, too," Corey said and pulled out a fat stack of cash. Almost too big of a roll to palm in one hand. "Help us hitch the trailer and we'll throw you a couple bills for your bar tab this weekend."

Ben smiled.

He and his sisters had grown up poor. They weren't poor anymore—their shitty habitual offender dad was out of the picture and their mom had finally gotten a construction business off and running with her own siblings and it was nice and stable now. But that shit never really left, so he always had a bit of a hustler in him. It was rare for him to turn down a buck or not take advantage of a way to save one. He wasn't quite at the level of the kid on the playground taking quarters to eat worms but he wouldn't have been above standing off to the side and collecting the admission fees so he could take a percentage off the top. I for sure had seen him pick up change off the street, and recently, too. Being a father of three had not helped to relax his money concerns, it only amplified them.

I was raised middle class. I wasn't spoiled but I never went hungry or lacked clothes or school supplies. I always got presents for my birthday or holidays and there was money for simple things like a Boy Scout uniform or karate lessons or a basketball, but not indulgent things like overnight class trips out of state or an instrument to be in band. I had a paper route when I was twelve but that was just so my parents could get me out of the house as their marriage dissolved around us. I wasted all the money on comic books, videogames and fast food. Whatever was within biking distance.

Ben had a paper route around the same time, too, and we didn't know each other yet, but I bet he scrimped and saved all that dough just to have normal shit, like new shoes for the school year.

So, as soon as I saw that too-large wad of bills, I knew we were going with these chumps.

"Cool," was all Ben said. Now I just had to figure out how to talk him out of it before we found Javi, or simply bail myself before we made it back outside.

"The Sea-Doos should only be on one trailer, but we've only got the pickup," Corey said. "No backseat. You'll need to pile into another vehicle. We'll meet you by your ride."

Ben frowned.

The perfect out. Ben's car is halfway across the city.

"Uh, we didn't drive," I said as casually as I could manage. "Guess you're on your own."

"No prob," Corey replied. "Javi's got his CRV. I saw it over on College in the Flagstar Bank parking lot, across Westfield."

"That's very specific," I said.

Two unreadable smiles.

"We parked right next to him."

"Alright," Ben said. We nodded at each other like this was all perfectly normal and they left.

We headed to the other end of the alley and back towards the front entrance. The line was smaller but seemed to be moving less. We bypassed it and went to another door a few feet down the block. There was no line but a bouncer. He hit our hands with the black light flashlight, curtly nodded and stepped out of way just enough that we could squeeze in past him.

Inside was the back of another bouncer who sensed us and turned and unclipped a velvet rope when we showed our VIP bracelets. He smiled and let us through.

It was more packed but less chaotic. Or it felt that way, maybe because I'd escaped my head and whatever I'd ingested had been forced out through cold fresh air and the adrenaline of the Redneck Twins presence. This fear tipped me well over into the sober territory and I wasn't even buzzing anymore.

Since we had left the alley, I was trying to talk Ben out of helping them. He wanted to, not just for the cash—*Did you see that stack, I think it might have all been hundreds?*—but also to get some facetime with Javier since we had barely seen him, let alone got any chance to talk with him.

"We're going to see him all day tomorrow and Saturday," I said. "Fuck. It's Friday already. You know what I mean."

He didn't budge.

I didn't say anything about how anybody—let alone some shady mother fuckers like his brothers-in-law—having that much cash they were willing to whip out in a creepy alley made me nervous as hell. I didn't say that I wasn't sure if they were fucking with me back there or sending me veiled threats.

Finally, Ben said, put off from me bugging him,

"I'll check with Javi and make sure they're on the level."

I didn't say *What is ever on the level about thousands of dollars of cash in a large redneck's hand in an alley at midnight in a city none of us live in?*

Maybe he read it on my face.

"You don't have to go," he said. "I can hook a fucking trailer up myself."

I didn't say *There might be things about me that they know that I don't want them or anyone else telling you, so I need to follow you around wherever you go to try and censor discussions and diffuse situations until this paranoia passes* which seems increasingly unlikely that it ever will.

We arrived at the VIP section and Ben leaned over and said something to Javier, but they were just far enough away that I couldn't hear them. Javi was all smiles and nods. He set his drink down and jumped up and politely (if that's even possible) patted a woman I didn't recognize on the ass and she scooted aside and he squeezed through the crowd and he clapped me hard on my back and we were turned around and leaving the venue again.

Everything with Javi always took forever and bars close at three in Indiana, so I couldn't imagine that we'd be back. I felt like there was some kind of plan for an after party—at a hotel somewhere maybe?—but I couldn't remember what the hell is was.

I thought of that bartender who would be at the Alley Cat. I wasn't delusional enough to think she'd be there for me, but part of success is just showing up. I tried my best to close off that part of me and to close off her smile and the way she tucked her hair behind her ear when she asked a question. Sayonara. We maybe could've had fun.

Sometimes, everything seemed to slow down and I focused on the details and recounted every word that had been said and collated everything into a narrative shape, a story from it that made sense and had clear roles and precise action and breathtaking scenery.

Other times, things slipped by like trying to catch water from a faucet with my hands, and it was not a story. It was just things that happened. And I was tossed around and through these events and there was no sense to be made and a deep primal part of me realized that this was always the way of my life and any parts that had a story-like shape, well—I reconstructed it that way after the fact.

We got to Javier's ride—which seemed identical to Ben's or Niedz's rides—in the bank's parking lot. The twins were parked over by the drive thru. They flashed their lights at us as if we wouldn't see their massive pickup.

"Is that a confederate flag license plate holder?" I asked.

Ben made a face.

"I don't call them the rednecks for nothing," he said.

"They're okay dudes," Javier said as we piled in. I let him ride shotgun since he was getting married tomorrow and it was his car, even if he didn't call it.

They drove past us and the one in the passenger seat smiled and pointed forward. They slowed when they got to the street.

"So, you've really been hanging out with them?" Ben asked him as we pulled out of the lot to follow them.

Javier nodded in the affirmative and looked out the window at the throngs of drunk people stumbling around and sitting on curbs and huddling around cigarettes and waiting in line for hotdogs and falafel and tacos.

"Yup," he said. "They've been helping me out with

stuff."

"I thought you were helping them out," I said.

Javier looked out the window nonchalantly as we drove, his head resting on a fist propped under his chin. He rubbed his thumb and first two fingers together with his other hand without so much as looking over at either of us. "We're helping each other. You know, mutually beneficial."

This vague money talk was not helping me feel better about this shit.

Ben and I locked eyes in the rearview mirror. I didn't want to be there—I hadn't wanted to be there since they asked and offered up cash, but now it looked as if Ben was maybe starting to get a clue.

He focused on the road and shifted uncomfortably in his seat.

"So, a couple months back I was up at the lake getting some shit out of my grandma's old place. Some stuff for my mom," Ben said. "Anyway, I had some meetings, or something fall through at work one day, like a Tuesday or something, so I just went up there. I didn't tell anyone. It'd been on my to-do list for a while. Figured this was the perfect afternoon to get it done."

I exhaled audibly. How the fuck can I get out of a moving car without breaking my neck? Or maybe I should just break my neck…

Javi was still staring out the window as if Ben's voice was an old, long forgotten song he couldn't be bothered to remember.

"So, I got some stuff Aimee gave me to put in storage and I do that and I root around for the crap for my mom and I find it and I load it into the back and I think shit, that made me thirsty and hungry," he continued. "And I think I'll go surprise my sister and take her and her kids for a late lunch or something."

Yes. Breaking my own neck by belly-flopping out of a moving SUV in the early morning on a cold Indianapolis highway seemed like the right choice.

"But you know those lake roads," Ben continued, "I don't wait for that drink so I go inside and grab a glass from the counter and I'm about to fill it from the tap when I notice I can hear the fridge cycling so I figure I'll check since it shouldn't be plugged in this time of year anyway—we don't get a lot of winter lake rentals as you can imagine—and I figured I might get lucky."

Alright. I'm interested now, I admit. Even Javier's shifted in his seat and is side-eying Ben as he weaved his tale. Is there gonna be heads in the freezer or what?

"It's full," he said, maybe not as dramatically as he intended to. "As if someone's living in my grandparents' house or at least using it regularly."

I panic, just briefly. But no, no. We've never used that house for a hook-up. Even she has lines she won't cross. Maybe. The lake, sure, but not that house.

"So, I start looking around, and yeah, it's definitely being used." he said. "I didn't notice before, but there's little things like the bed is made and the remote is on the couch—nothing super obvious, someone's covering their tracks or at least doesn't want a superficial exam to fail. If you glanced in the windows nobody's been home for a while, but how many dozen times have I gotten that place ready for renters in the spring? I know what it looks like."

He paused as we exited the highway. We were in Greenwood or somewhere equally south and weird. Fuck.

This little side trip was going to take all fucking night. I imagined I could see the sun rising already but I couldn't. I glanced at the dashboard clock. It was after 1:00.

"I figure I'll ask Meg about it when I pop over there. Then I check the fridge again. There's a lot of beer in there and it's Stroh's. Do you know the only person I know who drinks Stroh's?"

He waited for an answer but neither of us said anything.

"Your grandpa?" I guessed after it was clear he wasn't going to continue until someone threw out a hunch. "Is this a fucking ghost story?"

Javier laughed.

Ben flipped me off in the rearview mirror and I blew him a kiss.

"Nope," he said. "Corey, Meg's husband. Not even Dustin, the other dimwit, will drink it, shit's so nasty. It tastes like the first sip of beer your uncle let you try when you were six mixed with a bottle of old lady perfume."

"That sounds like a very personal tasting experience," Javi said. "You gonna tell me that one too? Maybe on the way back or do you need a whole day for it?"

Ben flipped him off and Javi laughed.

"So, I look behind the Stroh's and I find a more-or-less equal amount of Natty Ice. Now that's Dustin's brand of choice," he said.

"I don't get," I said. "So, they've what, set the place up as a man-cave or something? Don't they have garages and tool sheds and shit?"

He nodded.

"Right," he agreed. "What the fuck is it for? Now, I don't like either of them, but I don't really want to fuck their shit up by asking Meg or Ellie about it. If it's just a hide-away to get away from my sisters and drink a couple brews? Who gives a fuck? I understand—I waited eighteen years to get the fuck away from my sisters and I didn't wait one second longer."

This was true. Ben was the youngest of us by a few months and on his eighteenth birthday, he loaded his old Jetta with anything he could, picked Mark up and they rented an apartment that very afternoon. I was in college at the time, but it was my home away from home and school.

"So, on my drive to my sister's place I'm trying to make up my mind. Do I ask her or not? Does it make a difference? We all jointly own the property, and everybody has a key and I don't really care if anyone uses it whenever. But what if they're having problems or something and she needs someone to talk to?"

"Wouldn't she talk to Ellie?" Javier asked. "Isn't that shit sisters do?"

Ben shrugged.

"I would think so but how the fuck would I know?" he said. "What if it's more sinister though?"

"Sinister," I echoed because I couldn't help it.

"Yeah," he said and swallowed audibly. This was getting weird. "What if it's some fuck-pad for the Redneck Twins and whatever skanks they can pick up in Kendallville or wherever?"

"Gah," I said or maybe Javi did. We both made disgusted noises either way. No one wanted to think of those turds fucking anything let alone the aforementioned Kendallville Skanks, the skankiest, nastiest of all the varieties of local skanks.

Why was Ben so fixated on cheating this weekend? Was it my imagination or a guilty conscience? Push it down, push it away.

"Uh, I've been hanging out with these dudes a little recently," Javier said.

"So I've heard," Ben said, still weirded out by it.

"Oh my God," I said. "You're the poon they're fucking?"

He reached back and tried to punch me, but I dodged it.

"Fuck you. Anyway," he said laughing, "like I said, they're OK dudes, but I can't imagine them fucking anybody. I mean I barely comprehend how they landed your sisters, Ben."

"Yeah," he agreed. "Neither does my mom."

We chuckled. We were on some bullshit, black-as-night back roads now. If they were bringing us out to kill us, they were going to get away with it.

"So, I decided I wasn't going to do anything," Ben said. "For the reason you just pointed out. Who would fuck these guys? They probably just wanted a place to watch football and drink beer, and I'm no narc. Then I pull into my sister's place and Dustin's truck is there."

"That's pretty normal, right?" I said.

"Yes, but Corey's truck wasn't." he said. "So, I go in ready to confront them, like how could you sleep with your brother-in-law? How could you sleep with your best friend's wife?"

"Jesus," Javier said. "That was your first fucking thought? What happened to you when you were a kid?"

"My dad cheated on my mom whenever he wasn't in prison," Ben said matter-of-factly, and immediately moved on before we could process it. "So, I barge in and Ellie's sitting in the kitchen with Meg and they're having tea and are like What the fuck are you doing here? Is everything OK? Why did you bust in here like something's on fire?"

"She borrowed his truck?" I said. "Is that the end to this story? I swear I'm going to bury your body out here."

"No," he said. "Dustin drove them up here. Ellie had the day off work and apparently Dustin and Corey have been working together on some new job. Something very vague."

I was starting to get nervous again. Javi didn't help by pretending to look casually out the window again. He clearly knew these dopes better than either of us, so he knew where this was going.

Ben noticed it too.

"Do you want to finish this part for me, Javi?" Ben asked him.

He sorta shrugged and didn't look at us.

"Why?" he said quietly. "You seem like you're having a ball telling it."

"It's meth, right?" Ben asked him. I would have done a spit take if I had anything to drink.

Javier didn't even shrug this time. Just looked out that fucking window.

"Are you fucking kidding me?" I said barely containing the volume of my voice. "It's not meth is it? Tell me they're not fucking drug dealers. Tell me we're not following drug dealers into the middle of nowhere in the middle of the night."

Javier kept looking out the window or maybe he was contemplating his own reflection in the glass, searching for meaning there, trying to remember who he was supposed to be and what he was supposed to be doing.

There was a cat or some kind of small animal near the road and Javi rolled his window and bellowed at it. It took off.

He rolled his window back up.

Ben glanced over at him.

"They're, like, wholesalers," Javi stated flatly. "They know a couple guys up there that cook it. Small time dudes. Dudes that cook it so they can smoke it themselves. Guys drawing a government check or a pension or a disability, with time and a little money and access."

"Who the fuck knows meth cookers?" I asked.

"C'mon," Javier said, "It's all over the place. You're telling me there's no shady mother fuckers speed-walking through your Walgreens in the middle of the night? Wiry crazies missing a few teeth?"

I could easily picture handfuls. People with permanent 'colds' picking up Pseudoephedrine night after night, week after week, month after month.

"Of course," I said. "But I don't talk to them. I don't know them. 'Hey, do you weirdoes know of any good business opportunities? Like drugs maybe? I hear those are so hot right now.'"

Nobody said anything.

The Redneck Twins had slowed to a crawl and switched to just parking lights. Ben was doing the same.

"I'm not OK with this," I said as if there was any doubt.

"Wait in the car," Javier suggested.

"I told you not to come," Ben said.

"Oh, fuck both of you."

The Redneck Twins parked and got out of their vehicle and stood between the pickup and Javier's SUV. One of them had a dim flashlight pointed to the ground and the other scoped out the surrounding area while attempting to appear casual about it. They each had a hand inside their coats.

"We're not paying a guy for Sea-Doos, are we?" I asked.

Ben and Javier exited the vehicle, their doors slamming shut in quick succession like thunder echoing far off.

It's shockingly quiet and stiflingly stuffy inside the car by myself, like a plush phone booth or an elevator in a fancy hotel. Or an expensive coffin.

When you think you're a bad person, you kind of think you deserve it when bad things happen to you. You go along with it because you did something wrong or something you're ashamed of, so since there's cosmic justice you are receiving your comeuppances.

When I was younger, I would sleep with a girl and then immediately feel bad about it. There was a lot going on there to unpack, I think. There was a deep, puritanical part of American society that I never asked for and was trying hard to excise, but it remained ingrained. It was shame for doing something wrong according to some supernatural entity beyond space and time that would judge you forever for your indiscretions even if he built these into you and gave you the means to do something with them. Even then, it didn't make sense to me, even before I had sex it didn't make sense to me, but it was still inside of me making me feel a certain way. You can know you're feeling something, know you shouldn't, but that doesn't stop you from feeling it.

There were the women themselves who I didn't respect, or I respected so much I couldn't believe they'd just sleep with anyone, let alone me. Sometimes I didn't even really like them, I was just horny and they were there and they were willing. I didn't realize they were probably working out the exact same issues on me that I was trying desperately to work out on them or through them. We were two people spinning frantically in the front yard trying to get dizzy and sometimes our orbits would intertwine, and we'd crash into each other.

There was this girl I worked with towards the end of high school, Laura. We went to different schools, and she was probably the angriest person I'd ever known up to that point. I mean, we were seventeen or something so we (and everyone we knew) were pissed off all the time. She would rage at everything. She never took it out on me or other people—maybe her parents or siblings but I wasn't there for that. She just radiated rage, pissed off all the time. I guess we had a lot in common. We had the same job, we both worked on our respective school yearbooks, and we were pissed off all the time. She came over after school a lot. The first time she directed her rage in my direction was after I lost my virginity to one of her friends whose name escapes me now. She didn't matter. Not to me or the universe at large. She just blipped by, took her clothes off and winked out of existence.

Laura and I were friends. We were also very similar, single seventeen-year-olds who hung around each other nearly every day. So, naturally, I fell in love with her or lust with her or whatever. She's wasn't the girl next-door in either geography or temperament but if you understand that concept you understand my feelings for her.

I asked her out. After months of preamble. After months of eating together and shopping at the mall and hanging out with my friends and talking on the phone every stupid fucking day. Months of this. We were already dating in everything but name. So finally, I asked her out.

She said no.

I didn't remember how I asked her but I'm sure I was not straightforward or direct. I'm sure I made a joke out of it and I'm sure she at least partly thought I was fucking with her and when she accepted, I'd ridicule her with all my friends backing me up. No one is that angry and secure at the same time. What kind of persona did I project out into the world and how much did that affect how people responded to me which in turn affected how I tweaked my projection? Because I surely could not just be myself. This was before I realized that everybody was looking for somebody else and everyone's quirks were someone else's fetishes so yes you could be yourself and still get with chicks. Who knew?

Laura said no to me because of whatever horrible tangle of things were going on inside of her and around her at the time. I ran into this other girl that we worked with who was one of her best friends and I opened up to her just enough so she could see I was a human being and so was she and when was the last time anybody asked her out or told her she was pretty and suddenly we slept together and did I even like her fuck I didn't even know her I didn't realize you could sleep with people you didn't even know and I also didn't know it didn't make the hunger you felt towards the people you did know that you loved or thought you loved or you at least knew and they knew you a little bit, that it didn't push that away, it made it greater. It made you want them even more, even though you had someone else and somewhere else to get sex, you still wanted them. I learned this lesson many times over the years before I really learned it. I told Laura that I slept with her friend whose name and features have been lost to time (but not her smile or laugh or the pained face she made that first time). And suddenly all that rage was directed in my direction and I wasn't talking to her on the phone, she had materialized in front of me at my house she was parked crooked on the curb in front of my house in that chintzy Geo Metro that felt as if it was made of paper and she smacked me in the face on my front lawn in the middle of the day as if I actually meant something to her.

"You said 'no'," I told her with my cheek still stinging.

What else could I have said? I felt like I'd tried everything to get her to notice me, but if I was paying attention to that slap, she clearly already did, but how could I understand the shit going on inside her that she had to push aside just to get out of bed every morning, when I could barely deal with my own?

I think in the back of my mind I remembered something my father—probably drunk—had told me when I was a kid, *When you broke up with a girl, her friends would probably hate you, but some of them would want to get with you.* Clearly it had already worked once so why not try it on Laura?

It worked of course and probably fucked me up for

life. Success can be the worst thing for you.

I slept with Laura less than a week after fucking her nameless friend and then happily ever after, right? This was what I wanted so what else could it be?

But why did the story have to take these twists and turns to get to this point? I thought. Why did I have to sleep with your friend for you to notice me and why did that make you want me when nothing else seemed to?

Why would you even want to?

I hate me so you must hate me as well, even if I did everything to hide this. I'm going to try and trick you into sleeping with me and when I've cycled through the shame of my own end of that experience I'm going to hate you for falling for my tricks even though I'm glad you did and I tried very hard to make all of this come true.

Now, sitting silently in that car by myself in the darkness contemplating whether I had any choice or if those were all the convoluted consequences of a seemingly random string of events baring down on me.

The rest of it was still there of course but it was lessened. I looked out at them all huddled in the soft glow of the parking lights, and I saw the man whose wife I've slept with. It wasn't my idea. She approached me and I know that's thin. I know it's the X-rated version of a kid saying *But she started it!* isn't it? I went along with it. I didn't stop it. I was more than willing. I didn't think I had done anything to encourage her, but it isn't like I wasn't attracted to her before we began our affair. Was I putting out vibes, some kind of energy she could receive and process?

Does it matter?

Ben smiled at me that smile that said *Stay in the car*

if you want, nobody cares.

But that smile also said *You pussy.* Or it did in my imagination, but I guess that's where all of this was taking place anyway.

I was just projecting all of my shit onto them.

I didn't know what brought any of them here. I didn't even know the real reason we were here.

I didn't buy that Sea-Doo shit at all, not after hearing Ben's longwinded story of his brothers-in-law were maybe drug dealers, which was then confirmed by Javi—who was supposed to be *our* good friend—who turned out was deeply involved with this drug shit.

I was ready to leave the fleeting and relative safety of the SUV for whatever fate awaited me out there in the dark with people I thought I knew.

But I didn't believe in fate.

I was ready to accept this fate I didn't believe in because I was guilty of another crime, and part of me believed that I deserved whatever was waiting out there in the night.

But that's karma and I didn't believe in karma.

Or it was cosmic justice, which I also didn't believe in, because all you have to do is look at the world around and think of all the people that get away with whatever filthy thing they've done and don't even feel bad about it—the bare minimum.

I talked about influencing another man's wife with, what, vibes and energy?

Shit. I don't think I have to say *But I don't believe in vibes or energy.* I'm not even sure I believe in marriage...

I know. It's rationalization. She was a consenting adult. What have I done? If I hadn't fucked her, she would have found someone else to.

Hell, I'm not delusional—she probably has.

I didn't break their marriage or twist whatever's wrong inside her or make the world this way.

Were these the same things the redneck twins told themselves when they sold drugs? Somebody's going to, might as well be me since I'm not a piece of shit.

So I didn't even believe in any of that shit, but the point was, there was absolutely no reason for me to get out of that car.

I got out of the car.

I shut the door too softly, so it latched but didn't shut all the way. I leaned into it with my body until I heard it click.

It seemed deafening out here in the mostly dark of the predawn, the silence of the open outdoors with its infinite sky and endless land. The SUV was quiet because it was closed off. This was quiet because it was asleep, and tiptoes were required to keep it that way.

It felt much colder out there, too, even though it probably wasn't. If I checked my phone, I doubted if the temperature had fallen more than a degree. But there's the cold of being in the brick alley outside of a club radiating—almost living and breathing—with life and the cold of open farmland or wherever the fuck we were.

"Where the fuck are we?" I whispered as softly as I could and still be heard. I wasn't sure I even heard myself.

"Little south of Greenwood," somebody said, one of the twins. He spoke confidently louder than I had but still he whispered. "Kind of a trailer park."

"Kind of?" Ben asked in a tone of voice that told me he was liking this less and less as his confidence from the inside the car had evaporated at the same rate that the heat from inside the car had left his body. Nobody's teeth were chattering yet, but we were close.

Whoever was holding the flashlight flipped it up briefly so it was parallel with the ground and aimed towards the west. He lowered it back towards the ground immediately.

In that flash we saw, maybe fifty yards away, the edges of a trailer park. The grass where we were standing was uncut and long and ratty. The glimpse of the park was nice by comparison, trimmed and mostly fenced in. I didn't have time to count units, but there were several dozen trailers and twice that number of cars haphazardly parked around them.

Once I knew it was there, I could see it sort of—a blacker black against the lighter black of the sky and maybe a TV flickering here or there, and a light or two reflecting off the high gloss of automobile paint.

The flashlight flipped up again for another short burst, this time ninety degrees from what it had illuminated previously. North, if that first shot had indeed been west.

A lone trailer this time, not in the greatest shape, but who knew what a baller trailer would look like anyway? It was over in this part of the field by itself and two automobiles—a shitty old Saturn and an out-of-place and brand-new looking Hummer—were parked crookedly near it. I realized now that we had parked our vehicles to box these ones in and keep them from easily fleeing if anyone had those intentions.

And, in the last millisecond of light from the dim yellow of the janky flashlight, I thought I saw a flatbed with half a dozen Sea-Doos on it.

"Huh," I said, not intending for it to be out loud.

It was probably less of an actual word than a surprised grunt.

"What? What's wrong?" Corey said, betraying the actual state of his nerves more than anything else so far. A simple sound uttered by me threatened to undo all their carefully constructed coolness, causing their plan—or lack of plan—to collapse instantly.

When I didn't respond, Corey angled the flashlight towards me, stopping it just short of my face. It was one of those crappy red plastic flashlights from my childhood, the kind that took a couple of C batteries and required a vigorous shaking every so often to keep the damn thing lit. I could envision it winking out at an inopportune moment during whatever forthcoming fiasco awaited us.

"I, ah, didn't think there'd really be any Sea-Doos," I said. The flashlight hesitated on my chest and then lowered.

"Well, there are," he said. "And we're taking them back because our money paid for them."

"The dipshit in that trailer is one of our employees," Dustin said from somewhere in the dark.

"Right," Corey agreed, "He's like an independent contractor and we paid him up front for something he didn't deliver."

"Like he defaulted on a loan," Javier offered.

"Sure," Corey said. The flashlight bobbed slightly as he talked. I tried to focus on the words and not the movement of the small circle of yellow light wavering in the tall grass.

"These go a little way towards making things right,"

he continued. "But we also need to explain to him what's going on, so he knows and understands."

"Just talk," Dustin said in a way that made me think it would not be just talk or could easily slip into something that was beyond talk—and if it did maybe that wouldn't be so bad and just maybe he was hoping that it would.

The flashlight arced over the trailer park in the background again briefly.

"Most of these people know what's up," Corey said. "Or they know enough to mind their own fucking business. And Javi knows the guy inside."

"Yup," Javier said, and I could hear him nodding like this was the most normal thing in the world. Like he did this shit all the time and I became a little worried that he did.

"There's two vehicles," Ben said. He'd been so quiet for so long and he spoke in a tone voice so far from his own that I nearly forgot he was there. I quickly tried to figure out who spoke in the pause he took between sentences. "Does he have somebody else in there?"

I could hear Javier nodding in the dark, his dreads and thick beard moving about him.

"Yeah, I think I know who she is," he said. "This chick he's on-and-off-again with."

"Guess it's on tonight," somebody said.

"Javi's going to come inside with us while we talk to this dumbass," Corey said. "A friendly face to help him understand the situation."

"You two hook the trailer up to the pickup while we're inside," Dustin said.

I shook my head, then remembered that probably no one could see me.

"I'll go inside with Javi and one of you," I said.

The night somehow got darker. The air became more still. There was no sound at all.

"This woman has a kid, right Javi?" I said.

We could all hear him nod agreement. He spoke anyway.

"Yeah," he said.

"I saw the car seat in there when you hit the car with the flashlight," I said. "So, the kid's inside there, too."

More silence.

"Look," I continued, "Javi's this guy's friend, great. So that'll put him at ease. You're going to separate him from the woman and her kid, right? Who's going to keep them calm? One of you? C'mon."

"I have kids," Corey said, lamely.

"Kyle is sort of a ladies' man. He can keep her entertained," Ben said. His tone was sarcastic. I mentally flipped him off anyway. I dug through my brain for a good comeback.

Instead, I said, "You can hook this up yourself, Ben."

I didn't phrase it as a question, but he answered still.

"Won't be a problem," he said.

"So, one of you can stay out here with him and watch all our backs," I said. And added, "I assume you're armed with something under those big coats."

I regretted that last line, afraid they'd offer me or all of us guns and then I would have no idea what the fuck to do. Two were already two too many, if they were strapped. They said this was just going to be a talk, so let's see if they held to that.

"We told you," Corey said but his voice wasn't as sure as before, "those people out there won't fuck with us."

"Because you pay them, right?" I said and I heard Javi shift and maybe even Ben. One or both were starting to get it. "Do you pay them? Directly? Do you come down here and pay them or do you have this fucking guy do it that we're sneaking up on?"

I didn't think it was possible for the night to get quieter, but it had somehow. A motorcycle far off spoiled the effect.

"Look," I offered, "I'm not trying to fuck your shit up or step on your toes or tell you how to do shit. I just want to get the fuck out of here. As quickly and cleanly as possible. I assume that means you guys get what you want, and this guy and his girl and her kid don't get hurt."

More calm in the darkness. I could feel them exchanging a meaningful glance as they conferred silently in the night using whatever telepathic form of communication that was built innately into them. The flashlight never wavered from its fixed spot on the grass between us.

"Alright," Corey said, "that's smart. Kyle comes inside with Javi and me. Ben hooks up the trailer and Dustin keeps watch, helps if he needs to. I wanna be out of here in twenty minutes."

The flashlight moved away from our cars and towards the mobile home. It stayed low to the ground and swept slowly from left to right and back again as it moved.

Javier waited a beat and then followed. His eyes were doubtless fixated on the area of ground illuminated by the light.

I followed right behind him. I heard him breathing hard as he stepped carefully over the uneven, soft ground.

Dustin brushed past me and started pacing a tight perimeter. I heard Ben beginning to move around getting everything set. Now that we had tasks, everyone was itching to get to them. Things were happening quickly.

We got to the front step of the trailer and huddled around the door. Corey took a set of keys from his pocket, and using the flashlight beam, he selected one with a piece of masking tape stuck to it that read TRAVIS.

I wondered if they owned this guy's place, too, or if they forced him to cough up a key when he started working with them.

Either way, the Redneck Twins were more prepared than I would've given them credit for. I'd have to remember to tell Ben this once it was over and we were far removed from these events.

After he found the correct key, Corey turned the flashlight off, and I heard the key slide into the lock. It clicked and I felt the stuffy air of the place hit me in the face as he cracked the door. It was overly warm and smelled like a dozen different smells I could do without. I told myself to breathe through my mouth once we were inside the stifling heat of the place.

"Javi," Corey said and passed him the flashlight. He took it but didn't turn it on.

Corey rummaged in his coat for a second before coming out with something that radiated the cold more than outside air we had just left—I could feel its chill radiating off of it.

I knew it was a gun. As much as I didn't want it to. That never changed anything.

"Just talk," I whispered as softly as I could.

"Yup," he said.

We piled inside.

Javi turned the flashlight on for a second and took the lead. The way he moved through the cramped and cluttered space...they'd both been here before. I wasn't surprised.

The place was a shithole.

Maybe I'm betraying my middle-class upbringing biases, but I wasn't surprised by this. This is Indiana. Apartments were cheap and mortgages were even cheaper. Outside of the main cities in the undesirable suburbs? A place like Greenwood? You could get a two-bedroom apartment for under $800 a month. A three-bedroom, one-bathroom house—we're talking mortgage payment of less than $600 and probably below $500 without much difficulty.

Trailers are for losers and deadbeats and weirdos.

The stacks of magazines and pizza boxes and piles of foam to-go pops and half-crushed cans of more pop and more than one tube-style nineteen inch TV and a tangle of videogame consoles and huge towers of teetering stacks of DVDs in front of equally precarious stacks of VHS tapes and mounds of laundry and more mounds of laundry and big piles of bags of unopened off-brand chips and generic cereal—the kind that comes in huge dog food sized bags and not a box—and stacks of packages of store-brand cookie knock-offs and huge plastic bags full of more wadded up plastic bags.

No wonder it smelled like a stale Walmart in here.

I did notice and was surprised by the absence of beer cans or drained bottles of booze and wondered briefly if maybe we had the wrong place. I also didn't smell any old tobacco or see any overflowing ashtrays and I thought this guy was a fucking drug dealer and aren't they all the same?

Corey followed behind and to Javi's right. We weaved around the furniture and shit strewn about the floor.

Whatever had been carrying me until this moment set me down and I faltered. I did not want to be in this place. I did not want to do these things. The reasons I had for coming inside with them, I seemed to remember that they were good reasons, logical and just reasons, but my head couldn't find them anymore. They'd evaporated as soon as we started moving through this guy's nightmare home, stepping over his mounds of garbage that he hunkered down and was somehow comfortable in, that he brought people to, that he had his girlfriend come over and fuck him among, while her kid was shut into the bathroom or left in the car or outside on the porch.

If only he'd had some booze lying around maybe I could snag a swig for courage or at least understand him, because if he wasn't smoking and—goddamn did I want a fucking cigarette right now worse than the first day I'd quit or any day following it—if he wasn't drinking then what the fuck was this guy doing out here selling drugs? And I began to picture this Travis as a completely separate species of human, something I had never seen before or even dreamt of, something entirely other that looks like a person but couldn't possibly be, because how could you live like this and not conform to my every prejudice about you? How could you not have the vices I projected on you and your kind?

Why was I finding this sad, rather than disgusting?

I followed behind them somehow even though my

body was screaming at me to run, to hit them both over the head and run and bar anyone's escape somehow and burn the whole sad fucking thing down and fishtail wildly through the ashen remains in a stolen vehicle.

But I followed and the night stayed quiet even as my brain would not rest.

I lived alone in a small one-bedroom apartment beneath and beside other small apartments, but this place, with all its clutter and narrow dimensions, was something else entirely. It didn't feel as if there were thin cheap walls separating us from the outside—so thin and cheap that I could feel the night air leaking in from all around me and from all directions—it felt not as if the wide-open outside waited for us on the other side of walls I was certain I could push through with my unaided hands. No. It felt as if we were in a tight cave deep inside a mountain. It felt as if the cold that radiated in, that leaked and leeched its way in wasn't air but something much older, like it was packed earth, so far underground it had never seen the sun, and all it had ever known was the damp, compressed earth of the grave.

I knew these things were not true.

I knew we were in a shitty trailer south of Indianapolis.

I knew this man was a drug dealer who owed these other drug dealers money. There was no other reason to be here. This pathetic creature had nothing anyone would come here to take, even though right now Ben was hooking his shit up to the pickup so we could take it.

Yes. Yes, yes. I knew these things that were true and these things that weren't, but that's not how it felt. And that's why your feelings are not real things and cannot be trusted.

We stopped at the foot of the bed.

There were shapes under the blankets. A plethora of blankets even though the temperature in here had to be closing in on eighty degrees.

Javier went to the left and Corey went to the right.

I stayed at the foot of the bed in front of the doorway. I bizarrely felt no fear at keeping my back to this open area, even though I could feel it behind me like the edge of a tall building in a blackout. We hadn't checked the place for anyone else but where would they be? The child could be under the blankets with them. I hoped it simply wasn't here. I hoped it was with a grandparent or its father or Disneyland or the moon or anywhere else.

Javier hit the flashlight. It was pointed directly at a sleeping man's face on the left side of the bed. He'd either guessed correctly or knew which side of the bed the man slept on. Both seemed equally improbable.

He used no pillow. His head was back on the mattress, tipped far enough back that his mouth hung open comically. The flashlight hit him right in the mouth and it glowed pink and red from the flashlight beam.

Javier pushed down on the man's right arm with his free hand while keeping the light trained on him.

His tongue moved and he began to stir.

He made a sound that was still very far away.

His eyelids fluttered and he began to squirm under the pressure Javier was applying to his arm.

He tried to say something like *What the fuck?* but it came across as *Da fugg?*

At the same moment his eyes finally shot open, Corey hit a wall switch near him, and a bright overhead light blared on, bathing the whole room in a sickly compact florescent.

The woman next to him was already awake and alert. She moved her eyes calmly from Corey's face to mine to Javier's. Unlike her man, she'd been awake since before we entered the room. There was a comprehension in her eyes that the recently awoken did not possess.

Her eyes came back and rested on mine.

She appeared impassive but could've been memorizing my features. I was the only face in this room she did not recognize.

She glanced behind me into the dark of the rest of the trailer. There was no one back there and it was not a ploy to get me to look.

I had a flash of chilling insight: She was wondering where Dustin was.

The man beside her rubbed at his eyes with his free left hand and tried to twist away from Javier.

"Javi?" he said in a voice that told me he hadn't always been a nonsmoker. "What the fuck? What fucking time is it?"

"Early," Corey said and took a step forward. He had a gun in his left hand, but it hung loosely at his side. The woman was intentionally not looking at it.

The man jolted a little and blinked as he looked at Corey, realizing he was there for the first time. He tried his best to hide his *Oh, shit* expression.

"Corey?" he said. "What's going on?"

I got the impression that he wasn't as out of it as he was pretending to be.

"We need to talk, Travis," he said while looking at the woman next to him. "With a little privacy."

"OK. Alright," he said and tried sitting up straighter in the bed. He looked at Javier's hand holding him down on the mattress like he was just noticing something was impeding him. "Can I sit up?"

Javi waited a beat and then released him.

Travis pulled a pillow up from the ground next to the bed and put it between his back and the wall. No headboards in this trailer trash haven, I guess. He took a sip of something from a red solo cup next to the bed.

The girl had slowly and calmly pulled her hands from under the covers and folded them neatly on top of the blankets.

Travis seemed to notice me for the first time and nodded tentatively in my direction unsure of what to make of me.

"Where's Dustin?" he asked still looking at me. Maybe he meant to say, *Who the fuck is this guy?*

"He's outside," Corey said. "You know. He doesn't like to talk as much as we do."

Travis nodded like he was agreeing to something he hadn't really been paying attention to. He kept looking at me.

"I don't think we've been properly introduced," he said in my direction and stuck a hand out towards me.

I left my hands in my pockets where they'd been since we entered this sty and left him hanging.

"Forget about him," Javier said.

"He's not really here," Corey said. Which either landed more ominous than he'd intended, or he was going for a level of creepy I hadn't fully realized up to this point. I guess he was holding a gun in plain view even if he didn't point it at anyone.

Travis looked at him questioningly but asked nothing.

With his free hand, Corey lightly pulled the blankets away from the woman. She didn't argue or resist, even though she must be screaming inside, right? She must be. Her life couldn't be so insane that this kind of shit was so normal that she took it with a shrug and sarcastic roll of the eyes.

Please, please tell me there aren't people in this world for whom people with guns making them get out of bed in the middle of the night is no big deal. I said this to myself in my head, even though I knew that of course there were. There's nothing horrible I could be told or comprehend or even imagine that hasn't been done to someone so often that it's become pedestrian.

She didn't look at him as he uncovered her. She looked at me. Travis did, too, even though he was trying to hide it by taking quick glances at me sidelong. I was the unknown quantity in this room. I was the face they didn't recognize and the one they needed to be on guard against.

I'd miscalculated.

Why did I think I'd be a calming influence on the situation?

Why did I think I'd come in here and control anything?

She was in an over-sized t-shirt and maybe panties but that was it. It could've been a man's shirt but not this man. They were close in height and build which made Travis one scrawny mother fucker. I was more impressed by Javi's ability to pick him out based on their shapes under the covers. They would've looked nearly identical.

"You're gonna go in the other room with him," Corey

said to her, nodding in my direction and motioning at her to get out of bed with his gun hand. He just casually waved the thing around as if it couldn't kill everyone in this room in seconds. As if he didn't realize it was there at all, just a part of his body.

She moved to get up and Travis put a hand in front of her stomach the way a mother does to her child when they apply the brakes suddenly. There's danger.

"Hey," Travis said, "maybe we could all stay in the same room? Whaddya think?"

She made a noise that was either disgust or clearing her throat. She pushed his arm away without much resistance.

Corey leaned over her and pressed the gun into the blankets, pushing into Travis's thigh.

"We need privacy, Travis, remember?" he said with the first real hint of menace in his voice since we entered their home. Or maybe it was the use of the gun that punctuated his words.

"Ow, fuck. Yeah, man," he said and shifted under the blankets to get away from him. Corey leaned onto him with more of his weight before relaxing and stepping back. Travis ruffled the blankets as he rubbed at his leg and repeated himself. "Fuck. Yeah."

She stood up. I was pretty sure I caught a glimpse of panties when she did. At least she had that. I couldn't decide if I felt like more or less of a creep.

Corey was still in her way so she couldn't get by. She looked at him.

"Is your kid here?" he asked her, but he looked down at Travis as he asked it.

"He's in the closet," Travis responded.

"Jesus Christ, Travis," Javier said and shook his head.

"No, man," he explained. "It's cool. It's like a little room. He's got a bed in there and shit."

There were no doors in here besides the one I was standing in front of so the closet must be in the main area somewhere.

"You know," Travis said, a shit-eating grin on his face, "like you guys are saying. Privacy."

She made that disgusted noise again—either applied directly to Travis or indirectly towards her own disgust at herself for being with this loser.

But I was projecting.

For all I knew, that could be the way she laughed.

She pushed past Corey and came face to face with me.

"Take the blanket if you're cold," I said.

It was the first thing I'd said in front of them and I saw Travis flinch from the corner of my eye, maybe because he wasn't sure I'd say anything, maybe because I talked so quietly, to make sure that my voice didn't crack or betray how scared I was, and that freaked him out more.

She made no move to take a blanket. It was 100 degrees in here. I took her by the upper arm and guided her out of the room.

Javier took a step-and-a-half to the doorway and pulled the accordion pocket door closed. That shitty door made me sadder than the rest of the whole pathetic place.

We took two steps from that sad door to the couch. I fumbled with a lamp until it clicked on and lit the place in more of a sodium glow than that shitty flashlight the Redneck Twins had dug out of some distant past.

She stood in the middle of the room, arms folded, like

the queen of the trash heap. The lamp was short, the shade was crooked, and it rested on a low end table, so it lit her face—and probably mine—from underneath in an unnatural campfire glow. Maybe we'd tell ghost stories.

We could hear Ben and Dustin moving shit around outside. I heard the pickup start up and idle, softly rumbling like a big cat at a zoo. The SUV started after another few seconds and added its hum to the pickup's. An automobile orchestra tuning up for the evening's performance.

I hoped we didn't need to make the quick getaway they were planning for.

"I gotta pee," she said.

She hadn't spoken before and I tried to not react with the same shock Travis had upon hearing my voice for the first time.

I located the bathroom with a quick glance. It was closer to the bedroom than the front door and I was pretty much in front of that anyway. I shifted over a half step to the right.

I nodded consent and then, remembering the role I was playing, said, "Leave the door cracked."

"Whatever," she said. Her tone implied that she wanted to mutter *Pervert* but still wasn't sure how I'd react to something like that.

"It don't close good anyway," she added.

I heard Travis's voice go up an octave in the other room. She might be the brains of the pair.

She went into the bathroom, leaving the light out. I could see part of her legs through the angle of the door and her panties around her ankles.

They were nice legs and dark pink or red panties, but

this wasn't the time to be thinking about that.

I thought about it anyway.

As she shifted on the toilet, her legs rubbed together, and I looked away. She peed at what was probably a normal volume and amount of force, but with the door open and in this tiny space it seemed very loud, especially as the voices in the other room had reduced themselves to whispers.

Maybe they were hushed because they were listening to some strange woman take a piss as well.

There was a little rustling and I glanced back towards the bathroom. She was gliding the panties back up over her legs and this was not something I wanted to see.

I mean, I did want to see it and I wasn't looking away, but it was something I shouldn't have seen. It was too intimate and weird. I thought about women I'd been with yet had never seen them in this way, perform this simple act that they did multiple times a day.

I'd never seen Estella go to the bathroom and we'd lived together for four years. This was the other end of the spectrum—she was uptight about it. I pissed in front of her all the time.

Our bathroom had two doors, one from the hallway and one from the bedroom. One time, she entered through the hall and shut and locked the door as usual, but she didn't realize I was in the bedroom. She plopped down on the toilet with the posture of an NBA player benched towards the end of the fourth quarter—legs wide, hunched over with her elbows resting on her knees. The one and only time I ever saw her like this.

I made some sort of noise to let her know that I was there and in the sightline. She made some exclamation and swatted at the other door until it banged shut. She turned the fan on and was in the bathroom longer than normal.

She was embarrassed when she came out and asked me to forget about it.

Forget about what? I'd said, but she didn't get this simple joke and made me swear to try and forget it.

This clearly had the opposite effect, and I never saw what the big deal was anyway. I'm sure I would've forgotten it if she hadn't said anything about it.

I should tell her sometime that women I barely know have used the bathroom in front of me. Sure, she'd love to hear about that.

The toilet in the other room made a strange flushing sound as all toilets do in strange places and she came out of the bathroom rubbing her hands together with hand sanitizer. I could smell the alcohol scent from barely two yards away.

I must have still been thinking about Estella and it was plain on my face. She gave me a funny look.

"What," she said and frowned.

"I had this ex-girlfriend that would never pee in front of me," I said, and then realized how easy it would be to misunderstand my meaning, continued, "I mean, I didn't request it or anything. She was just weird about it."

"Well, I didn't have a choice," she said and then sat on the couch, moving a pile of clothes out of her way. She relented slightly. "Guess she was an uptight bitch."

"I guess," I said.

We heard some commotion from the other room. Travis's voice louder and then silenced. Maybe a hand over his mouth.

We both looked that direction despite ourselves.

"I saw her earlier tonight, actually," I said just to say something to distract us from whatever was going on in the bedroom, to cover the sounds of whatever mundane questioning techniques they were applying to him that morphed into absolute nightmare torture as it made its way across the distance and through the flimsy accordion door and into our ears and infected our minds with the most awful of imagined scenarios.

She looked away from the door and tried to focus on me, tried to distract herself with the same bullshit I was.

She nodded.

"Travis and me used to break up like that," she said, "and then fuck and then I guess we was together again."

I shook my head.

"It's not that," I said, and then because I didn't want to sound like I was better than her, "I've done that messy shit before. But this one... We just had drinks."

"Uh-huh," she said.

I pretended like she agreed with me.

"I'm with somebody else now," I said.

"That's never stopped anybody," she said.

I shrugged at the truthfulness of this statement. I've been that somebody. I am that somebody.

"It'd be kind of gross," I said. "I was with the other girl today."

She nodded, still half distracted from the strange noises emanating from the other room.

Then she went stiff on the couch and stared at me, her eyes bored into me. For the first time she looked something other than disinterested. She looked starkly terrified. I glanced at the door. I couldn't hear anything from there. Is that what was freaking her out? The nothingness? Her shit-talking man who was always running his mouth struck completely silent by something?

But no. She stared at me.

I reflexively reached a hand out to her.

She pulled away from me. She tried to tuck more of her legs inside the shirt. She was suddenly self-conscience. She was trying to make herself as small as possible.

I stopped extending my hand and held both up in a palms-out calming kind of way.

"What?" I asked. "What's wrong?"

She stared at me with crazy, unblinking eyes.

"What did you mean by that?" she asked hoarsely.

"What?" was all I could manage again. Maybe the confusion registered on my face, because she seemed to ease slightly.

"Being with someone else. Today," she said. "You don't mean me, do you? Do you think we're together? Is that why they brought you here? Some psycho to rape me and teach Travis a lesson?"

I couldn't say anything. I just stared at her.

"What the fuck?" I asked finally. "Jesus. What has been done to you?"

She pulled pieces of clothing from next to her off a pile and covered legs as best she could. I could see her bare feet and they were shifting and curling and tensing uncontrollably. I recognized it. My feet had been doing the same thing in Ben's car on our way here.

They wanted to run but had nowhere to go.

She must have registered the shock in my voice and on my face as genuine, or maybe the covering herself in clothes had made her feel safe, because she didn't seem to see me as this awful thing anymore. Her face had lost most of its concerned creases.

"Think I'm in this dump with that dipshit cause life's great?" she asked.

"Jesus," I said.

"If this kind of shit freaks you that much," she said looking at me with almost concern, "you gotta get the fuck away from these people. They're not good dudes. And that fucking brother..."

"Dustin?" I said, going cold.

"Yeah, he's a fucking weirdo," she said.

I wanted her to elaborate. Hell, I wanted to tell her things, tell her who I was sleeping with and why this was becoming more and more tangled by the second, but I couldn't do that and not even because anyone in the other room could easily hear me, hell they could probably hear me outside, but who was this fucking trailer girl? She acts scared for a minute and then suddenly I give her information for her to wield against me, to use with these crazy people that are fucking her man up right now?

She thinks the dumbass twins are scary monsters? And Javi? I've known him for fifteen years. Who the fuck is she? Living out here in this nightmare with this nutjob? Pissing in front of a stranger half-naked and then was suddenly bothered by it? How could it be anything other than an act?

And I remembered something else.

"Isn't your kid here, somewhere?" I asked with maybe a little more accusation in my voice then I intended. "Don't you want to check on him?"

"Yeah," she said. "As soon as you assholes leave."

And I believed her because it all tracked, and I didn't think she was putting anything on. I know—no one ever said they were bad at reading people, but I did... I believed her. That was it.

I became more scared for myself and for Javier and Ben and his wife and his sisters because we were all tangled up in this mess and I didn't see any way out.

We didn't talk any more.

She became too hot or regained her comfort level and brushed most of the clothes away from her.

She asked if she could turn the TV on and I said *Sure* and she absently flipped channels while I tried to keep an eye on her without looking at her legs too much.

I could hear Travis whimpering in the other room even over the TV so she could too.

The only thing I had to keep my thoughts from spiraling into sickness, to distract myself from the griminess of this place and the beating in the other room were thoughts about her legs. This was gross, but in a different familiar way. A way in which I was normally disgusted with myself. I tried not to think of them, but I mostly failed. I thought about how they felt. I thought about her spreading them and fingering herself in the flickering light from the TV. I thought about jerking-off on those panties.

She must have been able to feel this coming from me, because she stopped on some late-nite skin-flick on Cinemax and turned the volume up a bit and set the remote down. She stole glances at me now and again, relishing in how awkward it was.

Luckily, it was only another few minutes before Javi and Corey emerged from the bedroom.

The gun was tucked somewhere out of sight and Corey was rolling his sleeves back down.

Javi had a flat, cold look on his face. It was like he was powered down or shut off into standby mode.

He was holding a small backpack we had not brought in with us.

Corey nodded to the door as he strode past me and went out into the night air, Javi was on his heels.

Travis crawled from the bedroom and into the bathroom moaning. He didn't shut the door, but not because he was told not to.

I turned for the door and saw the woman stand up quickly and move to help him as he struggled in the bathroom.

No.

She wasn't moving to help him. She went to the closet and checked on her child.

The whole damn place shook when I shut the flimsy front door behind me.

It bothered me that I didn't know her name, but it also felt right somehow. Like she got to keep that piece of herself from me and these animals, although Corey and Dustin probably knew what it was, and Javier surely did. He probably knew her kid's name. He was good with names and faces and who-knew-who and all that bullshit.

I looked at the back of their heads as we walked to the vehicles and willed them not to tell me, not to slip into conversation tonight or later at some point, to just forget this whole thing had happened—yes all of it—slip Ben his couple of hundred bucks for whatever side-deal he had going with Javi, but do not give me anything or just give my share to Ben or something—anything—don't make me complicit.

And please, please forget that poor woman and don't tell me her name.

The headlights from both vehicles went from parking to full-on as we approached, and I shielded my eyes. I'm sure this was a much to identify us as to blind Travis or anyone else we didn't want out here.

Corey leaned into the passenger side window of Javier's SUV to say something to Ben and for a moment I worried that we were going to drive back into the city in a different combination than we'd arrived.

I thought of Travis and the woman's concern for where Dustin was and her hushed references to him as a weirdo and I did not want to be stuck in that pickup with him for forty fucking minutes.

But he simply said something to Ben, smacked the top of the door and got into the pickup. Dustin shifted to the other seat so he could drive.

I got into the back of the SUV.

"I can drive, if you want," I said.

"Yeah, me too," Javier said getting in the passenger's seat.

Ben shook his head no. He was gripping the wheel strangely, near ten and two as if he was an old lady. He even leaned forward in his seat, nearing the edge of it.

"Nah," he said. "I'm all keyed up. I need to do something."

Javi and I exchanged looks. *You're all keyed-up? You didn't even go in the fucking trailer. We're jumping out of our skins.*

Javi began futzing with his seat settings and vents and everything around him. I tried stretching out across the bench seat in the back. Maybe I could relax my body, which could relax my mind. My legs jumped and spasmed like I'd just been exercising. I felt my blood pumping through my body. I felt my veins. I felt individual nerves. I felt cells dividing and sloughing off.

"We're gonna meet them at a Denny's," Ben said and pulled out of the field first.

Javi glanced at him and then back out the window.

"I'm kind of sick of these fucking guys," I said. "Can't we do something else?"

Ben started to respond when we heard the shot.

He slammed on his brakes and we all whipped around in our seats.

The pickup was next to the hummer and Dustin had his window rolled down, his arm fully extended with a thin trail of smoke rising from the gun in his hand.

He'd shot one of the tires out. I couldn't see it and I was probably imagining the smoke from the gun barrel as well, but the Hummer sunk down on its back-right side now so what else could it be?

I couldn't be sure, but I thought they were laughing in the pickup.

The trailer door banged, and the woman came out, her face furious. She'd found pants and slip-ons. She was yelling at the truck and flipped them off.

She stopped when Dustin pointed the gun at her.

"No," I said or someone else said or thought or we all thought or maybe the woman said it or thought it and it was so plain I could read it on her face—I could read her mind in that instant because it was the only word in the world right then.

He shifted the gun and shot at the Hummer again. I couldn't tell if he hit it or not.

The woman jolted and shrunk down with hands over her head and face protecting herself. Travis was nowhere to be seen.

They were laughing.

I could hear them in the deafening silence that followed the gunshot as if shattering the quiet of the night had taken all the sounds with it, all the other sounds that were there but you didn't notice until they were gone, like insects and far off motorcycles and cars, like heating systems and electricity buzzing and not too distant dogs. Like the wind.

All there was now was the reverberation of the gunshot echoing off every surface near the gun. And those idiots' laughter or maybe I was just imagining that. They certainly looked pleased with themselves in the ominous red glow from our taillights.

Dustin didn't roll the window up or even pull his gun hand back into the vehicle but let his arm hang limply with the gun tracing lazy circles pointed at the ground.

It wasn't a driveway exactly, just a worn path through the grass and dirt. They could've gone around us if they wanted to get going, hell, they could've even if it was a driveway and a well-manicured lawn—I didn't think they cared much for those distinctions.

But they were feeling themselves now, really playing their part and getting into the role of pushing people around, so they flashed their high beams at us. *Get moving.*

Ben snapped himself out of it long enough to unclamp

his foot from the brake and drive the SUV out onto the road.

His mouth was a tight line and he was very subtly shaking his head back and forth from side to side as he drove. I might've even caught a grumble or mumble under his breath to complete the picture.

Before we got to the highway, they sped up and passed us. I felt thudding music coming from the truck, and the trailer full of Sea-Doos fishtailed wildly as they blew past us. At least they'd put the guns away and rolled up the windows.

"Did they throw horns when they went by?" Ben asked.

"I wasn't looking," I said. I'd sunk back into my seat as if settling in for a road trip.

Javier said nothing.

Ben fiddled with the radio but left it on low enough so we could still talk. But nobody said anything.

We drove up the nearly deserted highway. The pickup's taillights were long gone even though we were meeting them at Denny's. Something told me that they probably wouldn't wait for us to arrive to dig into their Moon's Over My Hammy or endless pancakes.

We saw flashing lights up ahead.

A cop car had a vehicle pulled to the side of the road. Looming, darkened shapes highlighted by police lights.

We all held our breath.

It wasn't them. It wasn't even the right kind of truck, and it wasn't pulling a trailer full of personal watercraft.

We all audibly exhaled and relaxed.

I couldn't tell if I was relieved it wasn't them or if I wanted it to be. If it was them, would they have pointed to us as we drove by and made us more a part of this? Would the cops have even believed them enough to stop us or at least take down Javier's plate number? It's not like they would find anything if—

Shit.

Shit, shit, shit.

I looked at Javier's reflection in the passenger side window glass.

"What's in the bag, Javi?" I asked him. There'd been no sounds in the car besides the quiet radio for a while now, so my voice sounded foreign and loud, even to me.

Javi shrugged. Not ignoring me or blowing me off but not quite ready to answer.

"You have a bag?" Ben asked. "From that place? What the fuck, man."

"It's my car anyway," Javi said.

"Well, I'm fucking driving it, asswipe," Ben said.

Javier turned away from the window and put up a reassuring hand, patting the air between them instead of Ben's shoulder.

"It's nothing," he said. "It's just cash and one of that dude's cell phones."

"What? What's the phone for?" Ben asked. He was strangely not focused on the money.

"I didn't ask, man, and Corey didn't say," Javi said. "Maybe so he wouldn't wig-out and call the cops when Dustin blasted up his ride."

"Forget about the phone," I said. "Give me my two hundred bucks and let me get the fuck out of here."

Ben nodded.

"Yeah, give me my couple of bills," he said.

"They want to do it at Denny's," Javier said.

"So?" I said. "I don't want to fucking eat with them."

Ben nodded again and added, "Yeah, fuck that."

Javier shrugged and looked out the window again as if there was anything other than blackness out there.

"Well, that's how we're doing it," he said.

"Look," Ben said, "we can drop you off at Denny's with that bag and your car, whatever. I don't see why we have to go inside. They promised us a couple bills, that's two each, so four hundred and we call a cab and call it a fucking night."

"More like a fucking morning," I said. The dashboard clock said it was almost 3:00.

Javi shrugged again.

"I don't know what deal you guys had," he said. "Nobody told me. But I do know that I don't want the tires on my car shot out on the weekend I'm getting married. So, all of us are going to Denny's. You can settle up there."

I sunk lower into my seat. I was tired and there was no sense in arguing. I know when I'm on the losing side of a discussion.

Ben wouldn't let it go. He kept at Javier, even going as far as to say he'd get the money from them later.

"I just don't want to see them anymore," he said. "Not after the wild west show back there. Not tonight. Mother fucker pointed a gun at that woman."

Javier hadn't raised his voice or changed his position and Ben was looking pathetic by comparison and before I realized it, it had pissed me off in a big way.

"You don't want to see them anymore? I didn't even wanna come out here," I said at Ben, not shouting, but I wasn't whispering or slouched back in my seat anymore.

I think even Javi jumped a little. "You didn't even go inside, man."

He looked at me in the rearview mirror hurt, and confused, but he saw in my eyes the same things. I was his friend. I was glad he didn't go in there. This passed between us in the mirror. I hoped it did at least.

"Look," Javier said, looking at us again, "If you don't go to breakfast, they're going to think something's up. Do you get it? If you're not at breakfast, you're at the police station."

"That's fucking stupid," I said.

"Yeah," Ben said and nodded. I was getting sick of him agreeing with me but contributing nothing of his own. Insanely sick of it. Like I was going to take it out on him because they were in another vehicle up ahead somewhere. Maybe he did get a glimpse of my mind in the mirror because he continued, "We're not going to the fucking cops. It's three in the damn morning. I wanna go to bed."

Javier let out a breath and finally agreed with us on something.

"Tell me about it," he said. "I gotta get married tomorrow. Man, it is a good thing I don't have to be home tonight. Staying with my brothers at their hotel. Lisa would fucking kill me."

I laughed.

"How many times has she threatened to kill you, Javi?" Ben asked, chuckling too. "Aren't you supposed to be married for a while before the wife wants you dead?"

Javi flipped him off but was laughing too. We all had the giggles coming down off whatever our bodies had pumped us full of to make it through the trailer park without exploding from the inside out.

"It's gotten better since I purposed to her, man," he said. "And stopped, you know, running around on her."

Ben laughed and shook his head.

For some reason Javi was the only person who ever got away with this kind of behavior in front of Ben. Maybe because his stories were so outlandishly cartoonish that they had a sense of the unreal to them. How could you be mad at this dipshit when he was clearly trying so hard to fuck himself over, and with a smile on his face?

"Her cousin going to be there, Javi?" I asked him while trying my best to hide a smile. He saw right through me right away.

"Oh, fuck you," he said and sunk into his seat.

"Which cousin is that?" Ben asked with the same impeccable acting skills I was displaying.

Javi put his head in hands.

"Goddammit," he said quietly.

"You remember," I said teasing it out as much as I could while knowing Ben couldn't have forgotten. "Lisa's younger cousin, the brunette."

Ben shook his head swallowing his mirth as best he could.

"Not ringing any bells," he said. "Anything, unique about her?"

"You guys aren't invited to my wedding anymore," Javier said quietly from the front seat.

"Yeah, yeah, there is one thing," I said. "Javi fucked her when she turned eighteen."

I thought Ben was going to drive the SUV off the road he was laughing so hard,

"Fuck you guys," Javi said, but he laughed too. "Yeah she's going to be there. She's handing out the rice or whatever the hell you throw around now."

"Oh shit, seriously?" Ben asked.

Javi threw his arms up in the air in defeat.

"What the fuck could I do?" he asked us. "Tell Lisa, 'No, I don't think we should invite your cousin cuz I fucked her one time when she was barely legal?' It might be awkward. They're actually fairly close now."

"Not as close as you," I said. Javi reached back and punched me from the front seat. "C'mon, you walked right into that one. I could've said something like, 'From cousins to Eskimo sisters…'"

"What about that chick from New Haven with the kid? The crazy one. What was her name?" Ben asked.

"Tracy," Javier said quietly into his hands.

"Right, Tracy," Ben agreed. "Is she invited?"

"Fuck off, seriously," Javier responded not as quiet.

"What was the deal with this Tracy, again?" I asked. "Don't think I ever met her."

Ben laughed.

"I think you still lived here, maybe you were in school," he said. "So Javi decided that he needed some 'strange,' which, you guys know how I feel about that, but whatever. Clearly, I'm the weirdo here. But instead of a one night or casual hookup, he gets himself another girlfriend in another city, so he has somewhere to stay when he's in town. Javi was traveling a lot for work then, back and forth."

I laughed. I knew this story of course. It was famous.

"Right," I said. "What was your work then? Why were you traveling from Indianapolis to northeast Indiana on a weekly basis?"

"Vacuums," Javier said plainly.

"Yeah, he was selling fucking vacuum cleaners," Ben said. "He rented office space and everything. But he forgot to make it large enough to sleep in, so he hooked up with Tracy, so he'd have a nice bed to sleep in when he was on the road."

He shrugged.

"She was fucking hot, too," he said. "I don't care what you say."

"She was fucking insane," Ben said. "That time she drove down to Indy to confront you, and Aimee and I had to keep Lisa busy while you sorted her out?"

"Wait, what?" I said, offended. "You do this for him, and you give me shit about my ways?"

Ben shrugged his *It's just Javi* shrug and moved on.

"But that's not the story," Ben said. "The story is, he came to me and said 'Ben, what do I do? I got these two bitches and it's driving me crazy. Tell me exactly what to do and I'll do it.'"

Javier let out a whistle between his teeth.

"The fuck I said it like that," he said. "And what's that fucking voice? Is that supposed to be me?"

Ben waved him off.

"So, I said, 'Well, Javi, break up with Tracy right now cause she's nuts. And you say you love Lisa, right? Then, it's gonna be hard but you gotta tell her the truth and then together the two of you decide where to go from there.'"

"Now you're doing a voice for yourself? That doesn't make any sense," Javier said.

We ignored him.

"So, I assume, since he asked you for advice and you

gave him pretty good advice, he followed it to the letter, correct?" I asked Ben.

"Hmm," Ben said, "that would be reasonable to assume, wouldn't it? This is not what happened."

I did my best *Home Alone* impression in the rearview mirror to register my shock. Javier ignored us.

"He did not break up with the psycho and he did not tell Lisa," Ben said, but the humor had died from him a little because this was the man's soon to be wife we were talking about and we wanted to tease him and poke at him and give him shit but we didn't really want to get in his business.

"I did break up with her," Javier added, "eventually."

We weren't laughing anymore. He didn't seem particularly offended or hurt by our razing, but we'd lost the taste for it.

Have you ever been excited about something, excited about something in your own mind and as you're telling someone else, something about it embarrasses you? Maybe they react in a way that is not the way you were looking for. Maybe it just doesn't make sense to you anymore why you were so excited, why you had to tell them, why you opened yourself up to them like this. It doesn't matter why but suddenly you want to stop talking and disappear inside yourself, if not disappear completely from sight and from the world, but it's too late and you can't simply stop talking now because they are paying just enough attention to you that they'd notice if you ceased speaking without ending the story.

So, you kind of trail off or cut the story short or shrug off the ending or try to make a joke out of it or, as a final attempt, make a joke about yourself.

It didn't make sense, but it was as if you finally glimpsed, in their reaction to you how they really felt about you and maybe they didn't like you very much and that was too painful.

So you sit there in that space and feel bad about yourself because maybe you're starting to suspect that the only thing you're good at is feeling bad about yourself, that the only talent you have for surprising others and yourself is just how shitty you can make yourself feel. You can make it from the slightest glimmer for the smallest sliver and even you can create it out of thin air and from nothing at all.

I didn't know if that's how Ben felt about it.

I didn't know if Javier was bothered by this talk.

I could ask them, and they could tell me, but I could never really know. I could only ever truly know myself and that was something I didn't even like that much. I liked it so little, in fact, I tried to never think about it, which made it—even in absence—the only thing I ever really thought about.

They could tell me, and I could even believe them, but I could never truly know.

We drove the rest of the way up the highway in silence.

Ten-plus minutes of frozen and faded blacktop zipped by in the bleak mid-February early morning. The inside of the car was warm, but we could see the exhaust steaming and the frosted windows of the other vehicles on the road, and we knew everything was only warm until the moment we let the outside in.

It was gray because the sun wanted to poke up, but the dark wanted the sky more and was winning. It was the end of winter. It was nearly over, and that should have meant it was easier to hope for spring, but, like always at this time of year, that's when it seemed furthest from any relief. When you'd been living with the cold so long that it felt like it came from within your own bones.

It was gray because it was the highway.

It was gray because it was Indiana

It was gray because it was February.

It was gray because it was us, because it was now.

We pulled into the Denny's parking lot so close to the highway that it seemed a part of it, as if it was a rest stop or had been opened in a particularly wide stretch of the median for some reason.

We had to drive past our hotel's exit to get to the exit for this stupid fucking Denny's, which was at exit three, just north of Indianapolis. This pissed me off. It felt like some intentional slight towards Ben and me, like it had been picked just to further inconvenience us by taking us out of our way just that much more, to show that they could.

Then I remembered Javi wasn't staying with us and there was no way he was staying anywhere near this far north and I felt bad for him instead.

There were dudes standing outside huddled around a cigarette when we pulled up. One looked like he probably worked there, and the other looked like he'd never worked anywhere.

We parked next to the twins' pickup.

I was mildly surprised that they were here before us. Of course, they should have been. They were far ahead of us on the highway and they were coming straight here just like us, but it seemed strange that this would all work out as it was supposed to when nothing else ever seemed to.

There were five Sea-Doos on the trailer, which seemed like an odd number. I mean it is numerically odd, but it seemed strange when six would've made more sense placement-wise and it looked like there was room for at least ten. But five. Fine whatever. I didn't care. I wanted to eat and get this shit over with.

"Don't forget that fucking bag," I said to Javier unnecessarily because he was holding it in his hands as he stepped out into the near morning. I said it with far more hostility than the situation warranted.

He said nothing.

I half expected Ben to agree with me again, the hype-man I never wanted or asked for, and I might have screamed at him right there in the parking lot in full view of the world.

He, also, said nothing.

Inside, we were immediately hit with a blast of heat, from the heaters, yes, but also from the 24-hour kitchen and the other human bodies. The smells also smacked us in the face—the coffee and syrup and bacon and the grease from the fryer, all mixing with that weird old-lady perfume smell unique to Denny's, that *We tried to clean the carpets but it didn't quite take* and *Hey, why do we have carpets in a restaurant anyway?* smell that IHOP or Waffle House or Perkins doesn't have.

"Fuck," I said.

They both looked at me.

"We should've gone to Perkins," I lamented.

"C'mon," Javier said and led the way over to them.

They had, because of course they fucking had, sat on either side of a booth that was made to hold no more than four people at once, and none of us, especially Corey or Javier, were small dudes.

Javier sat next to Corey, which further told me things about Dustin, if the second biggest dude would rather sit next to the biggest one than the smallest one. Ben walked past the table and grabbed a chair.

"I'll take the end," he said when he returned, aiming this statement at no one in particular.

I moved to sit down and Dustin said, "Hold on," and moved to get out of my way, even though he didn't move his coffee or anything with him. I didn't want to sit with this mother fucker, but I really didn't want to be boxed-in by him. But when he stood, Javi handed him the bag, and he took off towards the restroom.

I sat right on the edge of the booth and kept my eyes peeled for him.

The waitress popped over, and Ben and I agreed to coffee even though we needed to be asleep hours ago. Javier got a Coke, but I've never known him to drink coffee, so I didn't think he was intentionally being smarter than we were. Plus, that shit was sugar and caffeine.

She reappeared with our drinks as soon as we'd finished ordering them, within the same breath somehow. Impossible, but I was out of it—like, first-couple-of-weeks-working-third-shift out of it—and time skipped by. It must have taken her longer to get those drinks than it seemed and there were four dudes at this table so somebody was probably talking about something but at the same time, Dustin still wasn't back and how long could it take to do whatever he was he was doing?

She took our food orders and I didn't notice what my friends ordered, and I ordered last and I also didn't know—even more impossibly—what I ordered.

I tucked my hands under my legs to stop from smacking myself across the face to wake up.

Dustin came back and told me to scoot over but I stood instead and bowed for him to enter as sarcastically as one can perform such a task, and he looked at me for a beat before he sat and moved over without incident.

The food arrived. At a glance, it appeared as if everyone had gotten breakfast and there was no weirdo who got chicken fingers or a basket of fries or a dessert or something, but then again, I guess there were no women with us. Although, I have seen Javier order and then consume desserts in the unlikeliest of places. I saw him eat cheesecake in a strip club once and memory of that never failed to make me smile.

I didn't remember the specifics of what anybody ordered but I'm sure Javier made some crazy substitution or request or ordered two entrees but only wanted part of each. I'd been with him on more than one occasion where he'd hit multiple drive-thru windows to construct his current whim of a perfect meal. A Big Mac and a Crunch Wrap Supreme. A KFC two-piece and a biscuit and fries from Rally's.

I've long suspected that Javier invented the McDonald's McGangbang, which as everyone knows is a chicken sandwich between the patties of a McDouble with all the extra buns thrown out, but I've never remembered to ask him.

I also have no memory of what I myself ordered but I

received two pancakes, two eggs over easy, and two strips of bacon. A go to breakfast order for when I forgot to look at the menu or I needed comfort, or I was zoning out as I was then, deep into that foolishly long night.

"It's not morning until I've been to sleep and woken up again," is something Mark always said, and I realized I'd just said it out loud between mouthfuls of whatever I was eating.

Ben seemed to be the only that heard me as the rest were hunkered down into their food.

He nodded and got my reference right away.

"I wish Mark was here," he said and then started to correct himself, "Well, what I mean is I wish we—"

"I get it," I cut him off.

He wished we were somewhere else, wherever Mark was.

He was our friend. We hung out with him every week. Hell, sometimes every day. Yeah, we've known Javier for a long time. Ben's known him longer than he's known me or Mark or Jake or Niedz for that matter and these other two who are his brothers-in-laws. So, he shouldn't be as uncomfortable as he is. No one should be.

We were supposed to know these morons and they had been acting like people I didn't know—like people I would never want to know. Maybe if Mark had been here this wouldn't have gone down, wouldn't have shaken out the way it did.

At least I wouldn't be here, having breakfast amongst these familiar-looking strangers.

I glanced side-long at Dustin who was face deep in his eggs, and then to the right at Ben, who sat fully erect in his chair, chewing thoughtfully as he absently scanned the diner either believing himself to be above all this shit or willing his posture to make it become that way.

I was the same, only my mask hadn't slipped off yet.

I was living a lie and doing shit that would make this man never talk to me again.

I wanted to tell him.

For the first time, I wanted to tell him, to confess, to give him details that would make him write me off forever, that would give him no choice but to come at me across the table here in a Denny's, as the early morning breakfast crowd was just blinking their way towards their first cups of coffee. It wasn't a Waffle House, but I bet this has happened here before and for the same shitty, ordinary reasons.

I shifted nervously in my seat as if my thoughts were day-glow projections and my forehead was transparent.

This was not the place and these people were really, truly, not the company to have if I decided to tell him about this shit.

I wondered if Dustin still had his gun on him or if he'd left it in the truck.

I attempted to make my thoughts my own again and restrain them within the confines of my own skull.

Dustin's alarm beeped quietly on his phone and he thumbed it off clumsily through the fabric of his pants. He covertly popped a pill from another pocket into his mouth and washed it down with coffee.

Corey tipped something from a flask into his own mug without much regard if anyone saw him doing it.

He sipped his spiked drink and looked across the table at Dustin. I detected something passing between them on waves the others and I could not receive or process.

Corey very slightly nodded as he set his mug down.

Dustin sighed and rolled his head around on his shoulders, cracking his neck.

He dropped two folded hundred-dollar bills into my lap and flicked what I assume was the same amount at Ben's chest. The money caught in the folds of the fabric of his shirtfront before it tumbled out of sight and onto his lap. He calmly wiped it away with a free hand. I let mine sit there for a bit before I moved it to a pocket.

I didn't want this money. I never did. Now wasn't the time to make this point.

Nobody said anything and Javi pretended not to notice any of it either. If he was getting any coin, it was probably much more and at a different time and location.

Corey sat with his elbows firmly on the table and waggled two fingers at Dustin in the international sign language motion for *Gimme*.

Dustin handed him a cell phone.

Not a flip phone but still new-ish, though kind of beat up. What do they call that style of phone? Candy bar, maybe? Not what TV has taught me a burner phone looks like. Anyway, Corey fiddled with it for second and then slid it over to Javier face-up and open with the screen fully lit.

"What?" Javier said to him around some toast, not looking at the phone, like, *I'm done with this cloak and dagger shit. Just tell me what's going on.*

Corey tapped on the tabletop with a single index finger next to the phone with enough force or proximity that in wiggled with his taps.

Javi sighed and dropped his toast on his plate. He picked the phone up and looked at it. He glanced at Corey and then at Dustin. They were busying themselves with their coffee and remnants of breakfast.

"Are you fucking around?" Javi asked him and there was an edge to his voice I hadn't heard all night. I probably hadn't heard it in years, not since he was still a hotheaded teenager and shit could get to him and really flip him out.

They continued to pretend he wasn't there.

"What?" Ben said coming down from his cloud to see what all the hubbub was about. I tried to get his attention so he could see my *Don't play their games* shake of my head, but he was focused on Javier and the cell phone trying to see what was going on.

I was done.

I wasn't even trying to look at the screen.

Javier pressed something on the touch screen, and I thought I heard some tiny voices come from the little speaker, but it was hard to tell over the general noise of the rapidly filling restaurant.

He put the phone to his ear listened for a moment and put it down. He passed it over to Ben and stared slit-eyed at the Redneck Twins. He was fuming. Hate was leaping sharpened from his eyes and drilling into them. They kept pretending they didn't notice.

Ben listened for a second.

"Mother fuckers," he said and not under his breath.

He tried to hand me the phone while his eyeballs throbbed at his brothers-in-law.

I pushed it away. No games.

"Just tell me what the fuck it is," I said.

"The cell phone in the bag with the money?" Javier addressed me but kept boring holes into the twins with his violent laser eyes. "They were recording us in the car."

I thought back quickly.

We hadn't said anything too disparaging about them on that ride, had we? Nothing that couldn't be attributed to nerves or tempers or the time of the fucking morning, right?

Javier was looking at them, they were looking at their coffees and Ben was looking at Javi. I could tell he included him in his suspicion of the recording. He was in far deeper with them then we were, and he brought the fucking thing with him into the SUV. I elbowed him and shook my head *No* when he looked at me.

He swallowed and then nodded.

"I don't think they like us much," Corey said over his mug and speaking directly to Dustin.

"You're right," Dustin said, continuing as if they were having a conversation at a table alone as if there was nobody else in the whole restaurant.

"Fuck the both of you," I said and stood up.

Dustin tried to stand up too, but I pushed his shoulder down and he fell back awkwardly into the booth. He looked at me shocked. Corey sipped his coffee, clearly amused. I left my hand pressing into his shoulder. He succeeded in yanking his body away from me but didn't try to stand up again.

"Keep your fucking hands off me," he said without looking my way.

Ben and Javier were already standing up and ready to leave with me, so I probably should have let it go, but this twerp who had everybody afraid of him pissed me off.

I leaned down close to his face.

"Why?" I asked him without lowering my voice. "Are

you going to stick a gun in my face? Or do you just do that to defenseless mothers when you've already gotten what you wanted?"

"Kyle," Corey said quietly, but it was all he said.

Either Ben or Javier had an arm on me. They must have thought—and my tone of voice and posture suggested—I would do more than trash talk this prick. Hell, if he'd stood up right then I honestly didn't know what I'd have done.

"Fuck you, too, Corey," I said and pointed at him. "Stay the fuck away from me this weekend."

"Will do," he said, and smiled.

"Let's go," Ben said. He was the one holding onto my arm. Javier had regained possession of the phone. He dropped it into a mostly full glass of ice water. He turned and walked out. The twins were back to pretending they didn't notice things happening to their stuff and at their table.

Ben and I turned to exit and then he hesitated and turned back to the table.

"I'm talking to my sisters about this," he said. It was a weak threat and he didn't say it with any real force, but he committed to it. "I'm telling them what happened."

"What happened?" Corey asked his mug and then looked at us. "Do you know? Do you think they don't know more than you already? What do you think you could tell them that they don't know?"

He asked as if he was generally curious, as if none of this bothered him and I guess it didn't because he was probably right. This did not make things better.

"I don't know," Ben said and shrugged and walked away.

Again, it was pretty weak, but it was free from bluster or posturing, I'll give him that.

I followed him out of the restaurant while resisting the urge to flip them off or take a piss on their pickup.

Javier was standing by the SUV smoking.

"Are you smoking a cigarette?" I asked him. I'd seen him smoke cigars or weed but never a cigarette as far as I could remember.

He shrugged and offered me the butt-end.

I declined. It was, pathetically, the hardest thing I did all night.

"I was stupid enough to quit six weeks ago," I said.

Ben surprised me by taking a drag from it. It'd been years for him. I wondered if I'd give in by the time the weekend was over. It was thoughts like that where you could rationalize anything, where nothing mattered, and I was going to have one again sometime so it might as well be right now.

Mercifully, Javi dropped it to the pavement and ground it out with his shoe.

"Where am I dropping you?" Javi asked us.

Ben shook his head.

"We can call a cab," he said.

"Get in the fucking car so this night can be over with," Javi said.

We were barely a mile from our hotel. I blinked and Ben and I were getting back out of the car in front of it.

"Were we supposed to do something today?" Javier asked. "Before the rehearsal?"

I had no idea, but Ben nodded.

"Lunch and then pick up the tuxes," he said.

"Let's cancel that shit," Javi said. "Do you mind

grabbing my tux on the way to dinner? It's all paid for."

"Sure," Ben said.

"I'm gonna sleep all fucking day," Javi said and he sped off.

We shuffled in through the lobby as businessmen were strolling out or carefully selecting items from the continental breakfast.

Never one to pass up a deal as good as free, Ben swiped some fruit and a muffin as we snaked our way through the lobby to the elevators. Food is usually one of the foremost things on my mind, but I couldn't even look at any of this shit now. Sticky and burnt smells coming from the Belgian-waffle-maker-end of the table were threatening to make me gag out loud.

We made it through the lobby and the elevators and down the hall and into our room somehow without me throwing up.

Ben remembered to slap the DO NOT DISTURB sign out on the door and within seconds we'd brushed our teeth, taken a last piss, and retired to our respective beds.

I was a light sleeper and I brought earplugs in case the sounds from the hallway or outside the window were too much. Ben didn't snore the way Mark did, but even tossing and turning across the room would keep me up.

Light came in from under the door and around the black-out shade of the window and I put a pillow over my face and tried to be comfortable. I was either too hot or too cold and I couldn't get the hotel pillows quite right.

I put the ear plugs in, but I was still too awake, and I could hear and feel my heartbeat hammering in my ears as I tried and failed to relax and slow my breathing down.

I was hopelessly tired—crazily tired—and it didn't

mean a fucking thing because I couldn't sleep.

I thought Ben was out like a light but it's not like I was going to ask him.

I eventually—let's say it was five in the morning when we got in bed so call it around eight—drifted into a half-sleep where I was relaxed and my mind wandered but I was still aware of the room around me and the bed beneath me. It's a state I find myself in sometimes and usually it transitions after a while to legitimate sleep but that's not always the case. Sometimes, as with this time, the whole night (or day) goes by in this fashion and when I pull myself out of it, hours have passed where it only felt like minutes. Imagine daydreaming in a first period class where you woke up late and you didn't have time for a shower or caffeine to help wake you up and suddenly the bell rings and you're like alright, I zoned out for a whole class and got away clean but then you emerge and realize the whole school day has gone by and you somehow didn't notice. That's what it felt like.

Usually, I felt just as refreshed from these nights of half-sleep as from any normal night, but I would fade faster later in the day. And if it was a work night with nothing really to do? Well, I wasn't above taking a nap in the stock room and, using my particular brand of light sleep awareness, as I heard someone punch in the code to the door I would spring up and pretend to be looking for something or start moving shit around.

I wasn't at home and this wasn't my usual schedule and I was pretty sure if we were sleeping through the afternoon there'd be no built-in nap time for me later.

Hopefully, tonight wouldn't be as balls-out as last night was.

I always have half-dreams when I sleep this half-sleep but they're usually dependent on location or placement of things around me. If I kind of drift off staring at a doorway then I'll have a series of dreams about various figures appearing in that doorway to talk to me or menace me or simply watch me silently. None of them are ever quite nightmares as I'm keenly aware of this sort of sleep state and I usually know whatever is happening is not really happening. But if I become too aware one way or the other—that I'm dreaming and I'd like to continue doing so and see where this goes or if I become convinced that this is a real thing that's happening and I need to deal with it—well, then...

Poof.

It's over as soon as it started, and I'll slowly fade into the next one, maybe this time about a crack in the ceiling and how did I not notice that there's been this huge crack there this whole time and especially when there's something—no someone—inside there and they're trying desperately to whisper something important to me?

And like a living thing that is trying to avoid my direct gaze, it flutters away from the corners of my mind and fades into a nothingness.

The shower turned on and I realized Ben wasn't in his bed anymore and I glanced at the clock on the bedside table and it was after three in the afternoon and the sun glowed magnificently on the carpet at the bottom of the shade where it didn't quite adhere to the wall.

I checked my phone and I had a few different messages and one missed call from a number I didn't know. There was a voicemail, so I checked that first, but it was only a second long and entirely silent.

There were a couple texts from Estella, one from my manager, two from Mark and, of course, a few from Her.

Since Ben was in the shower, I could be fairly certain about not getting caught, so I checked those first.

wake up sleepy

from a couple hours ago followed by one that read

i need u. inside me

which, naturally, was followed up with an explicit photo. Another one shot low, her legs on sheets with a finger inside of herself and a bare out of focus breast in the background. Most of her ass, as viewed as if I was going down her, was also visible. I'd have trouble taking a better photo of her from that vantage point myself.

I considered my reliable morning erection and how long Ben would be in the shower, but I shook it off and deleted the picture. I texted her back.

had a really fuckedup night

I said. She responded right away with

yeah i heard

which of course she did, and it made me madder than anything has all weekend, maybe all month. Probably this whole year.

Why did this upset me so much?

Because she kept this from me as I kept things from her, and we kept our thing from the entire world.

so you knew they sell this shit?

I said followed by

don't you think i should know this?

She didn't say anything for a few minutes which is not like her at all. Then, finally,

it didn't have anything to do with us

Yeah, I got in their faces and I've known them for a

long time and I was probably not taking them as seriously as I should have because I couldn't picture—even though I saw shit with my own eyes—these dipshits as dangerous.

But they were, and she gave me a shrug or a brush-off or what? She tangled me up in this shit and, by coming over to my apartment and fucking me every couple of days, she positioned me into direct opposition with these unstable maniacs. Yeah, I nearly challenged them to a fistfight in a fucking Denny's at five in the goddamn morning.

But this. This was messing with their family.

I typed it and sent it before I could convince myself not to. I said,

don't talk to me at the wedding

and then I added, just to dig myself a hole I couldn't easily pull myself out of,

blocking your # you wanna say something say it now

There was another long, uncharacteristic pause. The shower turned off and I could hear Ben rummaging around in there. I told myself I'd give her until he said good morning to me and then I'd block her number.

He emerged from the bathroom in a towel.

"Morning, dude," he said and gestured to the window. "Care if I open this?"

"Go for it," I said and clamored into the bathroom.

I brought my phone with me and as I took a long, slow piss, I opened my phone to block her number.

She had responded.

nope

was all she said.

I deleted her message and blocked her number.

• • •

After a quick shower—during which I realized I hadn't showered since I had been with her and I tried not to think about this or feel her on me—I dressed and ate half a muffin and half of an orange and we got the hell out of there.

Rehearsal was at five and dinner was immediately following that and so we piled into Ben's SUV and swung by the place to pick up Ben and Javier's tuxes. I guess Mark was picking his up tomorrow or in Ft. Wayne and driving it down here or something and it didn't really concern me, so I tuned it out and concentrated on finding some tunes on Ben's iPod for the drive.

I waited in the car when Ben went inside and checked my other messages. Just bullshit movie quotes and the like from Mark, supplying no facts about when he was going to finally get down here and how many cars they were taking and if he was staying Saturday night or not. Ben had said we only had the room through tonight, because he and Aimee had something to do on Sunday, but if I wanted to stay longer, he was sure somebody could take me back. I wouldn't stay. I wanted to get back to my apartment and my shit and leave most of this weekend behind me. The whole reason I was here, the thing I had to look forward to, was a fucking wedding? Was I insane? Weddings suck and I was here for three or four days?

Gah, I really should have driven separately.

In the meantime, I got a text from Nina, who's this chick at work that I've been kind of seeing here and there, and I must have mentioned the wedding to her at some point because she asked me if I still wanted her to go. Which didn't make any sense—I knew I never asked her because I wanted to be stag at this thing so I could hang with my friends and be on the look-out for trim. Yeah, sure. I'm a dirt bag.

I told her *No*, that I was already in Indy for it and I was going with some of my friends and tried to keep it as vague and casual as I could.

She took it fine and we made plans for my week off next week to do something and that was that.

Estella had sent a couple ambiguous, pointless texts, but I went ahead and confirmed lunch for tomorrow and us using her place to get ready for the wedding. She said *Yes* and *No problem* and *Call me later if you get a minute* and I tried not to think about that last one because Jesus Christ like I need more women to think about right now.

Ben came out with a couple of garment bags and I helped him hang them in the back window and we headed off to find the church.

He asked me if I wanted a snack or drive-thru or anything, but I still wasn't hungry somehow.

"Yeah," he said. "Let's gorge ourselves on Javier Sr.'s ticket later."

Which made me smile because he was back to his old cheap self, so maybe everything could go back to normal, maybe even me.

We chatted and fucked around as we drove through town. I had few jagged memories from living there, but I pushed them away as best I could and played music on his stereo just a little too loud to hear myself think.

We soon left any part of Indy behind that I really knew. We were well past anywhere I had lived, or any friends of mine had lived, or where Estella finished school, or even exotic locales like downtown, where we'd kill a couple hours on a weekend once every couple of months, and say, *We live in the Big City*.

We might have been close to where all the shit went down last night, but I couldn't know for sure. It had been so late and pitch-dark, and I'd felt pretty out of it. We were only a few hours removed from that really, but it began to feel like it had been weeks ago, which I wasn't complaining about. The further I could put that in the rearview the better.

Ben didn't bring it up either, so I assumed he felt the same.

We got to the church. Javier and his brothers were milling around outside near the parking lot. One had parked his car across a few spaces with nearly every door flung wide open, but I couldn't hazard a guess as to why that would be.

"Which one backed into your pickup that time?" I asked Ben, gesturing towards the brothers. They talked animatedly about something, so much so they appeared to be bouncing back and forth, as if they were practicing boxing footwork.

"Jesus," he said and shook his head. "Look at those fucking idiots."

Javier leaned back and roared as if he was paid by the strength of his laughter. I swear, his dreads shook with mirth, but at what, we'll never know.

"There's no way it was that funny," I said.

Ben nodded in agreement.

"Anyway, it was Brad," he said. "The day I bought the fucking thing. We walk outside of Javi's parent's house and that dopey mother fucker is standing by the end of the driveway near my brand new pickup with his arms folded, fist under his chin, one finger running under his lips and resting under his nose as if he's in the deepest of thoughts."

"Yeah," I said, "trying to remember why his finger smells like that."

"Scraped right down the side of the fucking thing," Ben said. "Fucking moron."

"So, it was Brad, I couldn't remember," I said. "uh, which one's Brad?"

Ben shook the nostalgia off and smiled at me.

"Let's see if you can guess," he said.

"Oh, c'mon. Don't make me look racist."

He jumped out of the SUV and strode over. I followed him.

"What's up, assholes?" he said, all smiles.

They glanced at us, tears in their eyes from whatever was so goddamn funny. *Call us whatever you want—you can't spoil this shit.*

Ben hooked his finger back over his shoulder.

"It's nearly six months old but do any of you pricks want to back into it?" he asked.

The one in the middle blushed and went bug-eyed as Javier and the other one doubled over with more laughter.

"What's up, Brad?" I said mostly to myself as I shook hands with him first.

The rehearsal didn't last long.

I sat in one of the front pews and thumbed through a battered burgundy hymnal while they practiced walking slowly in a straight line.

"Enjoying our redneck songbook?" somebody asked.

I figured he was one of Lisa's relatives. Probably an uncle. I hadn't been introduced to anybody. No slight intended—everybody had shit to do.

I gave him a long, penetrating look.

Her family were small town folks from one of the Nowheresvilles just south or east or west of Indy. They all had that strange, nearly southern accent some Hoosiers have. Why do they sound like they're from far below the Mason-Dixon line?

Javier and Lisa were together for a solid decade before they got engaged, side-projects aside. From what he's told me, her family loved him immediately and welcomed him. He spent a fair amount of time with them.

Ben's brothers-in-law are, if I was to believe the timeline of events, new to the drug racket and the only person I knew for sure was also involved in some way was Javier. I knew he hooked them up with partners or at least individuals in some capacity down here.

We didn't exactly call Ben's brothers-in-law the Redneck Twins to their face, but we didn't exactly keep that nickname secret either.

One of us might have even said it on that recording they made of us in Javi's SUV last night or early this morning.

Enjoying our redneck songbook?

None of this seemed outside the realm of possibility.

Even Travis or the woman he was with could be one of Lisa's relations. Shit—they might be at the wedding.

But it seemed like a stretch that this fat, old slob would be ham-fistedly delivering me some kind of message, a white trash threat.

My stare made him uncomfortable.

Enjoying our redneck songbook?

Just coincidence, right? I was being paranoid. He was some old fart making conversation as the rest of the participating adults made with the rehearsing.

I smiled and shrugged at him and went back to flipping pages and scanning hymn titles.

"Seems pretty normal to me," I said.

He asked me if I was friend or family with Javier and where I was up from and I answered him and maybe even asked him a thing or two and it was very innocuous and I talked briefly to a couple other people, maybe Lisa's parents for a minute and Javier's parents for a bit and *No, I'm not in the wedding exactly, Mark was but he had to work so I'm filling in for him right now* which consists of attending the bachelor party and eating his rehearsal dinner meal and sure I can walk or stand somewhere if you need to make sure everything looks copasetic and I wanted to talk to Gina, Javier's youngest sibling but she was avoiding Ben because they fucked that one time and clearly she associated me with him and yeah, I would have fucked her too that's why I was trying to chat her up.

Fuck it—it wasn't worth the hassle anyway.

And then it was over and I was loading Javi's tux into the back of a car and Ben and I were driving away and we were either following people to the restaurant or Ben knew how to get there but that wouldn't be right because we were in the middle of fucking nowhere and I was pretty sure we weren't going all the way back into Indy proper just to eat.

We weren't. We pulled over soon in an almost quaint

kind of downtown area, like a single street, like it was made to look like it had once only been a post office and a barbershop and a general store and a saloon with some upstairs rooms for shenanigans and then in the 1950s someone had added a soda fountain and duck-pin bowling and other bullshit. Fuck, it was probably built in the 1990s just to make you feel that way. Johnny Rocket's as an entire street.

We pulled in behind a small restaurant and bar.

Javi told us we were a little early and the back room wasn't quite ready for us yet, so we thought we'd go in and have a drink at the bar while his family fucked around outside on the sidewalk.

And inside the bar, right past the saloon doors and next to a half-full popcorn machine and a claw machine with stuffed animals referencing cartoons from before I was born, was an Area 51 arcade machine with both gun controllers that worked. I grabbed a couple two-dollar PBRs while Ben pumped quarters into the thing because of course he carried change like a grandmother.

He took a swig of cheap-ass beer and nodded at me in acknowledgment as he blew a zombie-alien away.

"Finally," he said. "We're doing something this weekend that I want to do."

I agreed, gulped some beer, wedged the bottle between my hip and the claw machine and gave those aliens hell.

We finished the first mission—Ben creamed me, he had 76% and I barely cracked forty. And then the table was ready and we joined everyone else in a cozy back room.

The grub was mostly bar food that leaned in the

Italian direction, but it was hot and comforting and the service was on top of it. I'd barely finish a beer and another one would materialize in front of me. The weekend of magical beers.

I had a nice buzz going by the time we got to dessert which was cheesecake and I almost told everyone how I watched Javier eat two pieces of nasty-ass cheesecake in an even nastier-ass strip club but I didn't really know most of these people and I wasn't sure Lisa knew the story. They'd met in a club and started as a one-night stand if my memory wasn't also drunk but I let it go and focused on attempting to make eyes at Gina across and down the table, but she never once looked our way.

I settled on flirting with one of the waitresses which went fine but I didn't push it far enough to go anywhere.

At some point, Ben told me we were going to pick up where the bachelor party left off last night. I guess Javier told his brothers, who told Ben, and Javi's cousin that was hanging around.

I shrugged.

Whatever. Maybe it can make up for last night.

So we hugged and shook hands with the various parental units and other relations that were too old, too young, or too uncool to hang with us, and we piled into a couple different vehicles and headed back into Indy.

It wasn't even nine and we already had Javi with us so it couldn't be the disaster it was the night before, right? Plus, we had some ladies with us this time and, even if Gina pretended we didn't exist, if you had some dames with you it was easier to attach more. I didn't know why this was true. Must be a safety thing.

I thought about suggesting OPTs again to try to

reconnect with that bartender—fuck, what was her name?—but we were already headed somewhere downtown instead.

It was a classier change of pace.

We weren't in our wedding duds for tomorrow, but we were all sharply dressed, so we hit up Nicky Blaine's, a basement martini bar just south of the Circle, located down a carpeted flight of stairs.

A svelte woman in a tight black cocktail dress sat us at a couple of plush couches and another woman in an even tighter black dress came over and got us rounds of drinks and cigars and lit them for us with long hickory sticks. I had the thought that maybe I should grow up, just so I could date women, women like these, instead of the girls I seemed to attract. Gina and Lisa and other members of the bridal party seemed a bit uncomfortable by the pampering classiness of the place, by the way they were huddled around like shrews. I switched chairs so I couldn't see them, and I could enjoy my smoke and drink without their sour pusses ruining it.

Yeah, I had a cigar, but I was drawing the line there. Just one.

Ben went to the restroom at one point, Javier was talking quietly with his cousin as his brother were in the middle of some joke, so I found myself scanning the place and I caught Gina with the corner of my vision. She was watching Ben walk away.

Like, watching him like a fucking stalker. And when he rounded into the small hallway for the facilities, she excused herself from whatever conversation she was in and quick stepped in that direction.

I caught her checking herself out in the mirror and

primping before descending into the same corridor.

What the fuck was this about?

I sipped my martini and set it down. I couldn't get a better angle while seated but our group was large, and everybody was at least a drink in. We'd stretched out and taken over this area of the lounge so I got up and scooped my drink up and wandered over as if I was about to say something to Javier but he was otherwise engaged so I hung back as if waiting for a chance to talk to him.

But I was watching Gina in the same mirror where she'd given herself the once over. From here, I could see into the hall, and she had not continued on into the LADIES but had stopped and waited outside of the GENTLEMEN door.

I watched her as she watched for Ben.

She could probably see me if she checked the mirror again, but I could mostly see her back. She was focused on the door.

Ben emerged at a brisk pace and nearly bowled her over.

This was not a planned rendezvous, then.

He stopped. His eyebrows were up, and mouth was a small circle. His hands were faced out defensively, as in a *Whoa, you all right? I nearly ran you over* posture, but it became a more standoff position as his face crinkled with recognition of who she was and whatever she wanted with him. I couldn't see her face or hear anything.

His hands came down on her shoulders, his arms fully extended, and elbows locked as the rest of him leaned back and away from her. The hallway was narrow and there was no way he was getting past her if she didn't want him to and he wanted to remain polite.

The whole of his body language was pushing her away and trying to escape at once. He began shaking his head no, but he didn't seem to be saying anything.

She was moving sharply, and I couldn't hear any words from this distance or with the big band music pumping in through the speakers, but the way her head and hair moved, she was saying something to him. She was trying to shrug away from his touch and she might have even smacked at his hands but it was clear he wasn't trying to hold her or touch her inappropriately, only trying to keep her from lashing out or bouncing off the walls of the hallway.

Finally, she'd calmed or at least slowed down enough that he pulled his hands back gingerly and held them up in the universal sign for *I'm unarmed please don't hit me*. He shook his head with eyes half closed and said one simple word as he scooted along the wall to get past her.

No.

He left the hallway and exhaled deeply before the faintest of smiles crept back onto his face as he emerged back into the lounge.

Gina stood in the hallway. She still had her back to the entrance and the mirror so I couldn't see her face, but her posture and body language sung with tension and vibration. She was going to combust or shake her molecules apart and slip right through the floor.

She unclenched her balled fists and flexed them a few times before abruptly pushing through the bathroom door with enough force to knock the hinges loose.

Ben sipped a sparkling water and tried to make himself comfortable in his overstuffed chair.

He either hadn't noticed I was somewhere else or

hadn't realized what that could mean.

I ambled back over to him.

He nodded at me dismissively as I sat down, distracted himself with his phone.

"What's up?" I asked him.

"Texting Aimee," he said.

I nodded in understanding though he wasn't looking at me.

He snapped his phone shut and returned it to the inside breast pocket of his sports jacket.

"How much of that did you see?" he asked me flatly.

I shrugged and finished my drink. I set it on the coffee table and pushed it gently away from the edge.

"It's none of my business," I said.

He stood up and motioned with his chin to the bar.

"Let's get you another drink," he said.

I stayed seated.

"We have a waitress," I stated.

He gave me a *How stupid are you?* look and I relented and followed him to the bar. I ordered a Cajun martini—Absolut Peppar, dash of Tabasco, celery salt rim and garnished with a jalapeno stuffed olive. Yes, this one is for sipping only—and the bartender looked at Ben.

"You?" he asked.

I watched him struggle with himself, an entire battle raged inside that manifested itself outwardly as a single spasm of vein in his forehead.

"No," he said. And added, even though the bartender was now out of earshot, "No thank you."

We waited silently for my drink.

I was determined not to ask him. I meant it. It wasn't my business. I believed that. And not just because it absolved me of not telling him anything that wasn't his business but that did help decide matters.

My earlier, sleep-deprived desire to confess to him had evaporated this morning upon waking. It swung like a pendulum in this fashion. And at this moment I was at the far end of the parabola where I would do anything to keep it from him at any cost.

I thought of that flat

nope

she'd texted me before I'd blocked her number. This wasn't the first time I'd blocked her or swore her off for good. She'd even talked me into fucking her again under the threat of telling Ben all about it and I knew there was every possibility I would soon come to that choice again.

I told myself it was out of a resolve that he never found out—a strength as opposed to the weakness I knew it truly was.

Fuck.

How could I make ending this—for good—her idea so she'd leave me alone?

He flipped open his phone and showed me an open text conversation with The Wife as it was labeled, and I pushed myself through terror to read what it said.

just got cornered by G again

Ben had typed followed by a response of a thumb's down emoji and

oh good. is she still in *love* with you?
that's what she says. she's a dumb kid

Ben responded which was followed by

a kid you slept with

and an eye rolling emoji.

I handed him back the phone.

"There's more," he said and didn't take it.

I didn't want to read on. I didn't want this glimpse at his relationship, the way they talked together when it was just them. The intimacy of it embarrassed me. I would never want anyone to see this side of me, not even whoever I was sharing the moments with. I wouldn't even want to stumble across it myself later and rediscover it. It'd be like seeing an old photograph of myself with middle-parted hair and baggy jeans in an awesome 90s shirt.

I get it. I know who and what I am. That doesn't mean I want to look at it or dwell on it.

I flipped the phone back open.

c'mon. you know i'm not encouraging her

he said and followed it with a heart and eye emojis.

i know. see you tomorrow

and a kissing face emoji.

"OK," I said, practically throwing the phone back at him. "I read it all."

He slipped it back into his coat. I nodded thanks to the bartender and collected my drink from the bar. Ben angled me further down the bar where nobody else sat.

Ugh. He wanted to keep talking about this shit.

"So, you told Aimee," I said. "Good for you. Is that what you want?"

It came off only slightly more hostile than I intended. He brushed it off and smiled at me.

"You're such a fuck-up," he said but with a grin. "You have intimacy issues. Seriously, dude"

"Fuck off," I said without any force.

"I'm half serious," he said, "if you can't bear to read a small exchange between a happily married couple—"

"Gross," I interrupted and made a puking face.

He ignored me and finished his thought. It was basically the same one I had while reading it, only from the opposite point of view. Openness was the key or some such shit. I flipped him off.

"Seriously," I said, "fuck off. Tell me what you want to tell me so we can talk about something else. You're making me wish there were honest-to-God televisions in here. With sports on them. That's how painful this is for me."

He laughed.

"You'd rather watch baseball than read that?" he asked but already knew my answer. "You are fucked up."

I nodded as I gulped my drink. I needed to slow down. I was more than half-finished with the thing already and they made drinks strong here.

He shrugged.

"You get the gist of it," he said. "The very few times I've run into Gina since Aimee and I got married, she's pulled this whiny, psycho shit on me. She 'loves me' and wants to be together. I don't know where the fuck it came from."

"You only slept with her that once?" I asked.

He threw his hands in the air, exasperated.

"Yeah, like four fucking years ago," he said.

"And," I asked, "I assume, she hasn't acted this way constantly since then?"

He nodded in agreement.

"Exactly," he said. "I don't get it. I dated around for a bit before Aimee and Gina had no problem with it as far as I know. We've never really kept in regular contact. Even when Aims moved in, nothing. It's only been since the wedding."

"Now that it's too late for her to do anything about it," I said.

"I wouldn't have left Aimee for her before," he said.

"Obviously," I said, but I felt like he'd been talking to himself and not to me. I laughed.

"What?" he asked.

I kept laughing. He got annoyed.

"Quit fucking with me," he said. "You don't have an answer, asshole."

"I do, fucker," I said. "It's actually fairly simple. Do you wanna guess?"

"You're stalling because you've got nothing," he said.

I had a tight closed lipped smile and I looked down at him as much as I could with my eyebrows arched high. If I wore glasses, I'd have been peering over them at him in a librarian sort of way, a math teacher sort of way, *I could give you the answers but it'd be better if I taught you how to find answers for yourself* kind of way, if that could be boiled down into a singular expression.

"Fucking out with it," he said, and I could see him regretting not getting his own drink. Mine, mysteriously, had been reduced to dregs on the bottom of the glass.

I chewed the olive obnoxiously.

"It's not about you, dipshit," I said finally.

He made a *Huh?* face but didn't say anything.

I elaborated, "Do you know what's going on in her life? Have you asked her? Has she had a messy breakup or something? Whatever's motivating this has nothing to do with you. I'm sure this is hard to understand, as an entirely self-involved person, I get it. Believe me. But this is coming from her, so it began with her. You're a convenient cipher for her to project this onto when she sees you."

He glanced across the room. I didn't tell him I had seen her exit quickly as we'd been waiting for my drink.

"That... makes a lot of sense," he said.

I put my arm around his shoulder.

"Well, I am smarter than you," I said.

"Uh-huh," he said laughed.

We returned to our seats.

"So," he said, "with your extra powers of perception and your fairly impressive track record with the ladies as of late, I take it you're using your powers for evil?"

"You don't know what my track record is," I said.

He brought his hands together, pinched his thumbs and forefingers together with his other fingers fanned out as if he was making mirror image OK hand gestures or like he was gripping the ends of a very thin piece of string. He pulled his hands away from each other at equal speeds until they were a few inches apart, as if he had traced an invisible string and pulled it taught.

"Panties," he said and smiled.

"C'mon," I said.

He shook his head at me.

"Nope," he said. "You're crushing it so hard lately that you didn't even know there were panties left on your floor."

If I argued with him, this would continue. How did I make it stop?

I spread my arms wide and bobbed my head slightly.

"I didn't know they were there," I said.

"Do you know whose they are, even?" he asked me.

I didn't think there'd be a follow up question, not the one I dreaded, anyway, and I could always just lie to him if it came to that. But if I played into what he thought my life was, this unfounded porno-movie he had me staring in... Well, maybe we could talk about something else sooner rather than later.

"I think so?" I said and crinkled my face a little, more in disgust at myself than in the phony tone of phrasing it like it was a question.

He shook his head in disappointment. But he was smiling.

"Jesus," he chuckled.

"So what?" I said. "I was in a monogamous relationship for nearly five years. I need to do something else. And you were right, though not as right as you thought you were, but the schedule is kind of built for it."

He cracked his knuckles.

"But you weren't exactly faithful during that five years," he said.

"I don't need your judgment—"

"Don't get defensive," he said, "I don't care. It doesn't effect me."

I tried not to choke or cough or laugh at this last part, because he had no idea what he was saying. It was probably good that I had finished my drink, because this would have been the perfect moment for a spit-take.

"You don't mean that," I said. "It's a moral issue for you and that's the problem. It's not just a personal code you live by, you move through world operating as such and you judge—you do—others that operate with less honor. Fine. I don't care. I don't have an excuse or rationalization for what I did to Estella. But how I'm living now is not the same thing. I have not misled these women or pretended to be anything or any better than I am. I wouldn't be surprised if—and I am in fact certain—that none of them think of me as their boyfriend and they get that shit from somewhere else."

"And that doesn't bother you?" he asked. "That you are complicit in their lying to or hurting other people?"

"But I'm not," I reasoned. "That's their shit. Again, it's not about me. It's them and whatever they are trying to work out."

"If it wasn't you, it'd be somebody else," he said.

"Right," I said. "Or something else. Who knows?"

He shifted in his chair.

"So, you're like the Redneck Twins," he said.

"How's that?" I asked, but I already knew. He'd sprung a logical trap on me, and I blundered into it blindly trying, vainly—even though I said I wouldn't—to rationalize myself to him. Fuck it. Play dumb, make him say it.

"I'm sure," he said, "unless they're just evil, which seems unlikely, that they tell themselves the same things. They probably tell my sisters these same things, and Meg and Ellie then repeat it to themselves until everybody's just echoing the same bullshit. They didn't invent the drugs. They didn't make anybody want drugs and if they weren't making money off the users then someone else would, and then that's less money for their families and it's not like you've suddenly solved the drug problems. They probably even tell themselves that it's better if it's them, because deep down they're good guys."

"So why did you take their two hundred fucking dollars?" I asked him. "Why did you go out there? You knew, more than I did, what we were walking into."

He looked at his hands a moment before responding.

"I've been trying to figure that out," he said, finally. "I dunno. I guess I didn't believe it, or it wasn't quite real. I just had to know. I had to know for myself."

"Well, it was pretty tame for an evening with some meth pushers, but let's not do it again, OK? Be comfortable in your state of not knowing shit for sure. It'd really help me out," I said.

"Sure," he said, "if you'll do me a favor."

"What?" I asked, sensing a bit but playing along.

"First," he said, "do you remember what you told me about cheating on Estella? And I'm pretty sure this was before you guys had even broken up. I don't think we were drunk but we could've been."

"I don't know," I said. "That seems unlike me. I'm not Javi or Mark. Not much for details."

He shook his head.

"No, no, not like that," he explained as if I was a particularly slow child. "This is back to the rationalization thing. I don't believe you were quite at your elevated mode of thinking yet, so you were still making excuses."

I flipped him off.

"I don't remember," I said, "but I remember that time well and if I wasn't lying to you then, I'm sure I could approximate the reasons I gave you."

"Please," he said. "It'll be an interesting experiment in bullshit."

"Fuck off," I said but I said it with a smile. "It's an excuse, but that doesn't make it bullshit. It doesn't make it right or justify what I did, but that doesn't make it any less true."

He said nothing so I continued.

"The last year or so, she got wrapped up in some shame issues or something in her head," I said. "I don't know what it was or where it came from. I know what she told me, but I told her my own lies so there's nothing that would keep her from doing the same to me."

He laughed.

"God," he said. "How about we just take everything at face-value and the liars can let the lies eat away at them later privately. Tell me what you know or were told, and we'll assume it's true."

"Fine," I said.

I paused and wished I had a drink or a smoke or something to delay this. I changed my mind.

"You know what, fuck this. She told me her reason in confidence, and I don't feel like sharing. But it manifested itself in her suddenly feeling a lot of shame about us having sex, even though we were adults and we lived together and we had been together for a few years at this point, and in a more traditional sense we were planning on getting married at some point. Or we at least told each other that we were and were also probably lying to ourselves or each other about it."

I paused again and rolled my sleeves up for lack of anything else to busy myself with.

"So," I began, "it would go like this: I would bug her about having sex, she would put me off and put me off and put me off and eventually relent and immediately afterwards would be like, 'Wow, that was great.' Yeah, so let's do it more often, but it went counter intuitive and more time would elapse between her giving in and giving it up. You put a month in-between and that's a long time that feels longer when one of the parties is pestering the other. Stretch that out to the two-month range and well, I'm not proud of this but I stopped asking her and started asking other people."

He shook his head.

"Yup," he said. "That's pretty much what you told me at the time."

I got up to hit the restroom.

"You still owe me a favor," Ben said.

"I thought that it was it," I said.

"Nah," he said. "That was just to embarrass you."

"It didn't work. What's the favor?" I asked.

"It's more for Aimee," he said, and I felt goose bumps on my arms and was convinced they were visible to everyone else.

"Fuck Gina for me," he said in all seriousness, "get her off my back."

I patted him on the shoulder as I walked past him.

"I could definitely make her forget you," I said. "But I've got enough problems."

After I hit the head, I skipped up the carpeted steps to poke my head out into the night air.

I didn't smoke anymore, but I needed to get out of this basement—no matter how plush and full of drinks and cigars and good friends it was.

And yeah, I'm going to keep mentioning that I quit smoking a heroic six weeks ago until I get some goddamn accolades. No one else seemed to notice.

Gina was standing outside smoking a cigarette in that way young woman do that makes it seem so unnatural.

It's the way they hold it in their hand more so than the way they inhale or exhale. Their fingers are too straight and appear as if they're pulling it away from their face at all times, like brushing at a loose hair that keeps sticking to their face or batting away a pesky insect.

"You can smoke inside," I said to her.

She angled a pack in my direction. I waved it away.

"Only cigars," she responded and blew a thin trail of nearly white smoke from the corner of her mouth.

Even when I smoked, I never dated smokers. Maybe I'm sexist but it's gross on ladies. I mean, since I quit, it's gross on everybody and people that smoke inside their own homes baffle me. I never did that even once when I smoked.

I could always ask her to brush her teeth before sucking on my tongue.

I leaned against the wall next to her.

"You're a hot lady," I said. "No one's one going to ask you to put out a cigarette in a room full of cigar smoke."

I almost said girl, but she *was* just a girl and I grasped that as being part of her psychology, hand in hand with fucking older dudes and smoking. She wanted to be taken seriously. She wanted to be seen as an adult.

Still, I couldn't bring myself to say woman, so lady would have to do.

"So, Ben sent you out for me and not Javi," she said.

I shook my head.

"Nobody did," I said. "I thought you'd left. I just needed a break. I quit smoking six weeks ago."

"Congrats," she said dryly, and inhaled down to the butt. She blew the smoke past me.

"I'm telling everyone," I said, "because then if I succumb to weakness and try to bum one maybe somebody will say 'I thought you quit?' and that will be enough to stop me."

She flicked the butt. It arced far past the sidewalk and into the street.

"Do you really think that will work?" she asked.

"No," I said. "It's too dependent on other people doing the right thing and other people are shit."

She looked at the ground and tucked some hair behind her ears.

"Yes, they are," she said.

I nodded at her purse.

"Have another one and tell me what's going on," I said. "And don't give me this shit about how you're in love with Ben and you didn't realize it until he got married. You're too smart to believe that."

She glanced at me with a wide range of emotions struggling for dominance on her face. She was betrayed, angry, shocked, and, with every degree in between those feelings also suffered, helpless.

She lit another smoke and she tried her best, but, man, it just didn't look right. It was like that guy who painted mustaches on famous paintings. It was comically, absurdly out of place.

"You're out here because your brothers don't know you smoke," I said, and knew it was true the moment I said it and felt stupid for not realizing it sooner.

"Javi doesn't," she said.

"He's protective of you," I said.

She made a face like *Duh* and seemed impossibly young in that moment. I wanted to smack the cigarette out of her hand.

I shrugged instead.

"I don't have sisters," I said. "But I get it."

She smoked and looked anywhere but at me. She wasn't going to tell me her problems and I really didn't care. The whole point was to get her to acknowledge to herself that all of this was coming from her and Ben was simply the medium with which she was making her feelings known in the world, even to herself.

"Did you tell Javi about Ben or did he figure it out for himself?" I asked.

"Did Javi say something to him?" she responded.

"I don't think so," I said putting the pieces together, "but last night he was kind of flexing his muscles and well..."

I trailed off. How do I tell her about last night without telling her about it? How do I explain that I suspected it was Javi's idea to rope Ben into last night's bullshit and I just happened to be standing near him when the trap was sprung? Javi has some kind of illegal operation going on with Corey and Dustin. Maybe it's just the drug thing, maybe it was deeper, but he wanted Ben to see it, to know not to fuck with them or him or by extension, his family.

It was a little thin and seemed too psychologically complex for the man, but I could find no fault in the new theory. It's not like Javier would need to be entirely hip to the reasons he was chest thumping in front of Ben for it to be true.

I continued, "Look, your brother's been puffing his chest up around Ben this weekend, is all."

"He kind of figured it out," she said. "And so I admitted to it. He's at least as pissed at me as he is at

Ben."

"I doubt that," I said.

"He is," she said. "He's like you and everyone else. Nobody believes that I could really love him. That I do love him. How the fuck would any of you know? Why would I feel like this if it wasn't true?"

I decided not to correct her and tell her, that yes, there was one person that believed her—Ben. Why twist her up more than she already was?

"You know our friend Mark, right?" I asked her.

"The red-head?" she asked.

"Yeah," I nodded. "So, he was in this shitty relationship for a long time with this chick named Kat. She made him feel bad. Not all the time, of course, and that would be his excuse if any of us would bring it up. He would say things like 'You don't see us during the good times.' Things like that. My retort to that would be it's not the good times that matter; it's how you handle the bad ones. Do you understand? I would see him after he got off the phone with her, nearly completely doubled over from pain in his stomach just from talking to her on the fucking phone. I'm not a great example. I always take the easy way out of situations. But when you see him or think about him or talk to him does it make you feel good or bad? Does it make you feel worse than good? How can something that makes you feel that awful be any good for you?"

She finished her cigarette and flicked it away. She fidgeted with the pack but didn't light another one.

"I wish I still smoked," I said.

She pushed the pack into the deep recesses of her purse and closed it with a snap.

"Don't ask me," she said. "I won't give it to you."

I smiled at her. Were we talking about more than just cigarettes? She was like a girl playing pretend. By the time she grew up, if that ever happened…who knew. I'd probably be long in the ground.

"Thanks," I said.

"I'm gonna take off," she said. "see you tomorrow."

"What do I tell Javi?" I asked.

"Nothing," she said. "Don't even tell him you saw me."

SATURDAY

W hen I wandered back inside a few minutes later, everybody was standing around and gathering their shit up.

"We out?" I asked.

Ben nodded but had this strained expression on his face.

"Strip club," he said.

"Fuck, c'mon," I said. "Seriously?"

"Afraid so, Buddy," he said and clapped me on the shoulder.

We filed out of the bar and I tried to think of some excuse to break away but couldn't come up with anything realistic. I checked my phone. It'd be near one by the time we got anywhere, so at least we wouldn't stay long. Maybe they hadn't decided yet and it would take a while to come up with a consensus and then getting a dozen people or so over there could eat some more time.

We turned left out of Nicky Blaine's and headed away from the vehicles.

Shit.

"Is there one down here now?" I asked

Javi and Lisa were leading the pack. He turned around and walked backwards so he could tell us.

"Yes!" he said with more enthusiasm than I'd seen him show all weekend. "Around the corner on Michigan, 'The Classy Chassis.'"

Somebody snorted.

"Seriously?" somebody else said.

He bobbed his head up and down like a kid telling us about a new toy store or arcade he'd discovered.

"Me and Lisa have only been, what, twice?" he asked her. She nodded agreement and he nodded at us in confirmation as if we couldn't see her head moving up and down right in front of us.

He continued as we walked, telling us how chill and nice this new downtown strip club was. As he continued, he walked backwards down the sidewalk and Lisa gripped his arm and steered him away from running into other pedestrians or getting creamed by a car.

I tuned him out.

You're either a strip club guy or you're not. I wasn't. Usually, girls I date are more into them than I am but that's not saying much since I would never choose to go to one. I've been, clearly—it's where my distain comes from—but only when I've been drunk enough to not object or in a social situation where I'm outnumbered.

Estella thought I was prudish. I didn't know, maybe.

Shame was a tricky thing. It was impossible to have

just the right amount of it, the correct balance. Too much and you were a buttoned-down repressive who was liable to snap at an indeterminate future moment, too little and you were an unfettered monster who spewed your filth into the world.

Earlier this week, after work, I was running a few errands and I came out of Target. It was in this strip mall with a bunch of other crappy stores and there were always weirdos bouncing around between places like some retail cross-pollination gone haywire.

In that tangle of concrete between establishments was this giant woman in a tube-top and workout shorts—in February—walking a dog so tiny I could only describe it as the fast-moving fetus of a canine trying to get away from her. She yelled into a cell phone—because of course she did—that was on speaker because, again, of course.

"Where are you?" she shouted.

"Just driving around," the voice on the other end responded. "Be there in a second."

"What?" she screamed. I couldn't understand how she couldn't understand when I heard it perfectly from a few yards away.

The voice repeated itself.

"Why would you do that?" she said even louder and gruffer and with a whine to the edge of her voice. "Why would you do that? I'm not paying for your gas!"

I was blissfully finally out of earshot and I didn't have to hear anymore. But I thought, *Just leave her there with her stupid fucking dog and her ridiculous outfit screaming into the air. Drive, man. Drive.*

She didn't act like this because she thought it was right or correct but because no one had ever told her not to. No one had ever told her to feel bad for what she was.

This woman had zero shame.

We made it to the strip club, and I tried to hang back and fade into the middle of our group where I could get lost.

It was noisy and hot and dark and felt sticky or humid or maybe that was my imagination. It was transactional, sad, and weird. I tried to get lost in my own head.

Jake and Niedz had joined us at some point or met us here, or they were always here all the time…? Maybe that's why I could never figure Niedz out and why he was closer to our other friends—he just took up space.

Javier was in his element.

When Javi worked for UPS he used to eat at strip clubs on his lunch break. That's a true statement. Wild, right? I could never decide if was more disgusting that he ate the food there, or that he had to go back and finish his shift all horned-up and sweaty.

We took up a couple tables and a long booth along one of the back walls. At least this wasn't a runway-type place. Well, they had that too, I could see it now that I settled into my seat, but it had more of a mingle vibe with scantily clad ladies weaving around. Ben immediately removed his phone from his pocket and hunkered down with it. No doubt letting his wife know every little thing that was going on. I tried to look around but not look *at* anything. I tried to make the same face I used to wear in school—something like *Don't call on me.*

I was trying to become invisible without looking like I was trying to become invisible.

There was a light touch on my right shoulder.

A stripper was standing next to me even though my

back was to a corner. How did she slink up on me? Did this place have secret fucking doors? I guess it wouldn't surprise me.

"Isn't it warm in here for this jacket?" she asked me while tugging at my lapels. It was but I wasn't going to admit to that. If I had an outer coat or a hat, I'd be wearing that shit, too.

I said something like, "Um" before she got distracted by someone else and swayed in the direction of a hand with cash in it.

With that encounter averted, I sank lower into my seat but they didn't make strip clubs so you can hide and be weird in them. I wanted a drink, but I didn't want to get money out of my pocket. I've made that mistake before. The last thing I wanted was to get swarmed.

Jakc leaned over to me.

"Let's get Niedz a private dance," he said.

"It's Javi's wedding," I said, deflecting.

He motioned to where Javier and Lisa had been sitting. They were gone. I followed his gaze and caught a stripper leading them into a back hallway, holding them both by the hands.

I felt dirty.

I'm not interested in other people. Maybe it's a fault. I didn't want to know private things about them. I didn't want to know what they do behind closed doors and whom they do it with. It's not my business and I didn't care—I didn't want to think about it.

I realized I didn't know what they were going to do back there, and my imagination made it worse than its reality had any right to be. It was hard to have an idea, maybe, but I've found that once you have it, it was even harder to get rid of it.

The glimpse as they rounded the corner.

Her streaming in front of them with a confident stride, her head held high, her arms held out behind her and gripping their hands in each of hers. That look that passed between Javi and Lisa as they disappeared out of sight.

I could read into that look that passed between them given things I already knew about Javi and other shit he's told me about Lisa. Christ. I didn't want to think about it. Why isn't this bass thumping through my brain keeping these thoughts out?

I returned my focus to Jake.

He shrugged at me.

"Niedz?" he said.

I was about to ask why that mother fucker needed a private dance and why we needed to pay for it, but I should probably stop thinking and worrying over shit and just agree to something. Try to turn my goddamn brain off for a few seconds.

I nodded and Jake clapped his hands together loud enough that I could hear it over it the thudding music. He jumped up and I followed him with less enthusiasm.

He grabbed Niedz by the arm and yanked him up. He had a *What the fuck, dude?* or *Watch my drink, asshole!* look on his face but he let Jake lead him.

We weaved through the crowd. Jake stopped at a small cluster of strippers and whispered to the skinniest, blondest one. He slipped her some cash. He hadn't asked me for any and I hadn't offered, and I hoped maybe that would be the end of it. She smiled and took Niedz by the arm.

Jake smiled a smile without teeth at me and nodded

slightly. We followed them as the woman led Niedz to one of those back halls. I really hoped we didn't run into Javi and Lisa back here or catch a glimpse of them somewhere.

We got to a small, carpeted room—like, every surface was carpeted. The floor, yes, but also the walls and the ceiling and benches along the wall.

She pushed Niedz gently onto the bench and he sort of sat or collapsed there with his back hunched and his legs spread wide. She leaned in close to him and then they both turned and looked at me. They had these *Huh?* expressions on their faces.

"What do you want?" she asked me like I hadn't been here the whole time, like I wanted anything at all, like we weren't just paying for our friend's lap dance. Niedz was looking at me with the same *What are you doing?* look.

Has this never happened before in the whole history of the world?

"We're just going to watch," I said as I turned so at least Jake could back me up.

He was not there.

"Fifty," she said to me.

"Bye," I said and got the fuck out of there.

I tried to look purposeful as I wound through the place to find the rest of my friends and avoided strippers and drink girls and everything else. If I could've floated or become intangible, I would have done that. But if I could've done that, then I wouldn't be there in the first place.

Javier and Lisa had returned and were having some sort of tense conversation. It was palpable whatever they were arguing about because strippers were careening away from them and Ben had put his phone away and was watching with rapt attention.

Javier's cousin was standing close to them awkwardly. He was involved somehow but didn't want to be.

I sat next to Ben and elbowed him.

"What's going on?" I asked and nodded at their direction.

"Javi's taking his cousin to Fort Wayne," Ben said. "Tonight, apparently."

I checked to see if he was fucking with me.

I looked at the three-way argument happening close by, but the music was covering whatever they were saying.

"Is he fucking serious?" I asked. "The wedding's tomorrow. Well, today. Why the fuck would they need to go up there?"

Ben stuck his bottom lip out and shook his head,

"No idea," he said.

"Why would Javi have to take him?" I asked. "Can't he rent or borrow a car or something?"

"He's from New York," Ben explained. "No license."

"Jesus Christ, can't somebody else do it then?" I asked.

"You'd think so," he said. "But Javier's insisting for some reason."

We watched them fight a little more.

"And I'm not fucking volunteering," Ben said after a minute.

Javier put his hand in Lisa's face.

He didn't strike her, and it wasn't exactly aggressive but there was a finality to it. She stopped talking and stared at him, seething.

He hit his cousin on the arm and turned towards the exit. The cousin followed him out the door and looked back at her once in some sort of apology.

It didn't take.

Lisa gathered up her stuff and two friends and they headed for the door.

"Do you ladies need a ride?" Ben asked but they blew past us. "Guess that's a solid no."

It was just us left there and it wasn't our scene, so we bolted, ducking and spinning away from strippers on our way out of the building like we were running football plays.

Javi and his cousin were long gone but Lisa was still pacing in the parking lot while her friends tried to calm her down and get her into a vehicle.

We got in Ben's SUV and when the doors closed—shutting out the distractions of the street made it quiet for the first time all night that my ears were actually ringing from the absence of sound—it clicked into place.

I laughed.

I get it," I said. "That fucking asshole. I get it."

"You get what?" he asked.

"C'mon, you get it," I said.

He looked at me blankly. If this was a *Simpsons* episode, this would be the part where Homer blinked twice out of non-comprehension.

"I'm not going to make you guess, because I'm not an asshole like you," I said. "It's Tracy. He's going up there to fuck her one last time before he gets married."

"He said he broke it off with her," Ben said.

"Well, he lied. Or it's somebody else we don't even

know about. Same principle," I said.

Ben looked at his steering wheel. He'd started the car, but we weren't moving yet.

"I hope you're wrong," he said.

I shrugged. That seemed unlikely.

"What else have you ever known Javi to travel for?" I asked. "Does he visit his parents or take vacations? Or does he fuck different women in different cities that aren't too far from home base?"

"Dammit," Ben said.

"Remember that chick in high school he met online?" I asked. "She was in South Bend or something. What did he do? He drove up there on a school night and busted inside of her three times. She tried to get him with that fake pregnancy…"

He waited until I trailed off and then he put his hand up so I would stop, even though I had already stopped.

He nodded his head in agreement, but also in an *Enough* sort of way, a *No more examples, please* kind of way.

I didn't say anything else.

I looked for Lisa, but they were gone now, too.

Ben put the car into gear, and we drove off and didn't say anything else on the drive to hotel. No radio either, just silence.

Ben was in the bathroom brushing his teeth or shitting or something when Estella texted me to
call me please
she said. Quickly followed by a
i'm freaked out

and then by

not about us. i'm scared

so, I called her. She answered before the first ring.

"Hey," she said quietly. "What are you doing?"

"Are you OK? What's wrong?" I said dispensing with the pleasantries.

"You know that guy I told you about who I dated briefly? That showed up at that thing I was at on Thursday before I saw you?" she asked.

"Yeah, I guess," I said even though I didn't remember.

"I think he's outside my house," she said.

"What?" I said and instinctively looked at the alarm clock on the side table. "It's almost three in the morning."

"I know," she said, even quieter somehow. "I for sure saw his car a few times today and then I think I just saw someone moving around back there. Outside."

"Did you call the police?" I asked.

"Can you just come over, please?" she asked.

Ben came out of the bathroom and gave me a *What the fuck, dude?* look. I held a single index finger up at him, but he didn't take it personally.

"Alright," I said. "I'm leaving now."

She thanked me and asked if she could stay on the line. I agreed and muted it.

"I need to borrow your car," I said to Ben.

"OK," he said. "What's up?"

I gave him the Cliff Notes version and he tossed me the keys.

I put my jacket on in the stairwell as I took the stairs down two or three at a time.

Outside, I couldn't remember where Ben parked. This

wasn't because I wasn't paying attention since he was doing all the driving—I mean, all of that is true as well, but I usually couldn't remember where I parked either so I always tried to park in the exact same spot whenever I went anywhere.

I hit the bottom on the key fob a few times until I located it from the little horn taps.

I did eighty most of the way there as I drove one-handed with the cell phone in the other. I took surface streets, but hardly ran into any other traffic. The streets were dead. Last call was twenty minutes ago and all the bars had just closed, but it was a cold night in February, so for a Friday night—well, Saturday morning—it was dead. I skirted any cool college areas I could and pushed the SUV hard.

I could hear Estella breathing over the phone. She hadn't said as much as two words the whole time I drove. When I saw her complex, I asked her where she thought she saw him last.

She told me and then immediately said, "Don't do anything, just come inside, please."

"What does he look like?" I asked her.

"Please, just come inside," she repeated.

"I will, but I should know what he looks like, so I don't keep one of your neighbors from entering the building, right?" I said.

She hesitated and then told me.

"He's about six feet, reddish hair and beard. Lanky," she said.

"What's he drive?" I asked.

She told me. It was something so common and prosaic, like a black Toyota Camry, that I immediately abandoned any idea about looking for it.

"OK," I said. "I'm gonna park and come inside. I'm going to make sure nobody's peaking inside your windows at least and that your car's fine."

She started to protest.

"You asked for my help," I said. "This is what that looks like."

I muted the phone again and slipped it into my shirt pocket.

I slid past her place and through the area of the parking lot any reasonable visitor to her building would want to use. It had an empty space and I drove right past it and hooked around to a side lot or an adjacent building.

There were no spots, so I parked on the yellow curb and got out and stumbled pretend drunk for anybody watching from the hallway of the nearest building.

I waited in the space between apartments for a couple of beats and then loudly opened and closed the door to the laundry room.

I ducked down and snuck along the corridor and came out the other end which was open to the backside of the complex. All the buildings were situated loosely around these back areas, vaguely tracing the shore of a manmade pond with a few crisscrossing jogging paths and an overabundance of NO FISHING, NO SWIMMING and PICK UP YOUR DOG SHIT signs.

There were trees and bushes, but they all hugged closely to the buildings, and if he was back here that's where he'd be. It might cover my approach, visually, but it'd also impede me from seeing him. Plus, I was no ballerina and I'd probably sound like a weed whacker tripping around through all that foliage.

The ground sloped gently down and away from the buildings and towards the pond. I touched the ground and it was hard and cold and mostly dead. It didn't feel wet. Well it did, but I was hoping that was the coolness and not any actual dampness. I was pretty sure it hadn't rained or snowed in a few days and it was too far off for morning dew or frost.

I laid out flat on the ground, completely prone, and pushed myself off with my weight, rolling across the ground. I had this terrifying image of rolling all the way into the water and then freezing to death in the open air before I could make it to her apartment. It would be like hitting something with your car even though time slowed down enough that you took in every detail, but your reflexes didn't speed up in time to counter the situation.

But I stopped my roll down the slight hill well out of reach from the pond. I pushed myself up on my elbows just enough to check my angle and I was, more or less, directly behind where I intended to be.

I had made a little noise, but I doubted he'd be able to see me down here or think I was much more than a cat or squirrel. But hopefully, there was no one here anyway and I could confirm that and get some goddamn sleep. These up-until-dawn nights needed to end sometime. I wasn't used to seeing the sunrise on my week off from work.

There was someone back here and he was in the trees behind Estella's building.

And he heard me, this jumpy stalker, or peeping tom or however you classify this particular brand of weirdo, because the shadows at the base between the trees and above the bushes shifted and coalesced into the clear silhouette of a bearded man in profile. It looked or listened for a few seconds and then returned its focus to Estella's building.

He was mostly hidden from the front by bushes. And since all the buildings formed a half-circle in the direction he was looking, I assumed he wouldn't expect to be observed from behind.

I stood up silently and scoped out the path to him to avoid warning him in any way.

When I was close enough to him, I could see his frozen exhales swirl, as lighter patches of dark twisting up and away into the black night sky. I said, "Excuse me young Christian man," in the raspiest voice I could muster.

He startled and leapt back from the trees and readied a stance that was maybe supposed to be intimidating but I knew he spent his Friday nights out in the cold spying on women's apartments, tugging himself off to it later while he listened to agitated voicemails from his mother. Or something. Yesterday, I went with some drug dealers to a dude's house while they pistol whipped him and stole his shit while I made sure his half-naked woman didn't do anything stupid.

This guy was nobody. He was nothing.

I continued, pretending not to notice his pseudo-aggressive posture.

"Do you have any change or food?" I asked him in my best imitation of this homeless guy I used to walk past whenever I'd leave the grocery store in college.

"What?" he said but had completely relaxed or been taken off guard. "No, I don't have anything."

All that, and stingy as well.

Maybe I'd have given him a pass if he'd reached into his pockets even vainly.

"God bless," I said and then half turned to go but I held up my left hand with the cell phone in it. "Could you help me with this?"

I thumbed the home button once and the phone lit up impossibly bright in the dark of the night. My muted call was still active, and the name ESTELLA shone vividly from the screen. He had time to read it and register it as I studied his face for recognition.

His face was slack, his eyes were bored—a nothing reaction.

"What is this?" he asked.

Uncertain, I glanced at the phone to make sure her name was visible, and he kneed me the stomach.

All the air in my lungs exploded from my body and I was suddenly on the ground trying to remember how to breathe.

I managed to snag fistfuls of his pants that kept most of his kicks from landing hard.

He bent down and punched me in the side, but my breath had returned, so I said the worst things I could imagine to him. He said the same kind of shit back to me.

I think—or hope—I got a shot or two in that he felt.

"I don't know who what this is, but stay the fuck away from me," he said, and half-heartedly kicked me once more in the legs.

"Don't come back here," I said, lamely as he walked off towards the parking lot.

After a moment, I pushed myself off the ground.

I went in through the back side of the building hallway and stopped outside of Estella's door. I didn't knock for fear I would wake the neighbors, or my knock would be so weak she wouldn't even hear it. My whole body was buzzing, shaking.

Was that even the right fucking guy?

I unmuted the call and said, "I'm at your door."

She opened it quickly and only gave me the briefest of glances as she ushered me inside and her eyes darted around outside.

"He's gone," I said as she frantically locked the door behind me.

"I swear I saw him," she said as she turned around. She then stopped and really looked at me for the first time. I vibrated with violent potential, charged with an energy barely realized. Outwardly, I'm sure it just looked like I was shaking.

And, you know, it looked like I was just beaten-up.

I thought for the millionth time in six weeks about wanting a cigarette. I would've settled for that stub of cigar I had crushed out earlier.

"Wait," she said, "You said..."

"He's gone," I repeated and then clarified. "I, um, ran him off."

She took a few quick steps until she was standing right in front of me. I could feel her all over me she was standing so close.

"Oh my God," she said and began fussing with me. I must have looked a mess. "Are you OK?"

I grasped her hands and lowered them until they were in front of her and between us. I was pretty sure I wasn't shaking anymore. Well, not too bad, anyway.

"It's just dirt," I explained. "I got low to the ground so he wouldn't see me coming."

"Jesus," she said. Her eyes were still moving all around me, all around the room, attempting to take in everything, to the see the whole world at once.

"Hey, don't worry about me. Are you OK?" I said.

She hugged me quickly and tightly and I held her back and despite myself I felt a stirring a long way off, although not as far off as it should have been. She rested her head on my shoulder briefly and I tried to relax my grip of her.

I released her. When we were together, she used to give me shit that I always stopped kissing her before she stopped kissing me. It was accurate—mostly a joke I think from her end, but there was always a little bit of truth in there.

I always suspected she liked me more than I liked her and that she knew it as well. I certainly treated her accordingly.

She stepped away from me and sat down on a narrow, cushioned bench she had in her front hallway. I sat down next to her.

I leaned against the wall and rested the back of my head on it. I splayed my legs further akimbo to relax my nerves and my leg touched hers and she didn't move away.

She never moved away.

I was always moving away from her.

She said something like thank you and put a hand on my knee and I put my hand over hers and she turned it over so I could hold it and I did.

Maybe she was looking at me, but I didn't know because I was still looking at the ceiling. Our hands were remembering how to do this, and I liked to imagine that she looked at the ceiling or the floor or anywhere else but at me.

I wanted it to be equal. I wanted our hands to hold each other because they were hands and they did that sometimes, not for any other reason that our bodies or minds might devise in the past or the present or the future.

I think she said something else to me, but I couldn't hear her words like I couldn't hear my own just moments earlier.

I tried hard to focus on her without looking at her.

"Thank you for telling him to fuck off," she said.

"Sure," I said.

"Do I want to know how you got rid of him?" she asked.

I shook my head. I felt every kick again.

"Probably not," I said. "Hopefully it sticks."

"Every woman you know has had a stalker of some degree at some point," she said. Her tone was accusatory, but I didn't dwell on it. After a minute, I couldn't let it go and I bit, even if that was what she clearly wanted. Fine. Let her have it.

"How could you know that?" I asked.

"Because everyone I know has," she said. "Every woman has."

"OK," I said. "I believe you."

She sighed and squeezed my hand slightly.

"I don't think he'll stop," she said.

"Then I'll come back, and I'll make him stop," I said. "Every time until it sinks in."

She shook her head.

"No, that's not what I mean," she said bordering on exasperated. "It doesn't go away—it moves around and lands on somebody else. He's going to do this to somebody else, some other woman. I feel bad for her."

"You can't feel bad for her," I said. "she's hypothetical. It's like when you're in an emergency on an airplane. Put your oxygen mask on first."

She thought about it for a second.

"That implies you will help others, though," she said.

"Then do. Call the cops," I said.

She sighs.

"They're all men," she said. "They don't get it."

"They're not all men, and I don't know what else there is," I said. "It's not perfect, it's not even very good, but what else is in place to help?"

"I don't know," she said quietly.

This time, I squeezed her hand.

"Well, we're not gonna kill him, no matter what horrible shit I said to him out there. Explain it to me," I said. "Try."

We sat silently for a while and I could feel her move her head or open her mouth to speak a few times, but they were all aborted attempts.

Finally, after a few minutes, she said,

"Imagine you're walking into oncoming traffic on 465 or just any busy highway."

"OK," I said.

"So, the person walking is a woman just going about her day," she said. "And all the speeding cars coming at you are men. The majority of cars will avoid hitting you if it's not inconvenient for them, but they don't slow down or make sure you're OK or try to stop anyone else from hitting you. Do you understand? This is most men—they let the bad shit happen around them and they don't really do anything about it."

"It sounds like most *people*," I said. "But I get it."

"So, there are a few that will stop their car and get out and even risk injury to themselves to help or to see if you're OK," she continued. "These are the good guys and there aren't as many as you would hope.

"Then there are the predators, the real evil mother fuckers, and they are the ones that would use the opportunity to hit you with their car, because no one would suspect they did it on purpose, or, at the very least, there are a lot of witnesses who saw you walking into traffic so how is it not your fault?"

"Do stalkers fall into this group?" I asked.

She considered the question carefully.

"Sometimes," she said, "but I think a lot of them don't move out of the way and don't try to hit you. They think of it like fate. Well, you're walking here and… I don't know. I don't know. It's falling apart. I can't describe it."

"You were doing great," I said and then added with a smile, "Even I could understand it."

"I don't want to talk anymore," she said.

"OK," I said. "But call the cops and report it. Tell them I was here or leave me out. Whatever you wanna do. Just make a paper trail, alright?"

She nodded.

Our hands moved from my leg to hers.

She was dressed for bed, so she was wearing a tank top and gym shorts. I knew that she would have been wearing this plus a robe earlier as she was getting ready for bed, but never socks, no matter how cold she got.

I felt like I should not know these things about another person. Not someone I didn't really know anymore. I felt you should never know someone so well and never know them again and yet they still live and move through the world and other people come to know them as well as you did or better and it branches out endlessly until everyone was connected to each other.

Which was the same as saying no one was.

No one knew anything.

My hand moved on her thigh now, around and up, and she was still touching me with her hand, but it was on the top of my hand and my forearm.

I heard her tongue click as her mouth opened wider when I slid my hand under her shorts and between her legs.

She wore no panties. I knew this before I touched her.

She pushed my middle finger into her easily. Her wetness was warm and ample.

She gasped and moaned very quietly.

I looked over at her. Her eyes were thankfully closed so I could look at her without her looking back at me. I didn't know why this seemed so important to me at that moment. I didn't know why I needed to see her but to be invisible and to have her know that I was there.

I was leaning in closer towards her. I was breathing on her neck. She arched it to feel my hot, slow breath on her skin.

She opened her eyes slowly and something was lost but it was fine. I still looked at her even if she looked at me. It didn't matter.

"Kiss me," she said quietly. "You want to kiss me."

I removed my finger. Her hand was gripping my wrist, but she didn't attempt to move my hand either way. We were on the edge of something. We were a frozen moment. We were a held breath.

"Kiss me," she repeated. I could feel her words on my mouth.

"Not here," I said.

I meant I didn't want to kiss her in the hallway, and not that I had any aversion to any part of her anatomy. But she understood. She knew me completely.

She stood up from the bench and, still holding onto my wrist, led me into her darkened bedroom.

"Turn the lights on," I said.

She did and stood holding my arm with her back to me and leaned back into me and pushed into me and I pushed into her. I kissed her neck and her grip relaxed.

I got my arms free from her weakened grasp and I rubbed her pussy from the outside of her shorts. I slid my other hand under her tank-top and pinched her right nipple.

She pushed off me and towards the bed, pulling the sheets back. Before she got in the bed, I stopped her.

"Take your clothes off," I said.

She stood with perfect posture in front of me and wiggled loose from her gym shorts without using her hands and they floated to the ground. She stepped out of them towards me as she pulled the shirt over her head and dropped it to the floor.

She stood naked in front of me. Different parts of her were flushed.

She was the same as I remembered, and she was different as well. It had been more than a year since I'd seen her like this. Was she different? Was I? Or was it merely that time had passed—and not even very much—but we were in different places now. I was more familiar with other bodies.

I took my jacket and shirt off and she reached out to touch me lightly, to maintain some physical contact as I took off the rest of my clothes.

She backed towards the bed.

"I have condoms in the..." she trailed off.

I pushed her back and down onto the bed.

She pulled me on top of her and I kissed her mouth and her neck and sucked her nipples.

I could feel her legs squirming beneath me and the heat radiating from her. Where it touched my stomach or arms or chest, I could feel its wetness.

I kissed her stomach and where her pelvis protruded.

I moved lower and kissed her thighs and circled closer and closer, but I wouldn't kiss her there until she asked me for it. I slowed the frequency of my pecks until she could no longer stand it.

"Please," she said from far away.

I slid two fingers inside of her. I kept my hand still as she pushed against it.

"Please what?" I asked.

"Please lick my pussy," she said. "Please."

I left my fingers inside her as I licked her clit. I began pushing them in and pulling them out and moving them inside her as the urgency of her hips increased.

It didn't take long but when she was almost there, I pulled my fingers all the way out and stuck my index in her ass to make it memorable.

She came fast and hard and shuddering with my finger in her ass and my tongue on her clit.

I rolled off her and scooted up on the sheets next to her. We fumbled with the condom like trying to open a bag of chips with mittens on. Somehow, we got it place. She rolled over on top of me and straddled me. She guided my hard cock into her. She braced her hands on my shoulders and I grabbed her just above the hips. She rode me with her eyes closed and I held onto her and bobbed her up and down. She leaned over me further and I sucked on her tits when I came deep inside of her.

After she fell asleep next to me, I pulled myself away from her slightly, just enough so she wasn't touching me, and I could get some sleep.

Later, after the sun was up but it was still early for a Saturday and the outside world remained quiet, we woke up and did it again.

I was on top and she wrapped her arms and legs around me and we went slower and longer and came within seconds of each other and afterwards we kissed.

None of this means it was better or worse than the other time. Things can be different from each other without being ranked or placed in an order.

Nothing means anything, anyway.

"Do you have time for breakfast?" she asked me as I put yesterday's clothes back on with more deliberation than they were removed.

"I have time for a bagel," I said. "Ripple Bagel?"

She sat up in her bed facing away from me and put on a bra from somewhere.

"I guess we're having lunch later anyway," she said.

"Shit," I said. "That's right."

She gave me a look like *Seriously? You don't remember? It was your idea, dummy.*

I shrugged.

"It's been a weird weekend. Long nights," I said.

"Don't you work third shift?" she asked rhetorically.

This is the part where I needed to ask her not to tell Ben about this. About anything. Where I probably needed to call off lunch and us getting ready over here and tell her that something could be a mistake even if neither party were wronged and nobody regretted anything.

But there was already something off about her mood this morning, and even though I may have done some very dumb shit and a lot of it quite recently, I wasn't entirely stupid.

"I think I have Toaster Strudels," she said after she was fully dressed.

"That'd be great," I said.

"Coffee?"

"Yes. Gallons, please."

I finished gathering my things and followed her into the eat-in kitchen. There was a small table by the window, but it had her laptop and mail and a bunch of other shit on it. In organized piles, but still. There was one stool by the counter near the coffee maker.

"Sit," she said and motioned to it.

Maybe I should have insisted that she take the stool, but I would've meant for her to take it if it was my place, so I sat down.

"Thanks," I said unnecessarily.

"I have another one in the closet I haven't put together yet," she said. She slid a coffee over to me.

I took a sip.

"I nominate Ben when we come by later," I said.

She smiled. She leaned back against the counter with her own cup. Maybe I should have said cheers.

I recognized the mug I was drinking from. It was part of a set that she had when we were together. Or maybe we bought it when we were together, or it was a gift from somebody. I didn't know but I remembered it. I'd drunk from it or one of its clones hundreds of times. I know I didn't take much with me when I left but she had to have mugs or glasses I wouldn't recognize by now, right?

I looked around the kitchen and the parts of the living room and the hall that I could see. I remembered most of the furniture and pictures and knick-knacks. Even the stuff I didn't know, it all fit somehow with her aesthetic and was familiar, even if I was seeing it for the first time.

Maybe this consistency of design and sense of herself would be comforting to some, maybe it should be for me, but it was making me seriously depressed instead.

"Is that a picture of me?" I asked her only realizing after I spoke that I had interrupted her, and she had been talking and I didn't know for how long or what she was talking about.

"I'm sorry," I tried. "What were you saying? Please finish."

She sipped her coffee. She was not going to finish.

"Yes, it's a picture of you," she said. "It was part of a photo essay I did my senior year?"

"Right, I remember," I said and tried to back out of this gently, or failing that, travel back in time and not bring it up.

The toaster sounded and two pastries nearly ejected onto the floor.

"One or two?" she asked.

"Just the one," I said, and she handed me a saucer with it and a little packet of icing.

"Right, so the whole photo essay is in the hallway," she said, sadly not forgetting what we were talking about. "You probably can't see the others from that seat. They're a nice shape for the hallway."

"OK," I said.

"Jesus—don't make it weird," she said.

I shook my head and tried eating my pastry and sipping my coffee to close the conversation off.

"Should I have blank walls?" she asked.

"No," I said. And then, because her tone was so self-pitying, like I was the asshole or like it was perfectly normal to have a picture of your ex-boyfriend on the wall of your apartment that you lived in alone I added, "Maybe just get some new shit."

She laughed or choked or exhaled loudly and took a bite of the other pastry. She didn't immediately respond so I figured it was over. Maybe she was surveying the place as well and was realizing that I had a point.

If she came to my apartment, she'd know nothing but my records and not even most of those.

"I didn't come down here to have sex with you," I said.

She started but I stopped her.

"I'm not saying you intended for it either," I said. "I'm just saying. You're important to me and it's important to me that you know that. Or that I told you."

"I don't want to get back together," she said, which seemed like a bit of a curveball.

"Good," I said. "We agree."

"For someone who doesn't care what people think about him, you seem to spend an awful lot of time worrying about what people think of you," she said.

I shook my head.

"I never said that," I said. "It doesn't matter what people think about me. But I still care about the opinions of others. Certain others."

She set her coffee cup on the counter.

"Are you going to break up her marriage?" she asked me after a moment of looking at the floor.

I stood up. I weighed the possibility of leaving without saying anything further.

"I don't know," I said.

"Don't you think you should figure that out?" she said.

"Probably," I said. "It's not my intention to. Whether you believe that or not."

She laughed and collected our dishes and took them to the sink.

"I do believe that,' she said and began rinsing. "You are just stupid enough for that to be true."

I considered hugging her as she stood there and giving her a quick peck on the cheek, but it seemed too much like a couple moment. We weren't a couple anymore even if we sometimes both forgot that. Even when neither of us could remember why. We were entirely separate individuals.

I said goodbye to her back.

I didn't check to see if he was still outside the apartment somehow. If he was frozen to the ground or lying in wait for me by Ben's car. I didn't look for his car to make sure it was gone or didn't follow me because I couldn't even remember what it was.

I didn't think to tell her to lock the door behind me when I left but she wasn't stupid, and if I was ever any good at making her feel safe…it was just more bullshit.

I'd like to blame it on the lack of sleep and the late nights and the unfinished weak coffee, but I didn't do or think any of these things. I didn't because I was too far into my own head.

So, I said goodbye to her back as she stood at the sink and I left like everything was normal.

I got back to the hotel and Ben was on the bed in a towel watching the news with the volume so low there was no way he could hear it. He was texting and sipping hotel room coffee. He was a better multitasker than I was.

"I got time for a shower and shit before they kick us out?" I asked kicking my shoes and shrugging out of my jacket.

He nodded.

"Yup," he said. "Checkout's at eleven. I made all the coffee if you want some."

"Fuck yes," I said as I poured myself a huge steaming paper cup. The carafe was nearly full to the brim even after Ben and my drink had been subtracted.

"You did make all the coffee," I said.

I sipped it gingerly, but it still scalded my tongue. It tasted of burnt and nothing else. It was awful and glorious.

"I cornered a maid in the hallway and charmed some extra out of her," he said. "There's powdered creamers and sugar over there too."

"What am I, an asshole?" I said and took my cup of bitter black with me into the bathroom.

He said something else about snagging some muffins or something from the breakfast, but I didn't really hear him. The congealed collection of preservatives and chemicals that is a Toaster Strudel was sitting heavy in my stomach.

I got the water as hot as I could and took a long shower. The pressure was brutal, and I let the water beat and scald me until I could no longer feel it, until it was no longer seemed new.

I had more terribly delicious hotel room coffee while I dressed and we haphazardly packed.

Ben left the key cards in the room, stuffed muffins and a banana in his pockets and we threw our bags into the back of his SUV and piled in.

"Do we need to check out?" I asked.

He made a *Nah* face.

"They'll figure it out," he said.

He was the kind of guy who could leave cash plus tip for a restaurant bill on the table and stroll out and assume the world took care of itself. I could not do this. I had to hand it to the waitress. I had to make sure it got where it needed to be.

We drove.

We had an hour or so before lunch. Javier wouldn't be joining us. He and Lisa had bunches of family stuff. Assuming, of course, he was even back in town.

I texted Estella. She sent me a thumbs up that she'd meet us there. Jake and Niedz were meeting us as well.

Mark texted. He was finally on his way, wouldn't make it for lunch and there was another hitch.

"Mark's solo," I said.

"What?" Ben said.

"I don't know," I said. "He says that Amy and Aimee aren't ready. And nobody's heard from your sisters yet."

He exhaled irritably and shook his head.

"Whatever," he said. "They know where it is."

Ben stopped at an ATM and I ran inside the CVS for mints or a pack of gum or something so maybe I could stop thinking about cigarettes for one goddamn minute this weekend.

None of this took very long. We still had forty minutes to get to a restaurant that was five minutes away and that was assuming the three other people we were meeting who were all arriving separately got there on time, which was crazy talk.

"You wanna get a beer?" Ben asked me. He looked as tired and worn out as I felt.

"I want a cigarette," I said. "Yeah, let's get a beer."

He had not asked me about Estella. He had not asked me anything about last night. I hadn't brought it up and I appreciated it, but now it was starting to sag everything else around us.

Last night was over, but unfortunately today followed yesterday. They were not independent from each other. Dawn hadn't wiped the slate clean, a hot shower hadn't washed anything away, and hotel coffee hadn't burnt the taste of it from my mouth.

So, he hadn't asked, and I hadn't said, but it remained.

It weighed down our innocuous chitchat. It sagged between us and pulled us into its gravity. A blackhole distorts space and time. Soon, we'd be too far gone, and we'd never escape it.

Nothing mattered.

Beginnings came from endings.

You were where you were from.

There was nowhere to escape to.

We parked on the street near the army surplus store and somehow walked past Yats even with all it's amazing smells and ducked into the bar next door. It helped that we'd be back for lunch soon.

The bar, a jazz club, was dark and most of the chairs were still upside down on the tables. This place changed names and owners and atmospheres so much I could never keep track of what the hell it was supposed to be. There was a lady behind the bar. I wasn't sure they were even open, but she didn't throw us out and quickly poured us a couple beers when Ben asked for them.

"Ask me about last night. Let's get it over with."

He sipped his beer and looked straight ahead into the dim and dusty bottles lining shelves behind the bar.

"Tell me about last night," he said.

We sat at the bar and I told him about it. I gave him the short, PG-13 version.

"Shit," he said. "I just fell asleep watching cable TV. You had adventures."

"Exploits," I agreed.

We finished our beer. Nobody else came in while we were there. I wanted to buy another pity round to give her something to do but we had lunch to get to.

We settled on a one hundred percent tip.

We hopped over to Yats. It smelled even better somehow.

"They might have Jambalaya today," I said.

"Don't jinx us, prick," Ben scoffed.

"I think I can smell it," I said.

The line was short—even though everybody else could smell this right?—and we lined up. I saw Estella sitting at the booth along the back wall reading a NUVO. I waved her over.

She left the alt-weekly newspaper and her stuff on the table and got in line.

She and Ben hugged and exchange greetings.

"I thought we were waiting on Jake and Adam?" she said. She never called Niedz by his last name like everyone else did. She rarely used nicknames. I imagined even his own mother calling him Niedz.

Ben and I shrugged in unison. He pointed his watch face in her direction.

"We said noon," I offered.

The guy in front of us stepped out of the way finally and we could read the chalkboard menu. There it was at the top, Jambalaya. It's been known to sell out in minutes.

I pointed at the menu.

"We said noon," I repeated.

I ordered half jambalaya and half chili cheese etouffee with extra garlic bread and a pop. Estella got half B&B and half succotash. Ben went full jambalaya.

I filled my drink with Mug Root-beer and no ice and smiled at the sign taped to the fountain drink dispenser—REFILS ARE FREE (AND NECCESSARRY)—as I always did.

I sat across from Estella before Ben could and make me sit next to her. He sat next to her.

Joe Yats brought our food out and recognized us—or did a good job pretending to—and we spent the next few minutes when we weren't stuffing our faces talking about what a great guy—even beyond his culinary mastery—he was.

"Jake and Niedz aren't going to make it," Ben said looking at his phone.

"Their loss," I said and the other two agreed by saying no more of it and continuing to shovel food into their mouths.

The food was hot, delicious and plentiful like it always was.

The garlic bread was soft and fluffy besides the flat-top-seared crunch of the garlic butter side. It was the perfect accompaniment, and an even better makeshift scoop, for the main dishes.

The etouffee was thick, creamy and velvety over rice. The aged cheddar tang, the salty sea taste of the crawfish and the chili spices melded together like magic.

The jambalaya was chunky and sticky without being gummy or watery. There were competing textures that were all pleasant and a nice mild-but-lasting spiciness.

On the counter they had dozens of hot sauce choices. I never reached for one.

We ate and talked and laughed and had a good time. Estella seemed past whatever ennui was threatening to descend on her earlier and I pushed mine aside as well.

Ben thankfully didn't bring up anything I had told him.

We finished. Ben and I had cleaned our plates, but Estella asked for a leftover container. Joe took her plate and said he'd freshen it up for her. When she got the to-go container her leftovers were inside along with more food than she had left on her plate and an extra piece of bread.

All that for seven bucks a person. It boggled the mind.

I snagged a NUVO from the rack near the door on the way out, folded it and stuffed into my jacket pocket, reminding myself to bring it with me to the wedding later so I'd have something engaging to peruse when it got boring as shit.

We walked to the cars and talked up the incoming and inevitable sainthood of Joe Yats some more.

We followed Estella to her apartment even though I knew the way.

She offered us drinks. I took a tea and Ben took a water. We freshened up and got ready and tried to figure the fastening of various rented tux parts and they helped me decide belt or no belt and tie or no tie and this or that jacket.

"Eh. It's just Javier," I parroted back to Ben, but it went right over his head.

Estella told me she'd decided not to go tonight, and I figured since she wasn't getting ready and yes, I promised I'd say something to Javier and no, I knew he wouldn't mind.

And we were ready and it was time to get over to the church, so we hugged her goodbye and Ben went to the car and I hung back for a second and we thanked each other awkwardly and I hugged her again and she kissed me politely on the cheek and I kissed the top of her head and I tried to say something about how I do love her but that can mean many different things or different things to different people or some such bullshit and she squeezed my right hand and said it was *OK* and she *Got it* and *Have fun at the wedding* and *We'll talk again soon* or maybe even hang out but it really felt like I would never see her again.

I didn't want us to be messy.

My life's messy. I've done messy.

I wanted us to just be what we were but maybe that's not even a thing.

I left her on the threshold which I've done before, and Ben and I drove to the church.

Mark was there before us. His tux was rumpled and creased in odd places as if he'd worn it in the car when he drove down here. Which he probably had.

High-fives, handshakes and hugs went around. It was good to see him and catch up, but he seemed unreal, somehow or not entirely part of the group anymore. He'd missed the last couple of days, and we could tell him about it and sometime when all this shit was far in the rearview, we probably would. But even then, he wouldn't get it. Partly, the fault would be ours because how could we explain it to him, but it would also be his fault for not being here. For not taking time off work or standing up to his wife.

Jesus, I thought half the reason he didn't some down earlier was so they could drive together and she's not even fucking here yet.

It was like he was tuned slightly differently than Ben or Javi or me now.

What about Estella? How was she tuned?

"Javi's not here yet," Mark said in response to something Ben said while I was daydreaming.

"What?" I said. "He was supposed to be here an hour ago."

"Where the fuck is he?" Ben said

But we both knew.

Mark shrugged and went on with something he was talking about. I saw Javi's brothers fast-tracking through the church and motioned them over.

"Where's your stupid brother?" I asked.

They glanced at each other. They shared a look like they knew where he was but would pretend they didn't.

"I don't know," one said.

"He's always late," the other offered.

They were terrible actors.

Ben beat me to the question.

"Is that fucker still in Fort Wayne?" he said maybe louder than you should say fuck in a church but what do I know?

"Wait," Mark said confused.

I didn't wait. I pressed the brothers who were looking more guilty all the time.

"What'd he go to Fort Wayne for?" I asked.

"Why is Javi in Fort Wayne?" Mark asked, still miles behind the conversation.

The brothers shared a look again.

I stepped in closer and got right in their faces.

"Don't give me that shit about driving your cousin up there," I said.

Ben stepped up with me. Something was lighting a fire under his ass.

"Yeah," he said and poked one in the chest. "It's your cousin too. One of you dipshits could've taken him."

"Hey," I said. "Don't look at each other, look at us."

They leaned away from us. They really, really wanted to look at each other. I was close enough to see one of them swallow.

"Dude," one of them said.

Mark got in the middle of it. He hates conflict and will throw himself in the middle of a situation just to diffuse it. Christ—how the weekend would've differed if he had just been here.

"OK, OK," he said and pushed us apart with his hands. "So, Javier had to go to Fort Wayne for a few. He's late but the wedding's still a couple hours away."

I was ready to grab him and toss him onto their side.

Ben said, "You weren't here, Mark."

He looked a little hurt. Good, yes, look hurt. You weren't here and things went to shit. Be hurt. You hurt us by not being here.

Where was this calming force on Thursday or Friday?

The brothers slipped away.

We heard a door slam and some shouts from the opposite direction and looked. We saw one of Lisa's friends or maybe relatives from last night. She strolled by face buried in her phone. Ben stepped away and said they exchanged a few words. He was all smiles.

When he came back over the façade had dropped.

"Lisa found out he's not here," he said.

We shared a look like the brothers had and then shifted our gaze to Mark.

"What?" he said. "I didn't fucking do anything. He has hours. He's not going to be late for the wedding."

Javier was late for his own wedding.

An hour and a half passed while we stood around and shifted uncomfortably in our seats and Lisa's face got madder and madder in some back room somewhere. I did see her once. Someone tried to stop her from coming out and she screamed something about how Javier wasn't here to see her so who gives a fuck.

Everybody was all about swearing in church today.

In the meantime, we learned that Aimee, Amy and, Ben's sisters would not be making the short two-hour trip down for the wedding.

Mark and Ben were pissed but seemed to shrug it off rather quickly. How often did they get to hang out with their friends and drink for free and not have their wives around?

Plus, for me, it saved any more possible drama.

"I don't even think my sisters are in Fort Wayne," Ben said. "Aimee tried calling Ellie but got no answer. She got one text from Meg that said 'Not coming' and that was it. Fucking weirdos."

Jake showed up and would've been late if the wedding had started on time but what's that saying about a broken clock showing the right time twice a day? There must be a version for inconsiderate assholes getting lucky every once in a while.

Javi finally arrived fully dressed in his tux and his head and face completely shaved, the dreadlocks and huge beard the faintest of shadows on his skin.

Ben nudged me.

"That's why he's late," he said. "Can you imagine how fucking long that took?"

The wedding happened and—even with Lisa's forced smile and Javi's unapologetic posture—it was a nice affair.

The reception was just down the street and, because we were late getting there, everything was set up and ready to go right away so there wasn't all that awful waiting around that usually happens after weddings.

It was a good time. I just treated it like a hangout in a strange place I'd never be in again.

I was relaxed and had fun fucking around with my friends and the food was serviceable and the drinks were free and kept coming.

I considered staying the night in Indianapolis again, maybe seeing if I could stay with Estella, but Ben was ready, and he wanted to go back tonight. For the best.

The wives were beginning to bother Ben and Mark about when they'd be back—like *they* were the assholes here. You're the bitches that didn't show up to your friend's fucking wedding. God forbid you drive two hours for someone else that has nothing to do with you.

"We should get going," somebody said as the reception wound down. The dancing had mostly stopped. Most of the relatives had vanished hours ago.

"Let's at least say goodbye to Javi," I said.

"I wanna stop in Muncie," Ben said, out of the blue.

Muncie was on the way back, sort of, but we'd have to dip off the highway about twenty minutes or so.

"For what?" Mark and I said at the same moment.

"Let's get an Optimator at the Heorot," he replied. It was a great idea and he'd have no objections from us.

We said adios to Javi and Lisa who looked like they were doing better or at least postponing the fight until it wasn't their special day.

We asked around to see if anybody else was heading back to the Fort and wanted to make a pit-stop for some insanely dark stout beer in a *Beowulf* themed bar in a meth-ravaged college town on a Saturday night with us, but, weirdly, didn't get any takers.

Muncie's closer to Indy, so it only took us forty minutes or so to get to the Heorot. We found a couple of seats against the wall with the papier-mâché dragon at one of the long picnic style tables. It's a minor miracle to find a seat there on a Saturday night, but it felt like people moved out of our way. We were dressed for a wedding after all, and we were buzzed, so we walked in like we owned the place or like we still came in regularly.

Ben bought us each a Spaten Optimator. If there was time, I hoped to wash mine down with a Guinness, but the way they kept checking their phones, there would not be time.

We were well dressed, so some sporty college chick tried to chat us up.

"Can you believe they don't have Coors Light here?" she yammered with disbelief.

The Heorot carried fifty beers on tap and twice that in bottles. The owner flew a bartender over from a pub in Ireland to teach his staff how to properly pour a Guinness. Maybe it was our attire or our welcoming manner that brought her over here, but it was time to stop this shit. My friends were married, and I couldn't be less interested.

"I think you're in the wrong place, sweetheart," I said as condescendingly as I could and looked away from her dismissively.

Mark, as the diffuser of conflict, tried to placate her and brush my antics off with a chuckle and a hurried explanation, but she bounced.

"Well, at least I didn't call her a bitch out loud!" I shouted over the din of the crowd after she left but maybe wasn't entirely out of earshot.

My friends sulked briefly over the lack of female

company, but we were only here for one drink anyway.

"I don't understand you idiots," I said. "'We have to get home to our wives, so let's stop for a beer.' 'Don't be mean to that brat nobody wants to talk to.'"

"You don't understand us?" Mark said and left it there.

I downed the last swallow of my beer and popped over to the bar and ordered a round of Guinness before anyone could object. One of the bartenders recognized me from back in the day and winked at me and gave me a high-five when she dropped off the pints. I never slept with her, but we were always flirty. When I used to live around the corner, I would come in for the 'one-dollar pizza with a pint' Friday lunch deal and bum her cigarettes.

I turned around and the boys were behind me.

They thought we were vacating the premises and Ben was holding my jacket out to me awkwardly now that they knew the score. I glanced over their shoulders, but our seats had already been filled. Nature, or a bar on a Saturday night, abhors a vacuum.

It was fine. We huddled around the end of the bar and guzzled our stouts quickly, the way it ought to be. I caught up briefly and fleetingly with the bartender but it's not like we ever really knew each other, so I just told her I had moved and I was just down in Indy for a wedding.

We drained our glasses and I said I'd see her later, because who knows? I was surprised she still worked there. It'd been, what seven years since I was in school?

"So, you and her?" Ben asked and made a lewd gesture.

"Jesus, what must you think of me?" I asked. "No, I

used to be in there nearly every day for a couple years. Just friendly."

He seemed almost disappointed.

"She did used to wear the sexiest Halloween costumes, though," I offered.

"Nice," they said in unison.

I considered elaborating, but those stupid looks on their faces—why ruin it? Their imagination was better than any of my words.

We slipped down Walnut St. and into the ancient brick alley that led to the open parking lot behind the buildings. I often fantasized about getting mugged back here when I was stumbling to a vehicle or taking a suddenly needed piss. It'd be like *Beowulf* then for sure—some horridly disfigured monster would attack drunkards leaving the Heorot, just like in the epic.

We emerged into the parking lot unscathed once again.

Mark bellowed *Shotgun!* when were within sight of Ben's SUV, even though he drove separately. I thought maybe this was some Midwest Lutheran, passive-aggressive way to ask me to drive for him, but I was feeling drunk at this point and pretended not to notice.

Ben got a call when we were in the alley but thumbed it off in his pocket.

It started ringing again.

"Jesus, I told her I'd text her when we were on the highway," he said and glanced at his phone. He answered it.

"You coming over to Ben and Aimee's?" I asked Mark.

He nodded.

"Probably. I'm pretty sure Amy's over there hanging out anyway," he said.

Maybe it was the stout talking, but I foraged ahead.

"Why the fuck didn't they come to Javi's wedding?" I asked him point blank. "I know we fuck around and treat him like a bit of a joke but he's our friend."

He was shaking his head agreeing with me but also in a *Dude, I know* exasperated kind of way. He'd had this conversation many times before and rather recently from the looks of it.

"I don't know what the fuck they were thinking, it's..." he said and then trailed off.

I almost said rude or disrespectful, but I realized he wasn't searching for a word. He was looking at something behind me.

I had my back to the entrance to the alley.

My skin prickled as I imagined the horrors sliming and slithering their way across the concrete towards me.

But no.

No gruesome monster bringing death awaited me tonight.

It was just Ben. He paced when he talked on the phone, and he had apparently answered his phone or called someone back and had zigzagged behind me when I wasn't paying attention.

He had this look on his face I'd never seen before. Shock or horror or unbridled rage at whatever he was being told from the other end of the phone.

He was gripping his phone so tight in his fist I was sure it would explode into shards at any moment. I could see puffs of warm air condensing into vapor as they left his flared nostrils.

Mark got to him first.

"Are you OK?" he asked him.

He quickly put a single index finger into the air. It was as if the whole night sky was holding its breath. Nothing could interrupt him.

"Yeah," he said into the phone but stared at us with wide, dark, unblinking eyes. "I heard you. We're leaving now. I'll meet you there. Tell Meg. She'll tell mom."

There was an inescapable sinking feeling in my stomach as the ground threatened to fall away from me.

"What is it?" I asked.

He sprinted to the SUV. I leapt in behind him so he wouldn't leave me there and take off with all my stuff.

"I'll call you," I shouted to Mark before the passenger's side door slammed from the force of the acceleration.

In the window, he stood there frozen, looking as bewildered and useless as I felt.

SUNDAY

When we got to the highway, Ben cranked it to 90 mph and set his cruise control. I didn't say anything.

He stayed in the left lane but actively swerved into the right to pass any cars over there. As we approached clusters of vehicles, he flashed his brights and tapped his horn a couple times. *Get out of the fucking way.*

When I lived in the rapidly receding Muncie for college, there was this bright red muscle car that, in place of a bumper, had an unfinished plank of wood that had the word MOVE painted backwards across it in aggressive black letterforms. I used to wonder about that guy and how often he got pulled over.

I was mildly worried that I associated that mystery man with the way Ben careened down the highway.

We hit a stretch of I-69 where you're between cities and there seemed to be an absence of other cars on the road and Ben slowed down enough that I felt comfortable asking him what the fuck was going on.

He told me.

I called Mark and relayed it to him with an eye on Ben, who, with a curt nod or a terse shake, would confirm or deny any details I gave Mark. Mostly he shrugged. He had no idea.

Mark asked me two dozen follow-up question that I didn't have any answers for, so I cut him off as politely as I could and told him we'd see him at the hospital.

The road flickered by, cold and hard. Everything appeared colorless in the dim of the night, even Ben's profile as he stared ahead and drove on and on.

When we finally got back to Fort Wayne, we blew right past all the usual exits for my apartment or his house and kept speeding north.

Finally, he slowed a tad and signaled, and we were exiting at Dupont Road, just north of town.

The exit was devoid of movement or light, but we could see the glow of the hospital up the road.

We tore through a red light at an empty intersection and I told myself that he checked it on our approach, but I'd never be sure.

He pulled to the curb and jumped out and looked at me helplessly.

"Go, go," I said. "I'll park it."

He nodded a quick thanks and turned and bolted for the doors.

The visitor's lot was barren, so I took a spot right up front as soon as I sussed out the confusing signage. I wanted to make sure Ben wouldn't come out here later to find a ticket or his car towed away.

I got out and paced around the car a minute. I buzzed with potential energy. I could either go inside or flee. The respective pulls were equal and excruciating.

Unsure of what to do, as if I had entered a room and forgotten why I was there, I was frozen next to the car. Another more familiar pull yanked at me.

I looked at the SUV.

Ben quit before I did, years ago, so there was no way. But I did see him take a few drags this weekend at Denny's. Was that out of nowhere?

I got back into the car and checked the glove box and under the seats. No cigarettes.

I leaned on the car waiting for Mark to show. Considering how comically befuddled he looked when we drove away from him, I was surprised that it only took him about ten minutes to catch up to us. He pulled up next to Ben's SUV and got out.

He was puffing away on a cigarette and I smiled ruefully at him.

He tossed the pack at me.

"I figured any cops would've pulled you over before I got close to you, so I mashed pedal," he said.

There was a little plastic lighter with the safety notch bitten off inside the half full pack of Winston's. I lit one without hesitation and let it fill me.

It felt like coming home.

Well, I didn't like going home. I was antsy and never comfortable there, but it felt like descriptions of coming home that I've read. Whatever. It felt right, anyway.

I took another drag and held it as long as I could before I exhaled it slowly through my nose.

I flicked the cherry off the thing, and it bounced and

sparked across the pavement. I blew off as much ash as I could and dropped the half-smoked thing into my breast pocket.

Mark cracked his neck. He was practically bouncing on the balls of his feet, ready to box somebody. He was crackling with energy.

"What the fuck, man?" he asked. "Update?"

I shook my head.

"You know everything I do," I said. "Does Amy know anything?"

"No," he said. "She's inside."

"Alright," I said. "Let's go. I wanted to give Ben a minute."

"I get it," he said whether he believed me or not.

Did I believe myself?

Was I giving Ben and his family a minute, or did I not want to go inside and deal with it? Did I think that I'd somehow make it real by seeing it? If a tree falls and all that.

We walked inside.

Mark tried to get the room from the receptionist.

"She thinks she might still be in the ER or ICU," he said and headed towards an elevator. "She told me where the family will most likely be waiting."

We rode up two floors in the elevator with the most tired looking woman in scrubs I've ever seen. She didn't press the number for her floor so much as lean into it. Nobody said anything.

We exited onto the floor just as Ben and a loose collection of worried relatives were bustling towards the elevators.

"She's been moved to a room," Ben said as he was

carried past us in a throng of nervous people in motion. In that moment they gave me the sense that they were like a flock of birds as if they were being carried from wherever they had been to wherever they were going in some sort of swarm or herd behavior as they undulated past us.

Amy peeled off slowly from the flock with a hand outstretched, and Mark took it and sidled up next to her and they reformed the outer layer of the mass all in one series of fluid motions.

I stepped in at the back but didn't feel much like one of them. I didn't have a wife or husband to grab onto. We were headed in the same direction and for the same reasons, but I was an outsider, at least only in my own mind. There were other, closer people that weren't here yet, but I was, and surely that counted for something.

It wasn't about me anyway, but the only thing I knew was myself, so that was how I related to and projected onto the world. Most people did this. The fact that I was aware of it was either an advantage, as in the phrase "In the land of the blind, the one-eyed man is king," or a disadvantage, as in the H.G. Wells story of the same name, where the protagonist was completely unequipped to handle the world in which he found himself.

I suspected the latter.

We squeezed ourselves back into the elevator and I saw Mark shift uncomfortably by the doors. He rolled his head around on his shoulders and breathed in and out audibly. I either saw sweat breaking out on his neck and forehead or I imagined I did.

He was claustrophobic.

He usually avoided elevators if he could, and I knew it was only worry and haste that had gotten him in one with me only moments earlier. He never took one twice in succession if he could avoid it.

Amy pushed herself into him, talking softly while rubbing his back. She'd noticed too of course. I doubt if anybody else did, but his embarrassment over this mild freak-out would last for days.

With nothing else to do, I surveyed the elevator to see who was here.

I was pretty sure the entirety of the car was taken with people here for our singular purpose, but I had been at the back of the pack and one or two in the far corners could have been extraneous bystanders sucked into our vortex.

Mark and Amy were here of course, and Ben and his Aimee, although they were separated and she was consoling some older woman, maybe one of Ben's aunts. I saw Ben's mom and maybe her new husband, but it could also have been her brother or brother-in-law. Meg was there, but neither redneck twin, nor the Baker patriarch, but this didn't surprise me.

Megan, Ben and Ellen's father would not be a welcome presence. I'd be shocked if anyone had told him about it, or even knew how to reach him.

We filed into the room in a kind of hierarchy dictated instinctually by our relational proximity to each other, and to the woman in the hospital bed before us.

But I of course knew this to be inaccurate and incomplete and that the threads that connected us to each other were not as straight or color-coded as some believed. I knew they were tangled, and some were frayed, and some had been strengthened and reinforced while others had either snapped from disuse or been cut with outright malice.

I wasn't fooling myself that I knew the whole story or that I could see the entire shape of the thing, but I knew of connections that others didn't. I was connected in ways that they couldn't know—and if they one day found out—they could look back in time and correct their understanding, but now was not that time.

Amy looked at me from past Mark's shoulder without his knowledge. Her eyes told me that she might know too, but, again, now was not the time to figure that out or even begin thinking about it. That was all distraction.

The various family members were swept or pushed or pulled by whatever their threads did to them, however their connections compelled them, and they visited her unconscious body briefly, then dispersed from her side. By the same unknown and unseen forces, I found myself at her bedside—I looked down at her, and I permitted myself a small display of public affection because no one could suspect its true origin, not here in this context.

I gripped Ellie's right hand and it remained slack. I tried to see the girl I knew better than I had any right to as I had the last time I saw her, when she walked barefoot out of my apartment a few days ago and left her panties on my floor for me to find later. But she was unrecognizable covered in tubes and bandages and bruises.

I set her hand back down onto the bed next to her and I had to step back before I lost it. I couldn't look at her anymore, not like this and not in front of these people or I would make our connections visible and our relationship known and palpable, emanating from our suddenly detectable auras as they sprang from us for all to see and merged above all of our heads, and everyone would know the truth and the lie wasn't even the important part or it never had been, but even the keeping of the lie wasn't important in that moment. She needed to get better, and anything that distracted from that was unacceptable.

And besides, she was so messed up, how could I look at her like this? Someone had ruined her. Someone had destroyed her.

I knew it was her, but it was a pile of bandages and bruises and tubes and blood, not the woman I knew. If I looked long enough, I would see her in all that misery and that would be too much. I couldn't let it start to feel like her or I would unravel.

There were other things to do, other things that needed taken care of.

Mark was talking with Ben and Ellen's mom and consoling her, and she was doing her best, but tears were coming now, and she was letting them fall freely as if she had any choice.

Amy stepped away from Mark only half a step and she was next to me. The room was tiny after all, but it was the enormity of the act that made us feel small enough to fit inside of it comfortably.

She placed a hand on my shoulder and squeezed my hand and I looked into her eyes and she knew.

She knew what Ellie and I had been up to, and she practically glowed with the knowledge. While the rest of the room's occupants were dull in their misery, I was vivid and filthy and angry in mine.

Rage burns, after all.

We shared our look and then Amy—either sensing

the mood of the room changing beneath us, or because she was just as scared as I was that my secret might somehow be projected onto the white of the hospital's walls, ceiling and every single surface—shook her head once subtly and released me, and when Mark turned back to her, it was if she had never moved and we had never shared a thing.

Her eyes said, *I know. But not here, not now.*

I was grateful for her touch and her understanding and I tried not to war with myself over it.

A couple nurses pushed their way in and pushed all of us out. They took names and relationship statuses and divided us into groups. Ben and Meg began to object, but Mark told them it was OK. We weren't family even if it felt like it, even if we should be.

"We'll be down the hall," Mark said and pointed in the direction that the nurse had just told us was a waiting room and he and Amy and I walked that way with one or two other people I didn't know who must be neighbors or other friends or something.

We divided up further in the waiting room, with Amy, Mark and I huddled in the far corner away from the TVs. We tried to sit but shuffled our feet and strained in our chairs.

After a minute, Amy asked Mark to get her something from the vending machines in the hall.

He got up.

"You want anything?" he asked me.

"Nope, I'm good," I replied.

He looked like he wanted company, but I knew why she had asked him to leave, so I sunk lower into my seat and seemed to turn further into myself.

He didn't ask me to go with him.

As soon as he rounded out from the waiting room, I sat up straighter.

"OK," I said, "when did she tell you?"

She smiled at me.

"I saw you two downtown," she said. "You were having lunch and I was across the street and I couldn't believe my luck that I had some friends I could join for a quick bite. I was waiting at the light and, I don't know, something stopped me. Something in your body language or posture, and I can't know this for sure because I just stood there not crossing the street, but if I had you would've seen me, and you two would've brushed it off like you ran into each other. And I would've believed you, but I stood there watching you instead, and Ellie put her hand on your leg under the table and left it there. So, I knew."

I placed the memory.

"This was outside at The Dash-In, wasn't it?" I asked.

She nodded in agreement.

"Dammit," I said and leaned back against the wall. "I told her we shouldn't eat outside like that. God, we argued about that day a lot."

She looked at her feet.

"Amy," I said, "no way. You confronted her about it? And she never said a word to me? C'mon."

"I wasn't a hundred percent," she said and shook her head. "But I was pretty sure she hadn't. You didn't act any different around me and she seemed way more concerned at the time that you'd find out her and I talked."

I bit my lip.

We were lying to everyone. I was lying to everyone. I was lying to her. Why should it bother me that she was keeping something from me?

"Did she tell anybody else?" I asked.

She shrugged.

"I really have no idea, but she didn't seem overly concerned that I knew," Amy said.

"Have you told anyone else?" I asked her.

"You have to tell the police when they get here, you know that," she said.

"You're evading my question," I said.

"I didn't tell Mark, idiot," she said. "Why else would I send him on a bullshit errand?"

"You still didn't answer me directly," I said getting nervous, thinking about an earlier, vaguer run-in this weekend with Niedz.

"No, you're avoiding," she said. "You have to tell the police. It could be motive."

"You can't put this on me, I was out of town," I said.

She looked around.

"Who's not here, Kyle?" she asked me. "Who hasn't been here that you'd expect to see? Her creepy husband, maybe?"

I concentrated on my breathing.

It was true.

Neither of the Redneck Twins were here. Did that mean Dustin had done this to her? After I stood up to him, maybe she told him about us, and he took it out on her and did this horrible shit? I saw him point a gun at a woman twenty-four hours ago. Could he do this?

Maybe. They were also drug pushers, so they kept—as I witnessed firsthand—very odd hours and were not ones to have cell phones turned on or even on their person.

"I'm not saying this is your fault," she said, "but I'm saying we—"

She stopped and sank back into her seat a bit more. I was about to ask her what she was going to say when Mark came in from the hall.

Our heart-to-heart was over.

He handed me an A&W.

"I got you something anyway," he said.

I thanked him.

He had a couple more drinks and an armload of snacks as well. Chips, mini doughnuts, candy bars, beef jerky. Amy knew that his need to please would have him hemming and hawing in front of the machine for a few minutes before he simply bought the widest possible array of products and would give us time to talk.

She was right of course, but I still wanted more time with her. I wanted more clarification, I needed her to tell me it wasn't my fault again.

I needed something. I needed anything.

I needed to find Ellie's husband and start beating on him before I even asked him if he did it.

I looked at the clock on the wall.

How long had she been here? When was she found? Who brought her here? How much time would pass without her husband showing, until it tipped the scales from *Could he?* into *How could he!* territory.

"I'm gonna get some air," I said, and realized I was standing by the door to the waiting room and my voice sounded strange to me, quieter and muffled within the echoes of my own skull.

I wasn't claustrophobic like Mark, but I couldn't bear to be inside anything like an elevator right now. I needed my feet moving beneath me. I needed my own power propelling me.

Besides, I didn't want to double-back past that room. I didn't want to catch a glimpse of her. I didn't want to see her mom crying. I didn't want to see Ben, her brother and my friend, standing there and projecting helplessness out into the world. I didn't want to run into her husband if he did show. I didn't want anything.

I almost wanted to be home, which was only a few miles from here—I was closer to the place than I had been in days, but I felt so far from it. I knew it'd be hours until I could sit on my own couch, among my own familiar things, or lie down on my comfortable bed that I had last been in with Ellie. I was hours from these things, but it felt like days. I was only down the road, but it felt like I was farther from home than I had been in Indianapolis. It was as if we had traveled south instead of north, and I was somewhere foreign, like Kentucky or Tennessee, and I might never make it home again.

So, I went left out of the waiting room and I didn't even look right, I pushed through the door to the stairwell and I stomped down each step in turn. They echoed in that concrete-and-steel way that only barren, terrifying stairwells can.

I encountered no other people.

I didn't actually know what floor I had been on, and I kept descending until the stairs stopped at an underground level. I wandered the empty halls of the basement floor for a while, until I heard approaching voices, and I knew, I knew inside me, like stupefying dream logic, that I had to get out of there before the voices discovered me.

I burst back into the stairwell and ran and pulled myself up to the first flight of stairs with my hands on the rails, but I heard steps and voices above me as well, so I exited immediately.

The ground level.

I could see the darkness of the outside, the expanse of the sky.

I could only equate the feeling I had with going for a run and imagining some beast was chasing you as a motivation to run faster, and how you knew it wasn't real, because you created it in your mind for just this purpose, but your body thought maybe it was really back there, maybe it was really chasing you, and despite the logic that told you it wasn't true, you felt your arms pinprick with goose bumps and you started to believe it anyway.

I looked behind me and there was nothing but the hospital.

I let the cold air fill my lungs, and I felt the briefest of hitches from my half a cigarette earlier, the poisons of the thing still clinging to my throat.

I started to calm down.

I still had Ben's keys, so I went to the SUV and popped the lighter on his center console and held the glowing thing up to my face as I lit the half butt. Half my face felt hot, like it'd been turned towards the sun. I'd nearly burnt one of my eyebrows off in college with a cheap plastic Bic disposable lighter that must have been twice the distance from my face than this incredible red set of rings was now.

But nothing caught fire except the crumpled end of the cigarette. I finished it in three long drags. I hastily exhaled as if I didn't want to be doing this, as if I just had to get through it, and I didn't want to absorb any of it into me, not like I did last time.

And yes, of course, it was habit. Even though it was one I thought was weeks behind me. You were right not to applaud me for my fleeting six-week hiatus. I was a failure and a fraud.

I had this list, in the back of my mind, situations in which I would be allowed to take up smoking again.

I find out I'm dying.

I'm drafted for war.

The apocalypse.

This was not one of those situations. Your best friend's sister, who you're sleeping with, and who's also married to someone else—someone dangerous, is found raped and beaten and barely clinging to life.

Obviously, this is one of those situations, because I was currently flicking a butt into the gutter, but it never occurred to me that this even had the possibility of happening.

The spaces around Ben's SUV had filled up, but I barely registered this, until a window of an adjacent car rolled down and a voice spoke to me from inside.

The voice asked me something normal and it sounded somehow familiar, but it was so out of context that I just blinked and stared at the voice like a slack-jawed idiot. The window rolled back up. The door opened and Ben's father stepped out.

I must have said *What?* or *Huh?* or made some sort of noise because he repeated himself.

"You're of my son's friends, right," he said. "Which one are you?"

"Kyle," I said.

He nodded and filed the information away for later use. He produced a cigarette and lighter from somewhere and lit up.

"Smoke, Kyle?" he offered.

I looked into his eyes without blinking.

"I quit," I said.

He exhaled calmly and moved his eyes in an arc and rested his gaze somewhere far off, vaguely where I had just flicked my butt.

"Sure," he said.

"Right," I said.

His was already to the filter and he let it fall to the ground before pivoting the toe of his right boot across it soundlessly.

"See you inside, Kyle," he said, and walked off towards the hospital in no hurry, as if he had all the time in the world.

I watched him disappear inside.

Ben's keys were in my hand. I grasped one between my thumb and forefinger and scratched a single thin line into his father's SUV, right above the gas flap. I saw, or imagined I saw, little sparks from metal on metal contact, or light bouncing off paint shavings as they jettisoned into the night air.

I walked back towards the building.

Away from the entrance and recessed from the light I could see a figure and I could see them bring a glowing ember to their mouth every once in a while. I could see the small trail of smoke that they exhaled. I walked towards it like it was a magnet and I was an iron shaving, or as if there was a groove cut into the ground and I followed in slavishly because to fight the rut would take too much work.

"Can I get one of those?" I asked and realized she was pointing the open end of the pack in my direction already. I guess I was easy to read. I rolled with it. Maybe it was because I didn't know this person that I didn't mind being what I was, wearing my vices in the open, naked on my chest.

She thumbed the button of a butane lighter and held the blue dagger of flame at a slanted angle for me and I touched the cigarette to it.

The lighter disappeared and there was nothing but the red glow of our cigarette tips and the sound of them burning as we inhaled.

"That bad, huh?" the woman asked me. She was in scrubs. She wasn't condescending or prying me for information. She was giving me a forum in which to say *It's that bad* without judgment or hindrance.

"Yeah. Worse, even," I said.

She didn't press me further. She didn't ask for details or proof or how I defined bad from worse. She didn't need to. Maybe it was on my face already, but she believed me, and I appreciated that much.

"The girl, right?" she asked.

I nodded and smoked more.

"Somebody," she said and trailed off.

I looked at her and waited for her to finish. I didn't want to have to ask her to, but I would if she made eye contact before getting back to it.

"You family?" she asked and stamped her cigarette out.

I tilted my right hand back and forth in the air.

"Kinda," I said.

"I'll let you decide who to tell this to, but somebody bit her," she said. "Multiple times. That's why her face is bandaged."

"Jesus," I said. "Fuck."

She touched me lightly on the arm and smiled sympathetically.

"Why'd you tell me that?" I asked her. Hopefully, I conveyed my thanks in that question, because that's how I meant it. It's hard in places like this to get anybody to tell you anything.

She understood.

"I would want to know," she said and spread her arms out to encompass the whole hospital campus. Maybe the whole of the world. "It's always bad and sometimes it's worse. And there are always things more dismal still."

Before she turned to go, she asked me if I wanted another cigarette for later. I found the fortitude to decline. This was either my last one or I'd be buying my own pack tomorrow. Wait and see.

After she left, I savored the rest of it in inverse proportion to the way I had sucked and spit out the last one. It was either taking hold of me or it was an extended goodbye I didn't want to finish.

Bit her? On the fucking face? That's crazy shit. That's hate. That's like a guy pointing a loaded gun at a half-naked mother while her child slept in a trailer for no reason at all. Crazy hate.

It could be no one else.

I smoked the fucking thing down to the filter and went back inside. I felt the door might come off in my hands.

I found a bathroom and washed my hands and face like I was living at home and hiding my smoking from my parents or sprucing up to see a lover. I guess it was the latter, but just not in that way.

I asked the receptionist what room she was in since I couldn't even remember the floor and I headed back up.

Ellie, Meg and Ben's family and friends were taking up most of the waiting room now. Mark and Amy were talking to somebody I half recognized from a wedding or graduation or something. A cousin or somebody similar.

I didn't see either redneck twin yet.

A lot of other half-remembered faces were dotted up and down the hall. She had so much support. I didn't see their father anywhere.

There were cops too.

Ben was talking to one and caught my eye. He nodded for me to come over.

"Kyle," he said. "This is Detective Russo."

I shook hands with him. He asked me for my full name, and I gave it to him.

"So, you were in Indianapolis with Mr. Baker here last night?" the detective asked me.

"Yeah," I said and then insisted on calling him Ben because Mr. Baker was somebody else, it couldn't be my friend even though they shared a last name. Mr. anything was just too much. "Ben and I were in Indianapolis since Thursday night."

"And you guys shared a hotel room? And paid for various things with credit cards?" he asked.

"Correct," I said. "I never have cash. Ben paid with cash here and there, I think, but he hit up a few different ATMs this weekend."

Detective Russo was subtly boxing Ben out of our little half circle, asking me questions while angling him out of my line of sight. I willed myself to not look at him for any confirmation of anything. I couldn't even be sure he was standing there anymore. There was a lot going on around us.

The detective was staring at me as if he could see inside my head and see my brain working. It was a practiced stare and I'm sure he practiced it on himself in the mirror or to others in this life to the detriment of their close personal relationships.

I tried not to let it get to me.

I did not do this.

I was not in town when this occurred.

There were things I did not want him to know but everyone has something they didn't want cops to know and every cop knew that. Every cop knows that everyone is lying to them all the time and not always for reasons adjacent to any particular case they were working on.

He continued with his gentle prodding.

"Was there any time you and Mr. Baker were separated from each other for an extended amount of time?" he asked me, finally getting to the meat of it.

I nodded.

"Yeah," I said. "I borrowed his SUV around three in the morning Saturday and returned it a little before nine that same morning. I left him at the hotel."

He looked up at me, interested for the first time. I assumed it was fake. He must have already gotten all this from Ben anyway.

"That reminds me," I said, and took Ben's keys from my pocket and used it as an opportunity to locate him. He had moved farther down the wall and was standing next to his mother, offering her support as she talked to another officer. I got his attention and tossed him his keys. He caught them one handed and slipped them into his pocket in a series of flawlessly practiced motions. If only he'd been sliding over the roof of a sports car as he did this.

"I parked for him when he came inside when we got here," I explained.

"Is that where you were just coming from?" he asked.

"No," I said. "Cigarette."

"I quit eleven years ago," he said automatically.

"I quit six weeks ago," I said. "And here we are."

He smirked at me for the first time.

He glanced at his notes and paged back a page or two and then returned his gaze to me. I had no illusions that he was looking for anything or that this man ever forgot anything. He seemed too sharp for that.

"Getting back to early yesterday morning," he said. "Where did you go when we you were in possession of Mr. Baker's vehicle?"

"I went to an ex-girlfriend's place," I said. "Near Broad Ripple in Indy. I spent the night."

"And she will corroborate this?" he said nonchalantly.

"Yeah," I said, only slightly worried that it went poorly enough that'd she'd pretend I wasn't there or that she had never even known me.

Russo said that'd he need her name and number and address, and I rattled them off to him after checking my phone. Who can remember that type of shit anymore?

"Did you go anywhere else on your way to or from Ms. Grey's?" he asked. "Food, gas, a wrong turn, anything?"

I shook my head.

"No," I said.

He nodded.

"Mr. Baker got an oil change the morning you left for Indianapolis," he explained. "The receipt was still in his wallet. I'm going to send an officer down with him in a few and do a rough calculation to confirm that you guys only made the one down and back to Indy."

"We were in Muncie finishing a drink when we found out about this and came back," I told him. "About fifteen, twenty miles off the highway."

He nodded.

"Mr. Baker told me," he said. "I believe you two, that's why I'm being so forthcoming."

I nodded since I couldn't think of anything else to do.

"All right," he said. "I've got your number if there's anything further."

"I'll be around," I said and turned to the less crowded area of the hallway to get some space.

"Oh," he said with all the fake haphazardness I credited him with earlier. "Your relationship to the victim?"

I smiled at the phrasing of the question, the out that it gave me.

"We're friends," I said honestly. "I'm friends with all the Baker kids."

"And their spouses?" he asked while studying my face.

"Aimee, yeah," I said. "The sisters' husbands I don't know very well. Don't really want to."

"Why is that?"

I shrugged and tried to appear as noncommittal.

"They're trashy lake people," I said. "You know the

type. Rednecks."

He maintained a stare for a beat, then nodded once and turned from me to some new business.

It was a gamble, but I couldn't imagine Ben had told him that his brothers-in-law were drug dealers and that his sisters knew about it. I'd have to get with him and figure out if he told the cops anything about Thursday night. Get that story straight. Javi would be a problem. He'd be leaving for his honeymoon any time now and I didn't really want to discuss it with him over the phone.

Jesus.

Javier was here in Fort Wayne that night when this happened.

This would not look good for him. Hope he had an airtight alibi locked down.

I remembered to breathe.

It was the bachelor party night. We were at a crazy club that was packed full of mother fuckers. No one would have noticed when we left, right? Or that we were palling around with the Redneck Twins right before departing.

Shit.

How far out of town was that trailer park? Forty minutes round trip? I think Javi has a GPS in the glove box, but I didn't think he ever took it out or turned it on. So that would be no help.

Stop.

Shit—what about all your texts? There were records of all that, right?

Stop, stop, stop.

It's fine. Estella would back you up, the miles might be off one way or the other, but there wouldn't be the 200-

mile round trip discrepancy they were looking for and not even looking for very hard.

They were looking for the husband. They had to be.

The statistics are there, right? It's usually someone you know.

Fuck.

How many people did she know in Fort Wayne? How many did I? What was the possibility that I wouldn't know who did this to her? Slim, razor slim. Even if they're caught, if I know them, then I clearly never *knew* them, and I'll never know why.

I'll never understand.

Even if they have all the evidence and they find them and then when presented with it they confess and give a detailed account that conforms to the known facts. I'll never really know why.

I'll never know.

Even told, I could never know.

Whatever they could say, it'd be too unbelievable. It'd be too mundane and prosaic or too outlandish and ridiculous.

There's no sound reason anyone could have for doing this, so understanding it is an impossibility and seeking understanding would be fruitless.

The weight of this, of no answer being enough, pressed down on me as I trudged through the hallway. With every step I took my feet felt heavier, as if I was sinking into muck. It was more difficult with each successive footfall to take a step.

The weight of the world, of the horrendous act, crushed me, sat on me and pushed me into the ground. It was inescapable. It was gravity. It wasn't even a push, but it pulled me towards it, a force from beneath the earth tethered to me in some unbreakable way and would never go slack.

It would pull me closer to the ground until I succumbed to it and joined it under the dirt, in the grave.

I stumbled into the waiting room, pulling myself through the door, hands on either side of the frame as if I was drunk or as if the axis of the room had tilted. I didn't walk into the room—I clawed at the sides of a trapdoor.

I sat in the first unoccupied seat I could find, surrounded by strangers.

My weight lessened as I filled the chair with my bulk. I felt heavy all over, but maybe the chair could support me, or failing that, maybe at least the floor could, and I could rest there without collapsing through the ceiling of the lower floor, down and down until I was in the cold ground. Maybe, but I had my doubts.

Mark and Amy stopped by my seat on their way out of the room and said some things to me that I couldn't process and forgot as soon as they said them.

I nodded and agreed and tried to look up from their shoes but that's what kept filling my vision.

They were leaving to get some rest or food or something and I should do the same and did I need a ride and I probably should and I did need those things including a ride but if I accepted then they would see that my muscles no longer worked or my mass had become so heavy that I couldn't manipulate my limbs anymore more so I said *No* or at least shook my head just enough that they got the picture.

As they were leaving and as I was positioned facing the door, Amy looked back at me, and with a raise of her eyebrows asked me if I told the cops about my affair with Ellie.

I lowered my eyes, shook my head and mouthed *No* again.

When I looked back up at her she shrugged at me exaggeratedly. *Why?* she seemed to ask.

I shrugged back and continued shaking my head despite the enormous weight of it.

I hung around the hospital as long as I could and tried to stay awake that whole time. Magical thinking on my part. If I was here my very presence would be some sort of help.

Positively bullshit.

I used to think the same thing when I was little and alone in the backseat of my parent's car as they drove around lost somewhere.

In the time before GPS, before even the personalized printouts of MapQuest directions that took you door to door with *For Dummies* instructions, I was little and we would take vacations as a family. We would always get lost, and usually at night.

As my dad drove and my mom tried to figure out how to read a road atlas on the fly, they would scream at each other, and miss or misread poorly lit and scuffed highway signs, and I would sit strapped in the backseat and I knew we would be lost forever and we would wander the endless, dark roads until we died.

I knew this with the same certainty that I knew that if I stayed awake and if I stayed quiet and if I looked at every sign as it rushed past even though I couldn't yet read, I knew if I did these simple things I was helping and I would get my parents and myself safely to our destination.

I applied this same nonsense to staying at the hospital long past most. I would have kept on sitting there if Ben hadn't passed by the waiting area on his way to the stairs. Maybe he felt the same way about elevators that Mark always had. Maybe he wanted the exercise.

'Shit, you're still here?" he asked even though it wasn't a question. He saw that I remained. Perhaps it was he impossibility of it. You're *still* here? Yes, somehow.

"Yeah," I said and tried to explain it, so he'd understand without knowing why. "I just couldn't leave with everything going on."

He smiled at me and offered me his hand. He clasped it and pulled me to my feet and hugged me.

"Thanks, man," he said.

I almost told him right there.

There'd never be a good time, I realized that, and continuing to lie to my friend did him no favors and piled up eventual strain on our relationship. But...this was not the right time.

I didn't know. Was I a coward? Yes, but also, I would've felt like I was saying *See, I'm closer to her than you. I'm sadder than you. This is affecting me harder.* Grief shouldn't be a competition.

"Come on, I'll drive you home," he said.

I thought about declining, trying to get a cab or catch the bus. Maybe I was worried I would tell him about the affair but I'm not a blurter. I'm sure it was more magical thinking.

He asked if I wanted to get breakfast and I was

starving but I said no. I just needed sleep and he nodded, relieved that we wouldn't have to come up with idle chitchat over pancakes.

His dad's SUV wasn't in the lot. I wondered if he'd noticed the scratch yet.

I blinked a few times and the short trip was over and I was looking at the front of my apartment building. I was so tired. I was dead on my feet. I'd either fallen asleep in the ten-minute ride, or it was short in comparison to the jaunts we'd been on in the last few days, so it flew by.

I wasn't a hundred percent, but we hadn't said anything in the car. Again, was this because we had no words left to say or because the last time, we'd run our mouths in this vehicle someone had planted a recording device?

I shook his hand in a bizarre formality and grabbed my suitcase from the back.

I waved a single slicing wave through the air at him. He rolled his window down but said nothing to me. He nodded.

He waited for me to get into my building. Once inside, I head his SUV backing out of the parking lot and driving away.

I checked my mailbox, even though I knew it would be mailers and ads like always. I dropped them in the small recycling box near the door.

I fumbled my keys out of my pocket, unlocked my door and clamored inside.

The place smelled stale and strange like it always did when I was away for more than a day or two. It reverted to whatever its natural state was, purging me and my scents from its system. I inhaled deeply and tried to place it but failed. So instead I tried to hang on to it, but that faded after a couple deep breaths. That, whatever that real smell of the place was, was its true nature and I easily camouflaged it in seconds without even trying.

I kicked the suitcase into the living room enough to shut my front door and left it there and stripped my clothes off in the living room as well and left them in a pile on the carpet.

I tried not to picture Ellie doing a similar thing a few days ago.

I pulled a fan out of my bedroom closet and plugged it in. I adjusted the long, vertical blinds over the sliding glass door to my patio for maximum coverage. I turned the fan on high. It was Sunday and this was a working complex. It was easy to sleep during the week and generally quiet but there would be more comings and goings at different times on a weekend, so I needed the white noise.

I crawled into my unmade bed and pulled and piled the sheets and blankets and pillows over and around my naked body as if I was drowning in them or sinking into them like quicksand.

I tried to smell her on the sheets, but time had taken it away.

I let myself cry.

I gave myself over to tears and let them flow freely in huge racking sobs as my mouth made uncontrollable, alien sounds into my pillows. Muffled and distant, I maybe could've convinced myself there were coming from someone else, but I didn't attempt to.

I let it take me on a wave and crash me into shore and pull me back out and repeat. It battered my body and soul until there was none of it left inside me. Less than five minutes probably. There'd be more later, I knew.

I rolled onto my back and readjusted. I could feel the wetness from my tears on the back of my neck and shoulders like the ghosts of cold kisses.

I put a pillow over my face and slept.

I slept for hours. I woke and tossed. I fell back asleep.

I woke again and was hot, that temperature you get from sleeping naked as your body heat radiates back onto itself and has nothing to escape or disperse into. I stumbled into the bathroom, and the air and tile were pleasantly cool on my body, like a light rain in the middle of summer. I teetered and pissed into the toilet and got most of it in the bowl. My urine was a deep yellow and it stung a little when I peed. Maybe time for a glass of water.

There was a glass in the dishwasher. Sometimes I felt like I should rotate my dishes or get rid of most of them as I just drank out of the same glass all the time and ate off the same plate with the same fork.

I filled it from the sink and drank it down in a couple gulps. I refilled it and drank this glass slower and turned around and leaned my naked ass against the counter.

Ellie's new panties were hanging on my fridge.

Ben must have done this when I was distracted getting my stuff around. He'd affixed them with a magnet to the mostly empty surface and had no idea the morbidity of this little joke at my expense.

I refilled the glass and took it with me back into the bedroom.

I left the panties hanging there. As a trophy or a

eulogy, as a reminder or a sick joke. I didn't know but I couldn't touch them. Not right now.

I went back to sleep. Mercifully, the dreamless kind.

I slept off and on all day.

Huge multiple hours-long chunks and little spurts of a few minutes. I pissed and drank water and ate cold, past-their-prime leftovers from my fridge, standing naked in my kitchen as needed. And then I'd crawl back into bed and fall back asleep.

It was Sunday and my week off had started at eight a.m. and usually, I tried to stay awake as much as I could to jumpstart a normal sleep cycle for the coming week. This sometimes worked and sometimes didn't.

Today I abandoned it completely. It never even occurred to me that I needed to be awake for any reason.

During one of these brief trips to the bathroom or the kitchen I squatted down into my pile of clothes and retrieved my cell phone.

It was well into the late afternoon and I had a few texts and a missed call from my mom who hasn't figured out how to text.

Estella asked how the wedding went and Javi had sent me a shot of his cruise ship and I tried to respond to these things. I wrote out responses both noncommittal and verbose where I explained the horrors that await them when their future catches up with ours. I almost even called my mom back.

But I deleted the messages without sending them and snapped my phone shut without pressing that green Call button.

I made sure the phone was still silenced and lobbed it onto the couch and went back to bed.

I woke up around seven p.m.

If it was my week to work third shift, this would be sleeping in.

I was lying on my back and the sheets and blankets and pillows had rearranged themselves into a semblance of order as I had slept.

My eyes opened and I knew the great hibernation was over. I could no longer escape into sleep, not today.

I swatted at the fan near my bed until it angled close enough to turn it off.

Cutting off the white noise, the world was shocking in its quiet. Like I was the sole survivor of the human apocalypse. Slowly, sounds from the outside world began to creep in and I realized I'd been holding my breath until I audibly confirmed the existence of other people still alive in the world.

I got out of bed and stretched and popped and cracked as much of my body as I could. I could picture Estella's gross-out face she used to make when I would do this in the morning when we lived together.

I found some underwear and socks and an undershirt and put all of those on and they felt itchy and weird and ill-fitting, but you can't just stay naked in your bed all the time. I'd just tried, and I hadn't even made it twelve hours.

I dug around in my freezer and fridge and pantry and started pulling things out for a proper meal. When I had all the items piled onto the counter, I took one look at them and immediately returned everything to its place.

I wasn't eating this shit.

I went back into the bedroom and finished dressing. Jeans and a clean button down. I checked my phone but nothing new. It was almost seven thirty. Everyone I knew lived normal nine to five types lives. Well, the dudes that weren't drug dealers, anyway.

I shrugged. Fuck it. I'll pick up Rally's or Chipotle or something.

I found my keys, pleasantly surprised that they were in my pants pocket and not hanging from the lock on the outside of my front door.

I forgot to put a jacket on, so I cranked the heat when I got into my car.

I waited a few minutes for the engine to level out and stop sounding so angry with me. It always did this when I didn't start it for a couple days, especially in winter.

I petted the dashboard and told it was OK and a good boy like it was dog. I talked to my car an embarrassing amount. I knew a guy in college whose car was on its last leg, so he drove it to the Atlantic—from central Indiana—because (and I quote) *He'd never seen the ocean.*

Maybe I was crazy, but there was always somebody crazier.

I drove out of the apartment complex and turned right on Clinton and headed up towards Coliseum and changed my mind when I was almost there.

I saw the Bandito's sign and turned in past the bank. Fuck it. Margaritas with chips and salsa sounded like the perfect dinner.

It was across the street from the mall and behind another shopping center. There were soccer moms rattling over-filled carts out of the side entrance to Kohl's, but mostly it was dead back here.

There used to be a movie theater next to this—I'm being generous with this term here—Mexican restaurant. But the oldest part of the theater had been torn down and the rest of it was boarded up. I remember when I was in high school or home for break from college, if you were too late for your showtime, you couldn't find a parking space, and forget about two seats together.

It hadn't been that long had it? Have things really changed that much?

I bumped over the uneven pavement and parked near a few other cars. There weren't even traces of yellow parking spaces anymore.

I pushed through the huge wooden castle-like doors. The restaurant was exactly the same. In the waiting area, they still had, behind the standard vinyl benches, a claw machine with stuffed animals and the cocktail-table-style Pac-Man machine I loved when I was a kid. It had to be the same one, right? Where the hell would you find a replacement?

Even the faux church carpet was nostalgic.

There was nobody at the hostess stand at the moment, but I think I set off a doorbell when I entered, so I slipped into the cantina before I had to talk to anybody that couldn't directly serve me alcohol.

I sat at the barstool closest to the door and glanced around. There were a couple people scattered here and there. I didn't do any deep calculations, but given the few vehicles in the parking lot, I'd be surprised if there were any customers sitting in the restaurant proper.

I reflexively checked the status of my car through the

window.

I couldn't believe it wasn't even eight p.m. It was that cold darkness of late winter that makes every moment after sundown seem like permanent midnight.

A bartender I half-recognized slid a bowl of warm chips and an ashtray like container of salsa in front of me on the shiny bar top.

He raised his eyebrows and nodded at me. I liked his style. He seemed as chatty as I felt.

"Pitcher of margaritas." I said. "Rocks."

"Salt?"

I nodded yes.

"Menu?" he asked.

I nodded again.

He produced a menu from thin air like a close-up magician and handed it to me and pivoted from the bar to find my drink.

The menu was different but still familiar.

I noticed under the Bandito's logo it now said Tex-Mex, so I guessed they were embracing their true identity were and I applauded them for it. I imagined this bartender shrugging when some unhappy customer accused them of not being a real Mexican restaurant. He'd shrug, glance around meaningfully at all the other white people working here, maybe even gesture towards the Indiana Hoosiers flag behind the bar.

"So?" would be the most they'd illicit from him.

He set a pitcher and a decidedly not very margarita shaped glass in front of me.

I heard a couple drunk women from a back booth begin cackling about something. Yeah. I wouldn't want to clean up all those spilled top-heavy drink glasses either.

The glass was tinted green and sort of meant to be cactus looking or at least remind you of one.

"Food?" he asked.

I hadn't really looked at the menu at all. I grasped at the long-buried memories of this place.

"Stuffed jalapeños?" I said. "To start."

He gave me that curt nod again and disappeared.

I had a friend who worked here in high school. I remembered he hated making the stuffed jalapeños and that's probably why it flashed in my brain.

I ate some salsa and it was delicious. I knew after the first bite that I would eat this whole bowl of chips no matter how much else I ate or drank.

It was thick, but smooth rather than chunky. I guess more of a picante sauce but that's not a complaint. Maybe because I was raised on it, but it was my preferred type.

I munched on chips and salsa and guzzled margaritas and glanced at the muted TV behind the bar without absorbing anything or even seeing it. I tried to ignore the top forty hits from twenty years ago playing over the speakers, but it wasn't too loud, and it was better than whatever today's hits would be anyway.

I thumbed through the menu with about as much success as the television.

He returned with the peppers.

"Anything else?" he asked.

Two words. We'd doubled our sentence length. Shit, we were practically friends now.

"Seafood enchiladas," I said. Why not. I was already eating Tex-Mex in northeast Indiana. Might as well throw seafood of questionable origin into the mix with the alcohol.

The stuffed jalapeños were not poppers. They were grander than that. I recalled them now that they were plated in front of me. They were huge amounts of jack cheese and bacon bits formed into balls and draped with a pepper split lengthwise and held together with a skewer. They were then dunked in beer batter and deep fried.

I remembered why my forgotten friend hated making them.

You had to stand over the deep fryer twirling them by the skewer—with your barehand—until they floated so they would retain their shape and not sink to the bottom of the fryer basket and become an unruly mess.

"Sorry, dude," I said, either to the memory of that forgotten friend or whatever schlub they had getting tiny grease splatters on his forearms now. Maybe they'd made some advancements in the past ten years.

After a single bite, in the same inverse token that I knew I'd eat all the salsa, I knew I couldn't eat four of these heavy, grease-soaked things plus the meal I had coming.

I sawed at the thing with my fork rather than pick it up like a fried lollipop or a shank of meat. I wasn't feeling that animalistic.

The waiter scooped up my empty pitcher.

"Another round?" he asked.

I nodded through chewy mouthfuls of peppers. I probably shouldn't have but when has that ever stopped me?

My second pitcher and my enchiladas arrived at the same time. I pushed the peppers and chips out of reach and dug in.

I ate one of the rolled tortillas and half the rice and

beans, drank the entire pitcher and ducked out for a piss. I swayed and stumbled through the lobby to the bathroom and was pretty sure I got most of my urine into the urinal. I blasted the water into the sink for a few seconds but did nothing but look at it flow. I pretended to wash my hands even though I was alone in the bathroom.

I bellied back up to the bar and asked for a to-go container.

"Another pitcher?" he asked, and I was tempted. I could easily leave my car here or, let's be honest, make the one-minute drive home without killing anybody or myself.

I shook my head no finding some reserve of willpower that no one—not even I—would've thought I possessed.

I paid my bill and collected my Styrofoam container and bounced.

I drove around the back of the shopping center away from the direction of my apartment. There was a Best Buy over there and I thought maybe I'd waste some money on a couple of DVDs I'd probably never watch but would maybe make me feel excited for a few seconds before getting back into my car, when I'd feel guilty for spending money on nothing and then they would sit in my back seat for weeks. Retail therapy—it used to work for longer than a few blinks.

They weren't open. Weird Sunday hours, I guess.

I dug my phone out and called Ben before I could think about it.

He answered after a couple rings. There was some half-familiar music playing in the background, but not loud enough that I could place it.

"Your kids asleep?" I asked him after he said hello.

"Yup," he said. "It's a school night. Aimee's in bed, too. She got zero sleep last night and isn't recently used to it like me or you. Wanna come over?"

"Sure," I said and realized I was automatically driving his direction anyway. "What are you doing?"

I heard him exhale but in a matter of fact way. There was nothing pensive about him now.

"Smoking and drinking in my garage," he said. "Wine, so at least I'm being half-classy about it."

"I had two pitchers of margaritas," I offered lamely.

I arrived at their place and pulled past the driveway and parked on the curb. My car settled into the spot like it owned the place.

He had the garage door cracked, so I ducked and rolled in. It was filled with smoke, which I would've been repulsed by a week ago, but it was welcoming now.

He extended a hand and helped me off the ground.

He hit the switch and the door lowered all the way back to the ground. There were upper basement-like windows that opened outwards from the bottom and they were extended to their maximum forty-five-degree angle so we wouldn't die of smoke inhalation at least. Well, not tonight.

There was a mostly empty bottle of red on his workbench near an overflowing ashtray and six beat-up darts sticking up from the wood in attempts at right angles. It was not the only bottle nearby. He had a half-full glass in his other hand.

"Ah," I said and motioned towards the small CD boom box on the floor plugged into the wall with an orange extension cord. "Foo Fighters. I could almost hear it over the phone."

He nodded and turned it up slightly.

"My CD collection ends in 1998," he said.

I laughed.

"I was about to say, 'So? A year or two ago?' when I realized how much has time has passed without me noticing, entertainment-wise," I said.

He agreed.

"If I didn't have the kids, I'd have no idea I was even getting older," he said. "But I can literally see time passing before my eyes."

"Maybe that's my problem," I said.

"We'll be thirty in a blink,' he said.

I shrugged to brush him off.

"You maybe," I said, even though we both knew I was only three months younger than him.

"I can find you a glass," he said, but I shook my head.

"How's Ellie?" I asked him.

He took a sip, pried a dart out of his workbench, and launched it across space. It landed with a soft thump in the outer ring. Not a scoring number. The chalkboards were marked for a game in progress. I didn't know if it would forever be truncated or if he was playing some game against himself.

"She's fucked-up," he said and launched two more darts. He pulled them from the board without marking a score.

He dropped the darts into the top of the wood. Two stuck but the third hit wrong and bounced to the ground and rolled out of sight. He seemed unconcerned.

He half-heartedly threw one of the opposite colors towards the board, but it stuck in the wall. He wrinkled his nose at it and gave up on darts, leaning into the bench and draining his wineglass instead.

"She woke up for a bit today," he said.

"That's great," I said and tried to swallow a *Why didn't anybody fucking call me?* accusation.

"Yeah," he said. "She even talked a little."

"That's great," I repeated. "Did she talk to the cops?"

He nodded and set his empty glass down on the bench and poured the rest of the bottle into it. Without steadying the glass with his freehand, it wobbled preciously, teetering near the edge but didn't fall.

But his other hand wasn't free. He was holding a lit cigarette. Either I wasn't paying enough attention, or it had been smoldering somewhere close by and he was breathing life back into it.

"Dustin," he said. "Her stupid fucking husband."

He ground the butt into the ashtray and sent older butts scattering across the bench and skittering on the concrete floor.

He lit another cigarette one-handed with a Zippo lighter I hadn't seen him use in ten years.

"Shit," I said. "I can't believe you still have that."

He nodded absently. I wasn't attempting to take away from the bomb he'd just dropped or ignore anything. I didn't know. It was so heavy. What could I say about it? The lighter thing popped into my head and I mentioned that instead.

You know how gravity pulls you into itself, so the weight of the Earth holds you down, pulls you, so when you fall to the ground, you're not really falling, you're being pulled home. It's a big idea everybody knows and understands but we didn't talk about it that way because it's too big. It upends too many things, so we ignore the semantics and move on with our day. What Ben had just told me was like that. It was big and inescapable like a natural force and I didn't know what to do with it.

He handed me a cigarette without looking at me and I put it to my lips even though I was sure I hadn't told him I was smoking again.

Maybe he thought I would need one for the next part.

"Dustin's been on an antipsychotic for a while, along with some other stuff," Ben said. "He had a fucked-up childhood and early addiction problems. Ellie…they met in a rehab program."

"I didn't know that," I said before I could stop myself from saying anything at all. Just let him talk.

He shrugged. *Why would you?*

"My mom didn't want to talk about it, Ellie didn't want to talk about it," he trailed off briefly. "I didn't know too much of this, I knew some of it and I didn't really ask about the rest. I have a wife and two daughters. I grew up mostly with my mom and my aunts and my sisters. If the women don't want to talk about something, well. I do learn some lessons over time.

"Anyway, I guess he'd been falling behind on his meds and nobody knew, or they were ignoring it or whatever and maybe he sampled some of whatever him and Corey and Javi were moving. But he freaked out on her. He came back late and she'd gone to bed and of course locked the doors, and he tried the wrong key or forgot his key or something, so he kicked the fucking door down as a first response and Ellie went for this old sawed off oak table leg she keeps under the bed, because why would her husband be kicking in the door when he could unlock it or maybe ring the fucking doorbell at least? And he comes barreling through the house and she's hiding and keeping it dark because she's fucking terrified, and this maniac comes straight to the bedroom and she takes a swing at him and maybe glances one off his shoulder or arm before she realizes who it is and is like 'Oh shit what's going on?' but he loses it and he snatches it away from her and hits her with it, even though by now the lights are on and he knows who it is. Who else could it be in their own bedroom? And he knocks the wind out of her and knocks her off her feet and maybe gets in a shot at her head, because she doesn't remember the next part—which is probably good—but she comes to and he's raping her. He's holding her down and raping her, and she sees his eyes and she's never seen his eyes like that—maybe she's imagined them when they traded old war-stories in rehab therapy sessions—pinpricks, wild and shifty. Crazy eyes. And she tries to fight back and he beats her more and continues raping her and bites her on the face. He fucking bites her face and she passes out again or something and she wakes up and he's just gone, and it hasn't been long because everything's still warm even though the doors are left wide open and he's gone."

He paused and took more cigarette drags, He wasn't shaking, but maybe he was vibrating with something I couldn't begin to fathom. But I tried because I cared about her too, even if I didn't act like it. Even if we never did anything but fuck sometimes, I did care. Maybe I was using her, but it was mutual, and I did care about her. I'd care if I heard this story about any human, because this should never happen to anyone, but I did care a little more because it was someone I knew.

"Where is he?" I asked. "Do they have him yet?"

He shook his head no.

"Not yet," he said. "But they don't think it'll be long. It's all very erratic and impulsive. He's not planning or thinking anything through. He's running and somebody will catch him."

"Is Corey helping him?" I asked and then before he could respond I added, "That fucker had—"

He cut me off with a shake and a horizontal cutting motion from his cigarette hand. The tip left a trail in the smoke-dense air.

"No," he said. "They had him in custody before we even got to town. He brought her to the hospital. They already released him without charge."

I relaxed a tad and breathed a sigh of relief and smoke.

I didn't like Corey either, but I didn't want both of Ben's sisters to have married monsters.

"Is he cooperating then?" I asked. "How'd they clear him so fast?"

"More or less," Ben said. "I'm sure he hasn't told them anything about their small drug operation, but he told them about my grandma's old place and other hangouts. Also, he submitted to blood tests and DNA for the semen they recovered from the rape kit."

"They didn't believe Ellie's story?" I asked.

"No, they did. They had Dustin's dentals matched to the bite marks and his blood type was matched from his semen. They're running DNA, but that'll take a while," Ben explained.

"Jesus," I said.

He continued, "But there were two different semen

blood types present."

Shit.

Shit, shit, shit.

He could see it on my face.

He looked at me directly and with interest for the first time all evening, his distractions and sulking lifted in curiosity for the moment.

He could read it on my face with clarity, like it was typed there in a boldface font.

"What?" he asked anyway.

MONDAY

I told him.

I told him all of it. It spilled from me and I just told him without attempting to explain or justify or rationalize or sugarcoat any part of it.

I told him when it started and why and my attempts to stop it and her reluctance and my eventual surrender.

I told him more than he needed to know, more than he wanted to know. He listened and smoked and drank and watched me tell him and said nothing.

I told him about the first time I was with her and the matter-of-fact way she approached me about it like it was an appointment, like we were scheduling something and putting it on the books, and it was so business-like I thought maybe she was just messing with me and it was a joke or something. Then when she did show I thought that it wouldn't be any fun, there would be nothing here. It would be just casual, a purely physical act.

But it was more than that. She was voracious in her needs and wants and her explorations.

I told him of further meetings, the ones I could remember because this had been going on for a year, since I had moved back, and she started to seem so careless about it like she didn't even give a fuck that anyone knew and that was probably the right way to look at it. But I was weak, and the danger of getting caught and the sneaking around parts might be what I was actually attracted to.

I told him of any of the liaisons I could recall, any specifics of when or where we met, and any detail that I didn't think he would find disgusting because I was telling him about his younger sister.

I told him of the last time I saw her when she sprang a last minute session on me minutes before he was arriving to pick me up and drive us to Indy, and that yes, those panties were hers that he'd picked up gingerly off my carpet. That was the first time he really made any kind of disgusted face and even then it was subtle, more of a curl of the lip and looking down his nose than an outright retching or dry heaving of any sort.

I told him about texting with her.

I told him about her torturing me with sexy pics.

I told him about swearing off her again for the dozenth time and blocking her number from my phone again.

I ran out of things to tell him and I sputtered and slowed and trailed off and stopped.

We sat in his garage and we smoked and stared at the silent space between each other.

"Does Meg know?" he asked.

"I don't know," I said. "I don't have sisters. Do they talk about shit like this?"

"Maybe," he said. "Nobody ever tells me anything."

To try and keep him talking, I offered more.

"Amy knows," I said and clarified before he blew his top. "Mark's Amy. She saw us somewhere or something and approached Ellie about it. I just found out."

He nodded.

"And I told Estella," I said. "Thursday when I saw her for a drink. It's been weighing on my mind lately, so I told somebody that knew her and all the players but wasn't really connected to any of us anymore."

He continued nodding.

"I'm sorry she got hurt. Doubly sorry if it had anything to do with me. But I'm having trouble feeling bad about the affair," I said.

I put my cigarette out in the ashtray only half smoked. They were starting to make me jumpy and twitchy. I got up and paced.

I felt nothing from the Mexican food or the alcohol any longer in my system. I checked his garage fridge and snagged myself a beer. I didn't ask and I opened it and began gulping it to try and depress some of these frayed nerves.

He didn't care, like I wouldn't care if we were at my place and he helped himself to something.

I leaned against the wall, so I wasn't so close to him and I observed him sitting in one of the camping chairs he'd set up out here for this purpose. He was in profile from my angle and he concentrated on his smoke and stared into the middle distance.

But it really wasn't as ominous as all that.

He could have just been a guy sitting in his garage enjoying a final cigarette before bed after a long day of work once his kids and wife were safely tucked in for the night.

He didn't even seem as if he was really contemplating anything, not really. It was like he was smoking the last of the day away.

"And Niedz might know," I said. "but I'm not sure. He acted like it this weekend, but maybe I was being paranoid."

He looked at me.

"Niedz?" he said. "That guy doesn't know shit."

I nodded. Seemed like a weird thing to focus on but what did I know?

"Anyway," I continued even if I didn't want to. "I didn't say anything to that detective, but if they're actively looking for a second person... Well. I'll call him in the morning."

"Thanks," he said absently.

"Look," I tried, but he cut me off with a shrug and a palm up in the air.

"You're adults," he said. "I'm trying to remember that. I don't know. You know my thoughts on cheating. It offends me, but it doesn't really affect me, I guess."

I was still waiting for him to stand up and punch me in the mouth, but it seemed more unlikely as the seconds passed by and he made no such move.

"I shouldn't get a pass just because we're friends."

"Do you want me to be mad you? Then shut up. I was never overly protective," he said. "I don't know. People make their own mistakes and no one ever listens to me anyway."

I had a feeling we were talking about something else, something larger but I didn't want to press him. I didn't want to move on from these real events that had happened into theory or hypothetical jargon. I didn't want to get away from real things happening to real people, people we were close to, into life philosophy. I didn't want to abstract these things, to give them cognitive dissidence.

I tried to steer the talk back into the direction of the concrete here and now. I asked him what I came here to ask him and what he invited me here for in the first place.

"What are we going to do about it?" I asked him. I said it quietly or at least softly enough to give it the weight that veering the conversation in this territory deserved.

"What?" he said to me and, at first, I thought maybe he hadn't heard me. Maybe I'd spoken with too much reverence.

I started to repeat myself, but he stopped me.

"I heard you," he said, "but do what? I've done everything I can. I told her not to marry that asshole years ago."

I stared at him.

He was still looking in the middle distance of the smoky garage with a fizzled spent cigarette in one hand and an empty wine glass crookedly resting on the ground beside the other.

I didn't know him at all.

I told her not to marry that asshole?

How could that be his response to this?

Couldn't he hear those words as he said them?

Couldn't he hear the meaning behind them? The pettiness. The *I told you so* bullshit of that statement.

Who the fuck was this person I've been friends with all these years? There wasn't an ounce of compassion in that statement. That statement about his own sister. His younger sister.

I told her not to marry that asshole?

He said that out loud to me while slowly shook his head in contempt. He was blaming her for this. She was the victim. He wasn't defending her? He wasn't on her side? He said this thing was her fault. That was what he wanted to send out into the world. That was his statement of purpose. That was his intent. That was who he was.

He wanted that vicious, awful thought out there. He would rather be proven right than offer help. How could he think this about another person, about another member of his own family?

Ben still sat there and stared, lost in his own poison thoughts or the haze of the smoky air.

I didn't know what I had wanted but it wasn't this.

I didn't recognize my friend in him at all.

I just…I thought he'd be angry at Dustin, I thought he'd want to kill him. I thought he'd want me to help him kill him. I didn't think I could actually do that, but I could fantasize about it, sure, until the police caught him.

I thought I would need to help him feel better, but instead he had no feelings at all.

We'd been friends for so long, we've discussed so much. We've helped each other through all kinds of shit. So many discussions about morality and what to do about the perpetrators of heinous crimes.

I wasn't saying he should kill this man. I wasn't saying he should even want to, really, but the fucking thought should cross his mind. At least before the idea of writing off his poor, broken, hospitalized sister. He was one of my closest friends, my best friend. He'd told me shit he hadn't told his wife. If he didn't entertain the notion of revenge in front of me, even as a joke or an outlandish fantasy...

It didn't occur to him at all.

I told her not to marry that asshole?

I couldn't believe this was the sum of his thoughts on the matter at hand.

"They haven't found Dustin yet?" I asked him in some vain attempt to spur him into the territory I needed him to go, to show me that this was a fluke, that it was merely grief twisting him in strange directions.

"No," was all he said.

"But they think they will?" I tried.

He nodded.

"Sure," he said.

Ben, my friend, he was supposed to be this man of action. Whenever there was that moment among the group of *What should we do? Where should we eat?* He was always the first with an idea and the first with his shoes on, leading the way. He was always early to anywhere he was going. He always showed up with a plan and the will to see it through.

He helped her attacker out a few days ago for a measly two hundred dollars. And he was just going to fucking sit here?

I was sure we could find Dustin before the police did. I already had some ideas. If he tried, he'd have the same ones. He'd probably double my own output. Why had he been in this garage at all when I called him? Why wasn't he on his way to find this fucker and put him in the ground?

OK.

Maybe I was leaning towards killing him.

But I blame Ben. If he had reacted like a human being, like the thing he presents himself to be, maybe I wouldn't have to react so strongly in the other direction.

I crushed my beer can and dropped it into the recycling tub next to the trash.

"I'm gonna take off," I said. "I'll see you later in the week."

He nodded without looking at me and said goodbye and thanked me half-heartedly and I heard him lighting up another smoke when I slipped out the door. I wondered if he had any wine left or if he'd segue to beer or harder stuff.

Hopefully he'd just sleep it off.

I walked through the house to get back out to my car rather than getting back down on the cement and rolling around. I locked the front door and shut it behind me and got back into my car. I wound through the neighborhood and turned left out of it onto Coldwater Road and then another left onto Dupont.

When I got to Clinton, the street I lived on, I blew right past it and instead took the onramp to I-69 and headed north.

I drove about twenty minutes and took the Kendallville exit. I stopped at a gas station and bought a pack of smokes and a cheap plastic lighter.

I smoked one with the windows rolled down as I drove west through town and came out on some other two-lane highway. I didn't know the names of any of these roads, but I'd been coming up here a few times a year, usually in the summers, since high school. This was one of the first places I ever got drunk or fucked some of my early girlfriends.

I saw a sign for Noah's Lake, but I already had my turn signal on. I was driving on autopilot.

I was doing what Ben should have been doing.

I drove without my brights on down the backwoods, dark-as-night country roads and then the twisting, somehow even darker lake roads.

I pulled into their driveway crooked and boxed the pickup truck in place.

I saw movement at one of the windows and then the porch light blazed on when I stepped on the first step. It was either a security light or someone had great timing.

"He's not here," Meg said through the screen door.

"Where is he?" I asked.

"I don't know," she said. "Probably getting drunk somewhere."

I scoped the driveway. It was his pickup I blocked in, and there was Meg's car. I mimed real obvious looking so she would see me doing it.

I glanced back down the road.

"Which one was your grandparent's cottage?" I asked. "I'm having trouble recalling."

She hesitated.

I smiled at her.

"Meg," I said, "tell me which one it is so I don't have to walk around looking for it and make a bunch of noise. You know I'm going to figure it out."

I thought for a minute she wasn't going to divulge but after a second of looking at me blankly she told.

"The blue one. Three houses down," she said and

nodded in the direction.

I thanked her.

"I'm leaving my car here," I said when I'd gotten to the end of the driveway, which seemed obvious. I also had no illusions that they could get their vehicles around mine or simply scrape the side of it if they wanted. I didn't know. I wanted her to know I was thinking of everything, or trying to, I guess.

I walked down the gravel and dirt road and passed the dark shapes of other cottages.

Not many signs of life in a small lake community in February. From the lights and empty driveways, I'd say less than half the homes were currently occupied.

I was three houses down, but everything looked black in the cloudy sliver of moonlight. I guess this would have to be the blue one.

I could feel a slight heat radiating from this one, as if there was power and gas currently streaming to it, compared to the shut-up-tight, cold-as-earth of the other ones I'd passed.

There didn't appear to be any lights or TV on inside of it. No light turned on when I approached the porch.

Even the screen door was locked.

I thought about the gentle parabola the road made when I walked over here. I remembered coming by in high school. Ben and his sisters never walked along the road. They always took a straight path through the grassy lawn—the shore path. It reasoned their spouses would as well.

I touched the screen and through some form of osmosis I tried to remember what this cottage looked like on the inside or at least the bare bones of the layout.

I didn't get much.

I'd never stayed in this one as a kid. Ben's grandparents had still been alive, and we stayed in the one that had been his parent's before they split up and his mom had sold it on the cheap to Meg and Corey after their marriage.

Maybe something around back would jog my memory.

I'm sure in the few times I'd been to this one, I'd approached from the shore anyway.

I walked around the left side of the house and there was a larger screened in porch on this side. Storm windows were in place and it was just as dark as the front.

"You looking for me, Kyle?" a voice said from the darkness.

I was aware enough and on edge enough that I didn't overreact to hearing a voice from the black. Or, maybe, I started reacting so quickly, like when I heard his mouth open but before he started speaking that by the time his words were made audible, I'd already composed myself. It was like this old alarm clock I used to have. The click as it turned over would wake me and I'd slam down on it before the alarm could even sound.

"How you doing, Corey?" I asked him. "And no. I'm not looking for you, really."

I heard him shrug in his winter clothes and tracked the noise.

He sat in an old lawn chair with his back to the house, staring into the lake. Whatever little light there was glinted off empty cans at his feet. I smelled his cigarette as I saw the tip glow.

I couldn't believe I hadn't smelled it earlier. My sense

of smell must have been dulled from restarting the habit.

I approached him and there was a second chair, so I sat in it and tried not to yelp when I felt the absolute cold press from the metal through my pant legs and into me. It was more startling than his disembodied voice emanating from the gloom.

It was that type of cold that made you forget what warm was, that this world could ever be anything other than ice.

I lit one of my own cigarettes.

"Haven't you been telling everyone who will listen that you quit?" he asked. It seemed like he was merely making conversation rather than undermining me.

I shrugged so he could hear it since there was no seeing anything. Not in this pitch.

"You know what they say," I said but never followed it up with anything.

Neither of us said anything for a while. The only sounds were our cigarette papers burning and far off automobile noises and the gentle ambient weirdness of a large, still body of water in proximity. There was nothing to hear from it, really, but it's like human bodies are tuned for it somehow.

He sighed and said, "He's not here."

"I know that," I said and then shut up again. I figured I could wait him out. I read once about effective torturers and how they simply began torturing without asking questions and the victims would start telling them things without any direction or guidance to get them to stop.

My silence would be my implement.

"I don't know where he is," he said. "I told the cops that."

I exhaled. I tried to make it sound as disappointed as possible.

"I know that too," I said. "But I think you have ideas that you haven't told the cops. Related to you and Dustin's...side business."

He began to protest but I stopped him.

"I don't care," I said. "I have some of the same ideas. I know where I'm going to look."

I heard him swallow in the dark.

"I need a gun," I heard myself say.

When he didn't respond, I continued.

"Preferably, the one he fired at whatshisname's Hummer on Friday morning," I said. "He didn't have it with him when he attacked Ellie, thank God, and she didn't have access to it. That's why she was brandishing a broken off table leg. I figure there's a better-than-good chance it's in this cottage."

I rapped on the siding behind me and I heard him start in his seat.

"What are you going to do?" he asked me as quietly as he could. It sounded fainter than our cigarettes. Lighter than wind. Calmer than flat water.

"I'm going to go find him," I said. "Do you want to come with me?"

He was silent again. This time, maybe, it was out of shock.

"Why would you want me to go?" he asked.

"He trusts you," I said. "And you might keep me from doing anything too stupid."

"Like giving you a gun?" he asked.

I shook my head.

"That's nonnegotiable," I said. "For self-defense."

"Right," he said.

"He's unhinged. I'm not going after him with nothing but strong words."

"You think I don't know that?" he said. Finally, someone with an edge in their voice. "I picked her up off the floor. I carried her into the hospital."

"Thank you," I said. "That's why I'm here. I've got a pretty good idea where he might be. If I just wanted to kill him, why would I come to you?"

"For the gun," he said.

"Shit, it's Indiana," I said. "I can get a gun at Walmart. If I wanted to kill him, I'd be sitting at Ben's and asking him."

This was the tricky part.

Corey and Ben weren't close, I knew that, but I also knew tragedies like this could bring people together. I didn't know where either Corey or Ben were all day and they could have had this conversation already or Corey could have felt Ben out and realized he was nothing but hollow in there with no capacity for what we had to do.

What we had to do.

Say it, if you mean it. We were going to kill him.

I act like I had to convince myself, but I knew it the moment I saw Ellie lying there.

"That's true," he said, and I had him.

I figured if nothing else I'd get Corey to lead me to him, lull him into a false since of security and then kill Dustin. I didn't have it all worked out, but at that point, Corey's prints would also be on the gun and he would've led me to him.

I had to get close enough to make it look like he offed himself. Or something. I dunno—I was new at this.

"What about the old man?" Corey asked me.

I was confused. Maybe my silence spoke for me or his eyes were accustomed to my facial expressions in the dark.

"Mr. Baker," he said. "You know, their dad."

I was blown away by this suggestion. That drunken, violent mess? Maybe it wouldn't be that hard to talk Corey into offing him as I thought it'd be.

"Have you ever met him?" I asked. "I'm not trying to be a dick, but he wasn't even at your wedding."

Corey spat into the frozen grass.

"Meg reconnected with him a couple years ago," he said. "She never told Ben since he hates him so much."

"With good reason," I said standing up for my friend.

"Whatever. Not arguing that," he said. "I never knew him then. But, well, he's been nice to us."

Something was off.

"Nice how?" I asked.

He sighed like he didn't want to tell me, but we were in pretty far as it was.

"He helped us start our new business," he said.

"Jesus Christ," I said. "He's your drug guy."

"Money guy, mostly, and a few contacts," Corey said.

I stood up.

"Well, I ran into him at the hospital and I don't trust him," I said, because I didn't, and I didn't like not knowing how deep his shit went with Corey or Dustin. I'm not saying the guy was pure evil or that he'd be willing to let the assault and rape of his youngest daughter go unanswered because he was in business with the man who did it.

But I couldn't know for sure.

And there was the other side of the coin. He could take it far too personally and rough Dustin up or some other dumb shit.

I didn't care if Dustin suffered.

I didn't care if he paid for his crimes.

I didn't care if he escaped by suicide.

The point was to take him out, to remove him. This wouldn't take away what he did but it would take away any future hurt he might cause.

I could do this.

I could do this dispassionately.

I could do this without feeling a thing or losing control.

I could kill this mother fucker so that he would be dead and for no other reason than that.

"How about just you and me?" I said. "We go right now and grab him and end this fucking thing."

"Sure," Corey said and stood up. "But why don't you tell the police where he is? Seems like that would be easier. Cleaner."

He suspected that I was going to kill him, no doubt. I didn't know why he agreed to go with me if that's what he thought. But here we were. Maybe he thought he could stop me.

"He feels like our problem," I said. "And besides, I'd have to tell them how I knew and what I was doing on Friday morning."

"That reminds me, you kept your promise," Corey said.

"What does that mean?" I asked.

I saw the green face of a watch light up near me.

"You said you didn't want to see me all weekend," he

said. "It's been Monday for over an hour."

We drove separately back to Fort Wayne after Corey assured me that Meg would cover for him if questioned that he was with her all night.

He did not ask me why he'd need an alibi.

I didn't have anything as airtight as a wife's testimony, but I did have neighbors who worked normal hours and would all be asleep when I pulled into my parking space with the lights out. I had told Corey to pull over to the side of the main road and I'd double back to him.

On the way to his pickup, I texted Estella and then called her, knowing that she puts her phone in Do Not Disturb mode when she slept. Also knowing that the cell phone towers would ping my location as my own apartment in the middle of the night and it would jibe with the drunk dialing yarn I was spinning in my head for the cops if I needed to tell it. After she didn't answer, I turned the thing off and pulled the battery out and returned them both to my pocket.

I hoped Ben was doing something that would place him in his house at this time.

I hoped Aimee would back him up if she could.

But I couldn't worry about that right now.

All I could worry about was finding him.

Then killing him.

Then getting away with it.

I climbed into Corey's pickup, but Meg was sitting in the driver's seat. No Corey at all.

"What the fuck is this?" I said and reached for the

door handle.

"Relax," she said. "You asked the wrong one. I'm her sister. You think because you poked her a couple of times you want him dead more than me? C'mon, Kyle."

"Ben didn't feel that way."

She smiled.

"I love my family, but they're all fucked up," she said. "A year or two ago I asked Ben if he wanted to go see a movie. Just some dumb action thing like we used to watch when we were kids. I can't remember what it was. Something with Kate Beckinsale or Mila Jovovich or. A hot chick beating up monsters, you know the type. He was weird and hesitant, so I went by myself. I never get time to myself. Corey was working and my kids were at Grandma's.

"Anyway, it was a fun, forgettable way to spend a couple hours. When I saw him later, he asked me, 'How was your propaganda?' I was baffled. He had heard it had a feminist agenda. Whatever that means. That's why he didn't want to go. 'Not into the feminism thing at all' he said to me, his goddamn sister.

"I tried to tell him she just shoots a bunch of guns. It was just an action movie. But he was the one that fell for the propaganda. This guy has a wife and two young daughters. He was raised by our single mom with me and Ellie and he's not into feminism at all? What is he fucking teaching his girls? That they didn't deserve to vote or make as much money as boys?

"So maybe you were surprised that Ben blames Ellie for what happened to her, but I wasn't. I've been planning to go after Dustin since Saturday night."

I still had my hand on the door handle.

"I have what you asked for," she said, and opened the center armrest to reveal a handgun tucked in there. "Now buckle up. I wanna make good time. I got shit to do tomorrow."

We hardly talked on the way down. Meg played some god-awful music like country or something, but she played it low.

We sat in the pickup and she raced down the highway and I smoked cigarettes and we both sipped coffee from thermoses she brought.

She assured me she had enough gas to get us there and back without having to stop. If not, she had some cash and I was mentally going over out of the way stations we could stop at.

I hoped she didn't ask me to go in and pay for it. I'd rather dangle her out on the hook. Well, not really. I'd rather dangle Corey, but here we are.

"How do you know Corey's not talking to the cops right now?" I asked.

"He's not," she said.

"But—"

"Kyle, he's not, OK?" she said. "Settle down and get married and you'll know what I mean."

"Huh. When you get this close to thirty, everybody's trying to sell you on holy matrimony. But you're the first to pitch the alibi angle as a reason. Tempting, but I don't see a husband in my future."

She ignored me.

We rode for a few miles with nothing but the barely audible music for company.

Sadly, a woman getting beaten up and raped by her husband isn't news, and there was a very slim chance Travis knew about it. Not that that meant he wouldn't hide his meal ticket even if they knew.

"Does he have anybody on the side?" I asked Meg.

"I don't know," she said. "Doesn't seem like his style. Plus, he's too weird for most ladies."

Except for Ellie for some reason. Push it away. Analyze that shit later.

"Corey said there was a stripper he was mildly hung-up on," she offered. "But he told the cops about that. It was in Fort Wayne anyway."

Thank God. I'd had enough of fucking strip clubs to last me the rest of my life.

"There's another place he could be in Indy, too," Meg said, and I could tell from the tone of her voice that she didn't want to tell me, that it pained her to do so.

"Where?" I said.

She adjusted her hands on the steering wheel.

"Javi's place," she said after a moment. "We used his garage a couple times and Javi gave us the code."

"We?" I said. "How involved are you with this drug shit?"

"Don't worry about it," she said. "You're missing the point."

"I get it," I said. Javi's out of town on his honeymoon and likely doesn't know anything about Ellie's assault. He probably wouldn't have thought to change his garage code anyway.

"It'd be a good spot," I admitted. "But do you think Dustin's in a right enough mind to go there?"

Meg shrugged.

"I don't know. Cops ain't found him yet," she offered.

We drove on for a while in silence after settling on checking Javi's place last. It seemed the least likely of the places he'd be, and it that it was on the way back.

Even though I had no desire to go back to that trailer.

When we passed the Pendleton exit, which meant we only had about ten miles or so to go before we hit the northernmost tip of Indianapolis, I broke the silence.

"We're gonna kill him," I said. "Right? Despite what I said to your husband."

She shifted in her seat and gripped the wheel tighter, but only barely. She nodded rhythmically as if I was still talking. As if I was saying something that made sense.

"Of course," she replied. "It's why Corey tapped me in. He can't do it. Look, Dustin is probably the best friend he's ever had but he understands what needs to happen. You ever put a pet to sleep?"

"Yeah," I said.

"But you didn't do it," she said. "You had a vet do it. And when she came into the room with the needle, well. You didn't stop her, right? Think of it like that."

She sighed and continued nodding but said nothing more.

"I don't want to hurt him. I don't want to make him suffer. I don't even really have any desire to see him punished. Do you understand what I mean?" I asked her.

She increased the cadence of her nodding.

"Yeah," she said finally. "He needs put down."

"Right," I agreed. "He's a dog that attacked somebody and will again. We have to take care of it."

"We have to take care of it," Meg repeated.

We drove into the sleeping Indianapolis.

"You should've let Corey talk you into corralling my dad into this," Meg said.

"Yeah?"

"Yeah," she said. "He had this business partner, way back. Anyway, turns out this guy was a scumbag, a pedophile or something. Guy disappears after recently signing over his half of the company to my dad. A few months go by and dad withdraws a large sum of money and gives it to the missing man's wife and kid, so they don't have to worry. They move out of state. He and my mom get a divorce soon after that."

"I think I heard a version of this once," I said.

She nodded again, but more matter of fact. She'd lost the continued bobbing of her head finally. I worried it might come back in the same far-out way I worried when I sneezed, that maybe I'd become one of those freaks you read about who's been sneezing for thirty straight years. Although I doubted I'd make it a month before I threw myself off a bridge.

"I'm a couple years older than you and Ben," Meg said. "And I remember it real well. I remembered at the time, Dad referred to the missing man's wife as his widow. Even though he'd only been gone a few weeks."

I cleared my throat.

"Well, that's pretty tidy," I admitted, "but he could just be a pessimist."

She continued.

"He quit drinking a few years ago, before we reconnected," she said. "I flat out asked him and he admitted to it and told me he was sorry for a lot, but not for that, and I was his firstborn and he was putting his own life in my hands by telling me this. By trusting me."

"Jesus Christ," I said.

"Yeah," Meg said. "It sure was something."

We came out south of Indy and exited at Greenwood.

Meg drove with confidence and, since we were planning on killing a guy, no GPS or stopping for directions.

We got to the trailer park and nothing much about it had changed. Travis's Hummer was nowhere to be seen, but I thought I caught a glimpse of shattered glass in the grass and thought I felt it crunch beneath my shoes. His woman's car wasn't here either.

I slipped gloves on as we walked.

There was another car parked over to the side of the trailer, backed in and at a crooked angle. It was facing, by the shortest means necessary, a direct route over the grass and to the street.

"I recognize that car," Meg said quietly.

I took this to mean that she believed Dustin was here or had been here.

Something poked me in the arm I reached for it. It was the handle of a handgun, handed to me butt first.

Meg smiled at me.

"You tried to leave it in the truck," she said, but without judgement.

I didn't know if it was the one Dustin had fired off the other night. I didn't know if that mattered.

Meg took another one from her purse.

"You've fired one before?" she asked quietly.

"Yeah," I said.

"These are glocks," she explained. "So, no safeties. Just point and shoot. And not anywhere in my direction."

"OK."

We stepped up to the trailer.

It was completely dark and totally quiet.

Meg stood to the left of the door and knocked softly.

"Dust?" she called out. "You in there, buddy? Looking all over for you."

There were sounds no or signs of movement from inside or the vehicle next to it.

She shrugged.

She tried the knob and it was unlocked.

"I'm coming inside, buddy," she said. "Kyle's with me."

She turned the knob and the door creaked open. I followed behind her. The place felt even stuffier and more stifling than last time.

Meg hit the light switch and illuminated the place. Still no movement. She had her gun down and sort of hidden behind her leg. I willed myself not to jerk mine up and sweep the room with it.

We're here as friends, remember.

I looked around. Meg was heading towards the bedroom, still talking to Dustin as if he was here. I stopped her.

"You've been here before, yeah?" I asked.

She nodded.

"When was the last time?" I asked.

"I dunno. Six months ago? More, maybe," she said

"Well, I was just here on Friday," I said, "and shit's different. The TV's gone. And a few other things here and there."

When we were here last, I didn't pay attention to what all this clutter had been, but I pointed to big blank spots among the garbage. Whereas before every surface of every area was covered with crap you had to practically wade through, there were big splotches of areas where things had been recently removed.

"Hmm," she said.

"Guess Travis left," I said.

"Maybe. Or sold some of his crap. I'll check the bedroom," she said.

I nodded and headed to check the tiny bathroom. I figured if toothbrushes were gone maybe that would tell me something.

I was vaguely aware that the bedroom light had come on.

I poked around in the bathroom, but there were like ten toothbrushes in there and all kinds of other shit, bathroom and otherwise. I was no detective and I doubted even Sherlock Holmes could make any sense out of all this random clutter and decay.

I left the bathroom and noticed that Meg was still standing in the doorway, facing into the bedroom. She'd turned the light on and then just stood there frozen for a few moments.

"Meg?" I said and her back showed no reaction at all.

I got this deep sinking feeling in my stomach.

I repeated her name and grasped her arm—the arm with the gun in its hand in case she snapped out of whatever trance she was in and decided I needed shot.

She glanced at me with droopy, wet eyes.

She turned from the room and walked out of the trailer. I heard her get into the pickup. The truck did not start.

When she had turned and looked at me and then away

from this place, I thought maybe I had seen a pair of shoes on the bed and I didn't want to look there. I didn't want to see what he'd done to Travis or his girlfriend or *Please God no* not her child.

I looked so that I would know.

I do things sometimes because I know that whatever I am imagining is far worse than whatever will really happen or whatever I will really see. I know that I can concoct situations and scenarios superior in their terror than anything that occurs in real life.

Well, I used to think that until Ellie was attacked.

So, I looked because seeing can't be worse than having it happen to you. I looked so that maybe it could be tribute to Ellie or that maybe this horrible thing would supplant the horrible thing that had happened to her.

I had this professor in college. He was in his seventies and he smoked and drank and was an all-around good time. He told us that his father, almost one hundred years old, was still alive and kicking and his favorite thing to do in the morning was read the obituaries. He especially liked it when young people died because he thought it gave him better odds.

I didn't want to see the battered and chewed remains of Travis and his girlfriend and her kid filthy with blood and semen but maybe this evil would eclipse the thing that happened to Ellie, somehow. Maybe it would take some of that hurt away by hurting someone else more.

It didn't make sense.

I was ashamed of these thoughts as I was having them, and I knew Ellie would never want what had happened to her to happen to others. Only a maniac would want that.

So, I looked. For them, too, because they deserved to be seen even like this, in this horrible way, in this depressing place.

It was not Travis, his girlfriend, or a child on the bed.

It was Dustin.

He laid on his back on the bare mattress with his legs splayed and his feet askew. His left hand was limp at his side and palm-up. His right hand rested in his lap and cradled a small pistol. His eyes were partly open, and a trail of blood traced its way out of his mouth, down his chin and formed a small pool near his collarbone.

There wasn't anything epic like the back of his skull split open or his brains splattered against the wall. His head just rested against the wall with his eyes sort of open as if he was drifting off while watching TV.

I left the trailer.

I got into the truck and she started it silently and we drove away from there.

"He used some flimsy .22," she said. "He's lucky it even killed him. Probably bounced around inside his skull and turned his brain to mush before his body figured out how to die."

I didn't say anything.

What was there to say?

He saved us some trouble, but I didn't feel grateful. I'd said I didn't want him to suffer and I wasn't concerned about punishment. I meant those things when I said them, and I'd mean them again tomorrow. But right now?

I didn't know. It didn't feel right somehow.

I realized Meg wasn't driving back towards town.

"Where are we going?" I asked, interrupting her bad-mouthing Dustin's choice of methods and weapons.

"Gonna stop at Javi's," she said like that was perfectly normal, like we had just been to see a friend and we were going to drop in on another one.

"What? Why?" I said and added, "I think we found him."

I immediately cringed at my flippant attitude towards a dead person. A dead person that had done horrible shit, but still. That had been someone I knew and someone Meg had been close to.

She didn't take offense.

"Because I need to pee, and I wouldn't mind a drink, and we probably shouldn't stop somewhere where other people can see us," she said with escalating anger rising in her voice.

I wanted to tell her that when we were discussing killing him, Dustin was already dead. We didn't need alibis. We hadn't done this. Not even in the magical thinking kind of way of manifesting it. He was already dead before we'd brought it up, stiff as he appeared.

"Sure, makes sense," was all I said.

Meg told me the code and I climbed out of the pickup and opened the garage and she slid the pickup inside and I closed the door.

Javi lived in one of those McMansions that are mostly garage or at least look that way. It was a three-car monstrosity and Meg pulled in next to an SUV. I looked at Javi's mostly abandoned motorcycle gathering dust in the far corner of the third space.

Meg didn't recognize the SUV, or maybe she was pretending not to like I was.

We went inside.

I realized I was holding my breath. But nothing happened.

"Take your pee, I'll find two drinks and we'll get out of here," I said.

She nodded.

I heard the bathroom door shut and a fan turn on.

"Mr. Baker?" I said into the darkness of the house.

There was no reply. There was no movement. There might be nothing but an empty house and darkness.

I wasn't mistaken. It was his car in the garage, with a single key scratch above the gas flap that I put there less than a day ago.

I could turn all the lights on.

I could search the place from top to bottom.

I could find him and know for sure.

Instead, I grabbed two rocks glasses and dropped a couple large pours of Maker's Mark into them.

Meg returned and I handed her one. We didn't *Cheers* or clink or toast. We paused for a moment and stared into our respective glasses, nodded, and drank them down.

I rinsed the glasses out, replaced them, and we left.

I wanted Meg to see what I saw in the garage when we pulled out, but she was distracted or oblivious or simply incapable of it. She wouldn't have taken me here if she'd known, right? There was no sense in that.

I looked in vain for a shadow at any of the windows when we drove away. I saw nothing and told myself it wasn't what I thought. But some things just are as they appear to be—there's no interpretation.

He was here.

Had he been at the trailer, too?

• • •

Two hours later, Meg dropped me off on the road outside of my apartment complex and we nodded at each other again instead of saying anything.

No one saw me as I crept through the darkness back to my apartment and into my bed.

I visited Ellie at the hospital later in the afternoon and she was doing much better. She turned away from me as I leaned into kiss her, so I settled on her forehead.

There was a rotating police guard outside of her room and lots of her family around. No Ben, though.

Nobody knew about Dustin yet.

Her father arrived after I had been there for an hour. He looked well-rested and relaxed. He kissed Ellie on the cheek, and she smiled at him and held out her hand for his. He stared at me curiously when we were reintroduced, as if he was trying to tell me something with his eyes alone.

Ellie had that same look in her eyes.

The room filled up with visitors.

When we had a moment alone or our eyes locked across the distance of the crowded room, I saw her features change and her act dropped. I doubt anyone else noticed. Even if they were looking directly at her, they couldn't see it. They didn't know her like I knew her.

I saw her suppress the flinch she innately felt at her father's touch.

I saw her mask the giddiness she felt when the cops told to her Dustin was dead.

I saw her and her father's shared glance, stained with a secret—*they both already knew.*

These were only glimpses, only flashes.

I wanted to clear the room and ask her what it cost her, when she'd already lost so much. What it took to let this man reenter her life just to remove another one from it forever. I wanted to ask her what it cost and what it will continue to cost and if she really believed it was worth it.

I wanted to ask her this, but I never did.

The preceding took place from Thursday, February 08 to Monday, February 12, 2007. I wrote the first section in longhand on loose-leaf college ruled notebook paper the following morning, Tuesday the 13th, and then lost it. It was the last piece of any significant length I wrote with pen and paper. Since losing it felt ominous, I went full computer from then on.

Twelve years later, in February of 2019, I rewrote that first lost section from memory and then kept going and didn't stop this time until it was finished. The whole thing took three weeks to hammer out in a shed next to a washer and dryer in Phoenix, AZ. I wrote three books this way and an important part of me will always be in that place somehow, as if magic were real.

Also, like magic, as if I conjured it from its hiding place by finally completing the book, I did find that original longhand section afterwards. I never have reread through those wrinkled, faded pages again. But I keep them folded and tucked in the folder with the print of the first draft like they belong there or mean something.

I'd like to thank Jana Carlile and Nick Jackson, always the first readers of any of my stuff. Sorry 'bout all dem typos.

Thanks also to Jordan Lepper for editing this one and leaving my voice intact. Also, to Brian Skillman—we'll figure it out next time, buddy.

And, most importantly, to Veronica. Thank you for literally everything.

The people in this book are not real and never existed. The events depicted herein did not happen. Everything was made up.

Except for those parts that weren't.

Kris Lorenzen lives and writes in Indianapolis with his wife and their cats. They have also lived in Memphis and Phoenix. He knows the best places to eat in these cities.

Visit him at: linktr.ee/kris.lorenzen